PASSPORT
TO
SPY

PASSPORT
TO
SPY

A Kat Lawson Mystery

Nancy Cole Silverman

LEVEL BEST BOOKS

Historia

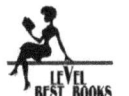

First published by Level Best Books/Historia 2023

Copyright © 2023 by Nancy Cole Silverman

All rights reserved. No part of this publication may be reproduced, stored or transmitted in any form or by any means, electronic, mechanical, photocopying, recording, scanning, or otherwise without written permission from the publisher. It is illegal to copy this book, post it to a website, or distribute it by any other means without permission.

This novel is entirely a work of fiction. The names, characters and incidents portrayed in it are the work of the author's imagination. Any resemblance to actual persons, living or dead, events or localities is entirely coincidental.

Nancy Cole Silverman asserts the moral right to be identified as the author of this work.

First edition

ISBN: 978-1-68512-327-7

Cover art by Level Best Designs

This book was professionally typeset on Reedsy. Find out more at reedsy.com

To Bruce

Chapter One

December 1999

Munich, Germany

As a journalist, I know better than to insert myself into the center of a news story. Especially when reporting on a murder. Getting into the middle of an investigation could have serious consequences. I could end up dead.

That's what I kept telling myself as I hid from my would-be assassin as he searched for my whereabouts on the icy Alpine slopes south of Munich. I had taken a chance and now had nobody to blame except myself.

Let me start at the beginning of my story, where hopefully, I can explain why I had a target on my back and what I needed to do about it.

My name is Kat Lawson, and up until a year ago, I had worked as an investigative reporter for the *Phoenix Gazette*, which had dismissed me because of an inappropriate workplace relationship with my boss. Him, they kept—me, they fired. Which might explain how I found myself working for *Journey International*, a travel publication and a front for the FBI. An excuse for the bureau to send select journalists undercover to retrieve information and pass it along.

My assignment was simple enough. I was to go to Munich, Germany, to meet with Hans von Hausmann and his sister, Erika Schönburg, celebrity curators for The Gerhardt Galerie, a new museum featuring a mixture of old-world masters and modern art. The Galerie was preparing for a show featuring *Fruits on the Table with a Small Dog* by Paul Gauguin, a French post-impressionist. According to my FBI handler, Sophie Brill, an art historian and holocaust survivor, the painting had been stolen in 1970 from a private gallery in London and recently bought by an American collector who, upon hearing about the unveiling, feared he had been duped.

The painting had an estimated value of between 10 and 30 million Euros. One of several the collector had bought over the years from Viktor Sokolov, a Russian art dealer specializing in finding rare works of art. But, when the collector heard about the unveiling of the same painting in Germany, he immediately contacted Sokolov and told him of his concern. Sokolov assured his American collector that he had nothing to worry about.

Yes, the Gauguin had once been stolen but later found and returned to its original owner in London. However, the owner, happy to have *Fruits on the Table* back on his walls, now wanted to sell it so that he might expand his collection and asked Sokolov if he could find a buyer. Which the Russian was happy to do.

As for the Gauguin about to be unveiled in Munich, Sokolov assured his client the museum had no doubt purchased a fake and was probably none the wiser—and if they were—they weren't about to say anything.

Whether the Gerhardt Galerie was involved in shady dealings, the FBI had no proof and, along with Interpol, had agreed to investigate any possible connections Hans or his sister Erika might have a link to organized crime. My job was to go to Munich, attend the unveiling, introduce myself to Hans and Erika as a reporter working for *Journey International,* and snoop around. Since I had no connections to the art world and was a new face for the Germans, everyone agreed I was a good fit for the assignment.

What I *wasn't* supposed to do, at least as far as the Germans were concerned, was to physically interfere with Interpol's investigation of Viktor Sokolov, of which I had no problem—thugs are not my thing. And secondly, and even more important, I was not to publicly expose what the FBI and those in the art world suspected was Gerhardt's Hoard, a hidden cache of masterpieces lost during the 2nd World War that Hans and his sister were suspected of

CHAPTER ONE

hiding and using to finance their wealthy lifestyle. If that sounded odd, Sophie suggested I consider Gerhardt's Hoard from the German's point of view. The war had ended better than fifty years ago, and any rumblings, much less proof of Gerhardt's Hoard today, would be an uncomfortable reminder of the German atrocities—a situation the Germans were anxious to avoid.

As Sophie put it, while the Germans were *'perhaps aware'* of Gerhardt's Hoard—and others like it—they were only interested in unpaid taxes on the sale of art either directly or indirectly through the museum or a third party like Viktor Sokolov. According to German law, while it wasn't illegal to own or sell stolen art, it was illegal not to pay taxes on the sale of such works.

Gerhardt's Hoard, Sophie explained, was the result of Otto Gerhardt—Hans and Erika's uncle—who had worked with the Nazis during the war to pull off the world's largest art heist. Gerhardt had helped the Nazis to steal thousands of masterpieces from some of Europe's most prestigious museums and the homes of wealthy Jews. At the war's end, Gerhardt was suspected of smuggling a sizable portion of what had been selected for the Fuhrer's museum for his private collection. While Gerhardt was never charged with any crimes, suspicion remained that Otto Gerhardt had helped the Nazis while successfully siphoning off many valuable works for himself.

Of course, Otto Gerhardt denied the existence of any such hoard and, up until he died in a car accident in 1956, claimed, other than a few family heirlooms that he had managed to salvage from his family's home in Dresden, that everything he had been forced to steal during the war had been destroyed by the allied bombings.

Hans and Erika, born after the war, maintained that the rumors of their uncle's hidden treasures were just that—rumors. And the German government, if they knew otherwise, wasn't talking. All I needed to do, was to get eyes on any possible secret cache and take a few pictures—proof the treasure existed.

I asked the obvious question. "And if I find Gerhardt's Hoard, what hope does the world have we'll ever see any of what was stolen?"

"The war ended fifty-five years ago, Kat. Times have changed. The cold war is over, the wall is down, and Germany's an ally today. Before that, the Germans were our enemies, responsible for the murder of six million Jews. People weren't thinking about art at the end of World War II. They were caught up in the atrocities of the war and the Nuremberg Trials. But we do have some hope." Sophie pulled a file from beneath her desk. "Here, you need to read this. Time is running out for survivors who might claim what was stolen from them."

I opened the report and thumbed through it. The first few pages were pictures of the outside of the Gerhardt Galerie, a neoclassical building in the center of Munich's Marienplatz, a photocopy of the Gauguin in question, and several pictures of Hans von Hausmann and his sister, Erika Schönburg. The family resemblance was strong—classically European with chiseled features, high foreheads, and square jaws. A masculine look that favored the brother while giving the sister a very hardened look.

"He's nice looking, Kat, and from what I understand, he has his uncle's charm and can be very charismatic. But you need to be forewarned. He could be dangerous. He's covering up one of the largest art heists in history, and we're not sure what he's capable of, but as long as you stick to the script and maintain your cover as a travel reporter, we don't anticipate any trouble. But you will need to be careful."

"And the sister?"

"Cold as she looks. But the good news is that Germany agreed to the Washington Principals on Nazi-Confiscated Art ten months ago. It's brand new this year, dated January 1999. Look at the back of the report. You'll find it there."

I flipped to the back of the report and skimmed the pages in front of me.

"Forty-four countries, including Germany, have agreed to eleven principles concerning the repatriation of stolen art. In theory, each country has recognized that art stolen by the Nazis should be identified and the records and archives opened. And whenever possible, any heirs notified."

"In theory?" I asked.

"Unfortunately, the agreement is up for interpretation. Leaving it up to each country to determine how to act within the definition of that country's

CHAPTER ONE

law."

"Which means they can return whatever they like or not at all."

"It's the best we have. Until now, very few masterpieces were thought to have survived the war. Popular opinion was that most were tragically lost or burned in the bombings. But the art community suspected differently. From time to time, word would circulate among collectors that a long-lost canvas had resurfaced and could be quietly purchased for the right price. The Germans have been slow to identify such hidden treasures. Their existence reminds the world of what happened to many innocent Jews whose collections were raided. And the longer these hoards have remained hidden, the more difficult it is for Germans to come clean. But now we have an opportunity. Find Gerhardt's Hidden Hoard, Kat, and we can force their hand."

Chapter Two

The Galerie's unveiling for the press and VIPs was scheduled for Thursday, December 2, at ten a.m. Sophie had booked an early morning flight for me out of Los Angeles for Tuesday, November 30. Which should have given me plenty of time to rest and adjust to the time change, but weather and mechanical problems delayed my flight. By the time I arrived at my hotel in Munich, it was the middle of the night or early Thursday morning. I set my phone alarm, called for a wake-up call, slept through both, and when I heard the sound of breakfast carts in the hallway woke with a start. Blurry-eyed, I checked the bedside clock. It registered nine-thirty-five. Panicked that I would miss my first assignment, I threw on a pair of black wool slacks and a sweater, brushed my hair from my eyes, grabbed my coat, hat, and backpack, and was outside the Hotel Schlicker within fifteen minutes. Not exactly a great way to start a new job.

Outside, it was still dark. The streets were wet and slushy with snow. Sophie had provided me with a guide map of the Marienplatz, marking the highlights and location of the Gerhardt Galerie, a brisk fifteen-minute walk from the hotel. With a little effort, I arrived just past ten, or in time to push past a protester who shoved a sign in my face with a picture of Gauguin's *Fruits on the Table* and hollered something in German. I ducked to avoid unnecessary contact and rushed through the museum's front door. Inside, I grabbed a headset and pamphlet, about the Gauguin, off the front counter. Then hurriedly signed the guest register and rushed down a long hallway packed with reporters and photographers until I came to the exhibition's center hall. I was just in time to catch Herr Hausmann as he posed next

CHAPTER TWO

to the museum's latest acquisition. I snapped a quick picture. Hausmann looked like a middle-aged college professor. His dark hair was mussed and greying, as though he had paid little attention to it or the clothes he wore, a loose-fitting jacket, and slacks, as he addressed those in front of him, looking over a pair of thin, round John Lennon-like specs.

I squeezed, best as I could, into the back of the room until I found space for myself next to a burly, heavyset man who reeked of onions and pickled herring. He was wearing a leather and lambskin winter coat and looked like he had just hiked in from the Russian front. I gave him as much space as possible, adjusted my headset, and glanced at the pamphlet. All of it in German.

Sophie had promised me my lack of German wouldn't be a problem. Most Germans, or those I was expected to interact with anyway, spoke English as well as they did their native tongue. But, if the pamphlet was any sign, I wasn't off to a good start. Still, I hoped I could corner Hausmann over drinks at the museum's soiree immediately following the formal presentation. But Hausmann's assistant, who looked like she was barely out of her teens, fielded him like a security guard. After a few quick introductions, of which I was not one, she announced Herr Hausmann was needed on an international call and rushed him away.

My frustration hadn't gone unnoticed. A tall, blonde, very Germanic-looking woman who could have been the poster girl for Pilsner Beer approached. Despite her heavy German accent, her English was impeccable.

"You must be new here. Hi, my name's Kirsten Muller." She offered me her hand and smiled. "I'm with *The Munchen Zeitung*. And you?"

"Kat Lawson. *Journey International*."

"You're American?"

"Is it that obvious?"

"Let's just say you looked lost. And from the way Herr Hausmann's assistant Inga brushed you off, I figured you weren't German." Kirsten reached inside her expensive-looking leather handbag and handed me her business card. "Here, if I can help, give me a call. Anything at all."

Journalists are a competitive lot. And I've learned to be wary. When

I started working as a newspaper reporter in Phoenix, I was assigned to cover a press conference for ASU's new incoming president. The briefing was scheduled to occur inside one of the university's new dorms, and I had gotten lost. Fortunately, I spotted a television reporter who directed me to another dorm across campus, which ended up being in the wrong location. She got the story, and I got a lecture from my editor about trust and favors in the business. There weren't any. Competitors were just that—competitors. Information and leads were proprietary information; no matter how trustworthy I thought the source, everything needed to be checked and verified. Kirsten, however, was working for the local paper. We were hardly competitors, and I figured I could use a friend who knew the city. I put her card in my pocket and planned to call her later.

* * *

"What do you mean you didn't meet with Herr Hausmann?" I held the phone away from my ear. Even four-thousand miles away, Sophie sounded like she was standing right next to me. "Didn't I give you a ticket and a cash advance to ensure you didn't have a problem?"

"Yes, but—"

"Excuse me." Sophie snapped, then paused. The silence was hot in my ears. I felt like a kid in school whose teacher had just slapped her desk with a ruler. She had my attention. "I'm still talking. You'd be wise to wait until you've heard what I have to say. Unless, of course, you don't want this job." I bit my lip. I needed this job. I wasn't about to get another job with a newspaper back home, and with the bills piling up, I didn't have a lot of options. Plus, I wanted to get back to Europe. "We're not playing games here, Kat. If you're not up to the job, you need to tell me now. I can't waste time on someone who's not committed."

Silently, I counted to three. I wanted to make sure Sophie had finished with her tirade.

"Don't worry, I'll fix it." I didn't imagine it would be all that difficult to return to the museum and talk my way into a private introduction. But

CHAPTER TWO

it wasn't *just* an introduction Sophie wanted; in her mind, I had wasted valuable time and lost an opportunity.

We both knew Sophie had hired me not so much for my talents as a journalist but partly because when it came to creating a believable backstory—should anybody ask—it would be easy. I had worked for ten years as an investigative reporter. And considering I was out of work and looking for a job, accepting a position with *Journey International* would appear to be a logical next step. Unemployed journalist accepts assignment with international travel pub for a chance to see the world. Sounded believable. At least, that's what we hoped.

But what Sophie really wanted was someone who had been around the block a time or two. Someone who wasn't a kid. A forty-something, middle-aged reporter who would be as good with women as she would be with a man and didn't harbor some romantic notion about love or some handsome European suitor.

In short, I was perfect. I had a good track record as an investigative reporter. I was widowed and divorced, happily single, and planned to remain so. My first husband, an Air Force pilot, had died in the Vietnam War, and my second had gone through my money like his own. I was intelligent enough to carry on a conversation with Erika and bait enough for Herr Hausmann, a man with a reputation for collecting fine art and tall, slim brunettes. Notably, women who had no problem being arm candy to one of the world's foremost art historians. Sophie didn't need to spell out how she hoped I would connect with either Erika or Hans. How I did that or chose to conduct myself was entirely up to me.

"Call me when you've met him. And do it fast. We're on a tight schedule here, Kat. Herr Hausmann is due for a conference in Bern, Switzerland, at the end of the month. We need you on the inside to know what's going on." Sophie hung up abruptly. If I had expected any handholding, it wasn't going to happen. What the woman lacked in warmth, she made up for in cold, calculating plans.

I didn't appreciate Sophie's attitude, but I was confident I could handle rescheduling a meeting with Hans. But first, I had a few plans of my own, and I saw no reason not to mix a little pleasure with business. After all, I had come six-thousand miles to do just that.

Chapter Three

I hadn't seen Sandor since I'd left Hungary, where I had gone at my father's request to find his downed B-24 a year and a half ago. Since then, Sandor, his wife, Aanika, and I maintained a long-distance relationship via mail and occasional phone calls. When I accepted the job with *Journey International*, I told Sandor and Aanika I'd be in Munich in December, and they suggested we meet. Sandor thought the timing would be perfect. His tour-for-hire business had slowed with the advent of winter, and Sandor was filling his time driving a long-haul truck for Aanika's uncle. We coordinated our schedules and made plans to meet in Munich on Friday, December 3, at eleven a.m., by the Fischbrunner, a 14th-century water fountain and popular meetup place for locals in the middle of Marienplatz.

But, when I woke the following morning, the temperatures had dropped, and the view from my hotel window was of a city blanketed in snow. White powder dusted the rooftops of the old town's neo-gothic buildings and the twin onion domes of the Frauenkirche.

I grabbed my heavy coat, not nearly warm enough for the near-freezing German temperatures, and braved my walk to Marienplatz, passing locals bundled in their puffy jackets with scarves and hats, their cheeks rosy from the cold.

A crowd had gathered in front of the Neues Rathaus, Munich's city hall, and I stopped as the Glockenspiel began to chime and looked up at the giant bell tower. It was just now eleven a.m., and from beneath the face of the big clock, a two-tiered balcony with colorful life-size figures began to move. Knights and jesters from a once royal court spun and danced in a circular motion, reenacting a scene from a wedding and a jousting match. When the bells completed their clarion chime and the figures stopped their dance, I waited while a golden bird emerged and chirped three times, announcing the eleven o'clock hour, then hurried over to the fountain where I planned to meet Sandor.

The fountain was covered with icicles, and Sandor was nowhere in sight. I danced a chilly two-step in the snow with my arms about myself, shivering, while I waited and hoped Sandor wouldn't be long.

"Kat! You're here." Sandor's voice echoed from across the Marienplatz. I turned to see him, his arms open wide. He ran to me and, pulling me off my feet, bear-hugged me. His round bearded face was cold and scratchy against my own. "Come, I have a table for us." Sandor tilted his head in the direction of a café. "Aanika's waiting. We have a surprise for you."

The warmth of the small café with its delicious-looking treats, each one like a work of art, and the smell of hot coffee was a welcome relief from the bitter cold. The tables were nestled close together, and Aanika struggled to stand as we approached. With her dark hair pulled in a ponytail, I noticed her face, like Sandor's, was fuller than when we last met. We embraced with one hand around my neck and the other beneath her very pregnant belly.

"Oh, my God, Kat, you're freezing." Aanika touched my face, so numb I could barely feel her fingers against my skin.

"And you're—" I stepped back and stared at Aanika's bulging stomach. "Pregnant!" She looked to be at least six months along.

"We both are." Sandor stood next to his wife and patted his stomach, which like his wife's, was bigger than when we last saw each other.

"We're as surprised as you are." Aanika touched her husband's arm. "It's why I wanted to come with Sandor. I had to be here when he told you."

Sandor signaled the waiter while Aanika and I sat down. "How about some peppermint schnapps to warm you up, Kat? We have much to celebrate."

When the waiter returned with three small schnapps glasses, Sandor took his and his wife's and downed them quickly while I let the sweet, hot taste of peppermint slowly coat my throat and welcomed the warmth that followed.

Aanika finished the last of her tea and put her cup down. "So, Kat, tell us

CHAPTER THREE

about this new job. What is it you're working on?"

I unbuttoned my coat and put my hat in my lap. The schnapps was already starting to warm me. "I'll be happy to tell, but you go first. It looks like you two have been working on something longer than I have. I had no idea. When's the baby due?"

"February." Aanika winked at Sandor. "And—"

"And we want you to be the godmother." Sandor smiled as though this was a done deal.

"Me?" I was as shocked by the request as I was to learn they were expecting.

"Yes, you. We've discussed it and can't think of anyone we'd rather have. And if this new job of yours gets you back to Europe more often, then maybe there's a chance you might be around for the birth." Sandor gestured with an open hand. "What do you say?"

Aanika interrupted. "Kat. I won't have this baby unless you promise to be her godmother."

I burst out laughing. "Her?"

"We don't know, but I think it's a girl. Call it a mother's intuition, but I'm dreaming in pink these days."

"And, if it's a boy—" Sandor nodded to his wife, "we'll love him just as much. But whatever it is, we want you to be part of his or her life."

I templed my fingers in front of my face. I had never given much thought to children. The timing and opportunity had never presented itself, but with Sandor and Aanika, how could I say no?

"I don't know anything about parenting and never thought about being a godparent. But, yes, I'd love to. And if there's any way I can be back here next February, I will."

"Good, then that's settled." Sandor took three menus from the center of the table and handed one to Aanika and another to me. "I think it's time we ordered. Aanika was hungry when we walked in here, and if I don't feed her, she'll likely eat me."

Aanika slapped Sandor with the back of the menu. "I'm not that bad. But I am happy to see you, Kat. So your turn now. What's this new job all about?"

I explained what I could about my job with *Journey International*, leaving out any possible connection to Gerhardt's Hoard, Hans von Hausmann, or his sister Erika Schonburg. "It's a temporary gig until I can find a job with a newspaper back home. But for now, it gets me back to Europe and gives me a chance to travel. I'm here on assignment. The magazine wants me to cover some of Munich's highlights and do a holiday feature on Germany."

"Then you'll be visiting the Kriskindlemart in Nuremberg. It's the oldest Christmas market anywhere. Sandor has business in the city, and we're going to shop for the baby. Maybe you can join us." Aanika looked hopeful.

"I'd love to, but I've some things to do here in Munich first, and by the time I'm done, I'm sure you'll be well on your way home. But—"

"When you finish, you'll come to Budapest for Christmas. I won't hear of anything else."

"That's my plan." At least, that was what I was hoping to do."

We enjoyed a leisurely lunch, reminiscing like old friends over leberkassemmel—meat sandwiches on a roll—with a side of kartoffelsalat, a potato salad served warm with an apple cider dressing when Sandor looked at his watch. It was almost three o'clock. Sandor said they needed to go. He was expected in Nuremberg by five p.m. to meet with a wealthy German businessman who had offered them his home for several days, giving Sandor and Aanika time to visit the Kriskindlemart before transporting the man's Maserati to Budapest in the back of Sandor's big rig.

I said goodbye to Sandor and Aanika and ordered a cup of hot chocolate to-go. The afternoon temperatures had risen, and it wasn't nearly as cold as earlier. Perfect timing for a late afternoon stroll around the Marienplatz.

I started with window shopping, taking note of the well-dressed windows with their Christmas wreaths and decorations. Then careful to balance my hot chocolate on a windowsill, I stopped and took my camera from inside my backpack so that I might take a few pictures of one of the window's holiday scenes. I was just about to snap the shot when I spotted the reflection of a man in the window who looked a lot like the photo I had seen of Herr Hausmann. I turned to get a better look. Wet footprints in the snow indicated the man had come from inside the Gerhardt Galerie, directly across the Marienplatz, and was headed for a bookstore. I put my camera away and picked up my

CHAPTER THREE

cup.

"Herr Hausmann?"

I hurried to catch up, but his ability to negotiate the wet, slippery cobblestones was much better than my own, and I fell behind. Even bundled in his hat and winter coat, I could tell this had to be Herr Hausmann—tall, broad-shouldered, and judging from the pace and intensity, he was on a mission. I watched as he stomped his feet to clear his boots of the wet snow, then disappeared behind the bookstore's door.

I followed, and moments later, as I opened the door, the sound of cowbells, a popular Bavarian door adornment, announced my entrance.

"Grüss Gott." An efficient clerk behind the counter nodded to me as I entered. Standing at the counter in front of her was Herr Hausmann.

I smiled and shut the door behind me. Then heard Hausmann ask the clerk something in German. She pointed to a section of books and said more of what I didn't understand. Not wanting to attract attention, I busied myself and pretended to be looking for something on the magazine rack. Hausmann went directly to the book section, where the clerk had pointed and selected a book. Whatever his mission, he wasn't browsing, and returned to the counter, prepared to pay.

I made my move. "Excuse me, Herr Hausmann?"

Hausmann put the book down and looked at me. He towered over me by at least six inches. I could see in his eyes his quick calculation as he switched from German to English. "Do I know you?"

"Yes...I, I mean, no. We haven't been introduced. My name is Kat Lawson. I work for *Journey International*. I was at the museum yesterday for your press conference." I rested my hot chocolate on the counter, and maybe because I was nervous or clumsy, as I extended my hand, I bumped the cup and knocked the drink onto the book.

"Oh, I am so sorry." I reached into my backpack for a tissue or something I might use, but I only worsened the matter as I bumped the cup a second time and knocked what chocolate remained onto the floor.

The clerk grabbed a rag from behind the counter and managed to sop up the spill. But the damage was done.

"It's quite alright." Hausmann picked up the book, said something in German to the clerk, then turned to me. "Where are you from, Miss Lawson?"

"The United States," I said.

"No, I mean, what part?"

"Arizona."

"Cowboys and Indians. Cochise and Geronimo." Hausmann smiled broadly, his cheeks dimpled like he knew he had surprised me and enjoyed doing so.

"Yes. But that was quite a long time ago."

"Are you familiar with the author Karl May? He wrote this book, *Winnetou*." Hausmann opened the slightly soiled book and pointed to a picture of the author on the inside back flap. "Every German child grew up knowing the adventures of Winnetou and Old Shatterhand. It's the story about a young German immigrant who arrives in your wild west."

I stared at the picture. "I'm sorry, I've never heard of him."

"Well then, perhaps you will now. This copy's in English. I picked it up for my nephew, who's struggling to learn. Consider it a gift."

"Please," I reached into my backpack for my wallet, "you shouldn't. It was my fault."

"It's my pleasure." Hausmann held his hands up and said something to the clerk in German. She nodded officiously, left us, and returned with a copy of the same book. This time, taking no chances, she put it directly into a shopping bag and handed it to Hausmann. "So, Miss Lawson, now that you know my story, what can I do for you?"

I explained my situation. How my plane had arrived late, and I had missed much of his lecture on the new Gauguin. "I was hoping I might be able to—"

"See it?"

"Why, yes. And perhaps get an interview, too?"

"On one condition."

"Which is?" My stomach tightened. Hans von Hausmann was as charming as I feared he might be.

"You agree to have dinner with me tonight."

The clerk presented the bill. Herr Hausmann paid with a credit card, and

CHAPTER THREE

as he scribbled his signature, I caught a quick look from the corner of his eye, followed by a smug grin. He didn't look up, but I sensed he had found our accidental encounter entertaining.

"Why not? It'll be a pleasure." Getting to know Herr Hausmann would be easier than I thought it would be. And judging from the look in his eye, this wasn't going to be all work on his part either. "You can fill me in on the museum and Karl May, and I can tell you all about our cowboys and Indians."

"Wunderbar." Herr Hausmann offered me his hand, and this time I took it without knocking over anything. "Meet me at the museum at six o'clock. We close early on Friday, and I'll give you a private tour. Afterward, I'll take you to The Augustiner am Dom for an authentic German meal. Have you been there?"

"No," I said.

"Gut. It's a short walk from the museum. I think you'll like it. Until then, Miss Lawson, auf wiedersehen."

Chapter Four

"Kirsten? Hi. It's Kat Lawson. We met at the museum?" I paused to give her a second to remember me, then continued. "It's last minute, but could you meet for coffee?"

After saying goodbye to Herr Hausmann at the bookstore, I was anxious to learn more about the curator and his museum, and I wanted to take advantage of Kirsten's offer to call. I was hoping she could provide me with a little more inside information about the museum, things a local might know that Sophie may have missed about Hausmann's habits and interests.

"Not a problem." Kirsten sounded friendly. "I'm just finishing up the museum story from yesterday now."

"Great. I'm staying at the Hotel Schlicker. There's a nice little coffee bar downstairs. It's a two-minute walk from the Marienplatz, on—"

"I know exactly where it is. I'll meet you in the lobby in an hour."

I was surprised when I arrived at the hotel's lobby to find that Kirsten wasn't alone. She was accompanied by a tall, somewhat gawky-looking man about her age, mid to late thirties, with dark hair, thick glasses, and a heavy coat. Her arm was linked through his.

"Kat, this is Peter Bergman. He's our new editor, in from Berlin." We shook hands, as is the way in Europe, and Peter started to introduce himself, but not before Kirsten added, "He's not staying. He's off to do some shopping. We're going to get together later, but I thought the two of you might like to meet. You know, being journalists and all."

Peter apologized for his abrupt departure and kissed Kirsten goodbye on the cheek. "Tschau."

CHAPTER FOUR

"I hope I wasn't interrupting your plans," I said.

"Peter?" Kirsten shrugged. "No. He's just a work friend. I tease him and call him my Lebensabschnittpartner."

"Your leben-what?"

"My Lebensabschnittpartner." Kirsten laughed. She was having fun at my expense. "It's slang for the person you're with today. You know how it is, nothing serious, just for kicks. But he's not bad between the sheets." Kirsten put her arm around me and led me to a small table. "So, what is it I can help you with?"

I nodded to the waiter, ordered two coffees, and then pulled my notepad from my backpack. Once our coffees arrived, steaming hot in clear glass cups, Kirsten took a small silver flask from inside her coat and dowsed her coffee.

"Schnaps," she asked. "Like some? Keeps you warm." I shook my head. "So, what can I do for you?"

"I have a few questions about the museum and Herr Hausmann. Things I'll need for my article, and—"

"Ahh, that's easy," Kirsten waved her hand dismissively. "There's not much I don't know about them or the museum. Hans and his sister Erika gave me my start. In a sense, I suppose I owe them."

"How's that?"

"Fate, I suppose." Kirsten took a sip of coffee and smacked her lips. "I had just started working on the paper when the museum opened. That was three years ago now. The paper's society editor, Agnus Seidel...she was a real bitch, cranky and opinionated. Nobody on staff much cared for her, but the paper's editor? He loved her, and I guess the readers did too. She was supposed to cover the museum's opening, but she had a stroke the night before, and the editor had no one to send but me, a rookie reporter. When I showed up, Hans and his sister were worried I didn't know what I was doing. Can't blame them. I didn't know anything about art. They basically wrote the entire column for me."

I tapped the end of my pencil against my pad. Not exactly how a reporter should cover a story, but I could understand why a rookie on one of her first assignments would have been relieved for the help and indebted to her rescuers.

"Hans and Erika saved my ass, and the editor loved it. The story launched my career, and they've been great to work with ever since."

"And the editor, he's still happy with you?"

"Oh, he's gone." Kirsten waved her hand like she was swatting a fly. "Retired, and I can't say I'm sorry to see him go. He had a heavy hand when it came to editing. He sent back as much as I ever turned in. A real pain. Know what I mean?" I nodded and took a sip of my coffee. Nearly every journalist I knew had a love/hate relationship with their editor. "But now that Peter's here, things are different. I don't worry about it anymore. Peter rewrites most everybody anyway, and he doesn't care what I write as long as I make my deadlines. And what Peter doesn't know won't hurt him. I'm always looking to pick up freelance work whenever I can. You know how money is for reporters. There's never enough. In fact, I was thinking, maybe we can help each other?"

I put my cup down.

"I don't see why not." From what I had just heard, Kirsten was quietly on the museum's payroll, and I planned to use whatever connections she had to my benefit. "I'll be happy to pass your business card to my editor."

"I knew I liked you." Kirsten put her hands up and wiggled her anxious fingers, a sure sign she thought she had struck a deal. "So, what do you need to know? How can I help?"

"Maybe you can give me a little background on the museum. The name, for instance. The Gerhardt Galerie? It's a little odd, isn't it?"

"Why?" Kirsten wrinkled her rose. "Because of all the rumors about Otto Gerhardt and his hoard?"

"I have heard a few—"

"Please, do you really think Otto Gerhardt was the only one to stash stolen artwork? There was a war, Kat. Things happened, and now there're rumors about people hiding stolen masterpieces all over Europe. Besides, if any of it were true, in my opinion, Otto Gerhardt saved a lot of art the Nazis would have destroyed. The man was as much a victim of the war as many people.

CHAPTER FOUR

The Nazis took his job. He was just trying to survive, and any art he tried to rescue was destroyed in all the bombings. Hans and Erika got nothing from their uncle, and most of the family's private collection was lost. Gerhardt's Hoard is nothing more than a rumor."

I wondered if I was listening to a pre-rehearsed script written like the story Kirsten had submitted to the paper for the Galerie's opening by the museum's curators themselves.

"Good to know. Just a rumor, then." I put my coffee down and picked up my pen. "And the museum? Anything special you can tell me about it?"

"Hans didn't think it would make it at first. The Galerie's small. More of a boutique, but their piece de resistance was the Matisse. *The Seated Woman*. It's what put them on the map. According to Hans, the world thought the painting had been lost at the end of the war. Then one day, about a month before the museum was scheduled to open, Hans says this Russian named Viktor Sokolov approached him. He told Hans he had a Matisse he was trying to sell and wanted to find somewhere he might show it until he was able to secure a buyer, and—"

"A Matisse?" If there had been a Matisse on the museum's walls, I wanted to think I might have noticed. Before leaving for Germany, Sophie had suggested I study the works of various artists, like Gustav Klimt, Raphael, Van Gogh, and Courbet, whose works were believed to have been stolen or destroyed during the war. One of my favorites was Matisse. I loved his colors and modern, post-impressionist designs. "I must have missed it."

"Actually, that's the problem. The painting's not there, at least not anymore, and Viktor wasn't supposed to be there either. I don't know how he got in. But I know Hans and Erika had a falling out with him, and they weren't expecting him at the unveiling. Inga, Hans' assistant, the young blonde you saw ushering him around, is close to Viktor and probably had something to do with him being there. Whatever, I stay clear of him."

I stirred my coffee. "What about the protestor out in front of the museum? He looked like he could stir up trouble."

"That guy? He's just some crazy. Nobody to worry about." Kirsten took a sip of her coffee. She was either avoiding the subject entirely or knew nothing about why the protestor was carrying a sign with a picture of the Gauguin. "So, what else are you going to write about in Munich? Anything I can help with?"

"I don't know, you tell me. The Nymphenburg Castle. Octoberfest. Do you have other suggestions?"

"This time of year? There's always a cooking class somewhere. Or Christkindlmarkt in Marienplatz. Not quite like the original in Nuremberg, but there are more than a hundred stands. Lots of gift ideas, lights, and Christmas ornaments. And tonight, you might want to take a walking tour. There's a torchlight tour with a guide who tells ghost stories. I could put you in touch if you like."

"Can't tonight. I'm busy. I'm going back to the museum."

Kirsten looked surprised. "You know the museum's not open."

"I do, but I ran into Herr Hausmann at a bookstore in the Marienplatz this afternoon. He invited me back to see the Gauguin."

The waiter returned and refreshed our coffee.

"Did he?" Kirsten added another splash of schnapps to her drink and left the flask on the table.

"It's one of the reasons I wanted to talk with you."

Kirsten picked up her cup and cradled it in her hands. "I like you, Kat, and I think I should warn you Herr Hausmann has a reputation. You should be careful. He likes beautiful women as much as he does his art. He collects them."

"Yes, I have heard that."

Chapter Five

It was dark when I left the hotel to meet with Herr Hausmann at the museum. I had changed my clothes—not that it mattered—most of what I had packed looked the same. Dark slacks, long-sleeved t-shirts, sweaters, scarves, and a black trench coat. Plus, a pair of flat black equestrian boots I hadn't worn since my riding days. I figured paired with thick socks, they might hold up against the cold. But what did I know? Coming from the Arizona desert, I didn't own anything close to cold-weather gear. I gave myself one final check in the mirror, added a touch of lip gloss, finger-combed my hair, and added a red scarf. Something a little festive and in keeping with the holiday spirit. Satisfied Herr Hausmann would like what he saw, I traded out my backpack for a thin black tote, transferred my phone, wallet, and reporter's pad into it, then grabbed my gloves and was out the door by six o'clock.

I walked the two blocks to the Marienplatz with my arms about myself, trying to fend off the chill, past the Fischbrunnen Fountain, where I had met Sandor that morning, and up the steps to The Gerhardt Galerie. I was freezing and did a little two-step as I knocked on the doors and waited. The doors, wood with etched glass insets, were locked, but inside I could see a yellow light as it spilled out onto the hallway's wooden floor from a small office behind the reception counter. Moments later, Herr Hausmann appeared in the central corridor.

Whether it was the cold or Herr Hausmann's eyes fixed on my own, a chill ran down my spine as he unlocked the door. I braced myself and smiled. Funny how excitement and fear can trigger similar reactions.

"Miss Lawson, please, come in." Hans opened the door and motioned for me to enter.

I stomped my feet to clear the snow from my boots, then stepped inside.

"Thank you. I appreciate you taking the time to see me, Herr Hausmann—"

"Please." Hans took my gloved hands in his own. So close I could smell his cologne. "Call me Hans. And may I call you Kat?"

"Why not?" I glanced down the long hall toward the exhibition room. The only lights inside the Galerie were the floor's dim running lights and the spill of yellow light from the office.

"Very good then. Shall we?" Hans led the way toward the exhibition room. His heavy footfalls echoed on the wooden floors, reminding me how alone we were in the museum. "By the way, I forgot to ask, is this your first trip to Germany?"

"It is. I'm here to cover the holidays. Plus, a few of Munich's highlights. Castles. Restaurants. That kind of thing."

"And the Galerie, of course."

"Absolutely."

"May I ask how long you've been with the magazine?"

"Not long. Germany's my first assignment."

"I'm sorry, you'll have to forgive me. I'm not familiar with your publication. *Journey International?* Is it new?"

Was it curiosity or suspicion I heard in his voice? I couldn't be sure and countered lightly.

"It's not new, but you wouldn't be the first not to know the name. There's a lot of competition with travel pubs these days. They all look alike if you ask me. I suppose that's why they hired me…fresh eyes and all." I glanced at the hallway's walls covered with art, a Monet, a Degas, and a small Renoir. "But I'm not here to talk about myself. I'm here to interview you."

"Humph." Hans stopped when we reached the exhibition hall and gazed at me over the top of his wireframes. "I doubt I'm all that interesting."

My mouth went dry, and I stumbled my reply. "M-m-my editor might disagree. She refers to you as the celebrity curator. She's in awe of you and insisted I get this interview." I laid it on thick. I couldn't risk Hans thinking

CHAPTER FIVE

I was here for anything more than a must-do interview to please my new editor.

"I hope you don't believe everything you hear. Aside from the charity galas I'm required to attend, I'm a hermit by nature and spend most of my time cloistered behind these walls or in my studio." Hans took another few steps into the exhibition room, then stopped and gestured to the Gauguin. The painting had been placed on an easel beneath a soft white light. "But here we are, *Fruits on a Table with a Small Dog*. This is what you came to see. Yes?"

"It's stunning." I stared at the painting. Beneath the soft white light, it glowed, giving the impression it was a much larger work of art than its actual size, barely two feet wide and less than eighteen inches high.

"It's one of Gauguin's earlier pieces. He painted it before he began studying with Pissarro. Gauguin had just left his job as a stockbroker in Paris and was determined to make it as an artist. I believe the painting shows his natural technique." Hans pointed to the plate on the table. "He used wax to smooth the paint, and you'll notice the darker outline of the objects. It seems to almost lift them off the canvas."

"I thought I heard that painting had disappeared." It was a question I wanted to ask, a chance to judge Hans' response and make a note of his reaction. A subject Sophie and I would discuss later when I reported in.

"Ahh." Hans clapped his hands. "So, you do know something of the art world."

I shrugged.

"Not really. The magazine hired me because I could write and wanted to travel. Not because I'm any kind of art historian. Far from it, in fact."

Hans paused as though he were digesting what I had said, then continued. "If the paintings in this room could talk, their stories would be as interesting as that of the artist who created them. But you're correct, Kat, the painting in front of you did disappear. It was stolen. Taken from a private collection in London almost thirty years ago and later recovered. My sister, Erika, was lucky enough to arrange for us to buy it. Beyond that, there's not much more you need to know. Come, it's getting late. I'll explain more over dinner."

I was anxious to hear more of Hans' story about the Gauguin, and followed him back to his office, a small room behind the reception desk. I waited inside the door while he went to his desk to get his wallet. Then suddenly, he slammed the desk drawer shut.

"What's wrong?" I looked over my shoulder to the open door and out into the hallway.

"Did you hear that?" The startled look on his face told me something unexpected had happened.

"What?" I asked. I hadn't heard anything.

Hans put his index finger to his lips. Then quietly went to the office door, pulled me behind him, and closed it tight, locking us into the office. "We're not alone," he whispered. "Someone's broken in."

I crouched back against the wall, my heart pounding. If someone had broken into the museum, why wasn't an alarm or security lights going off?

Hans pointed to a monitor on the wall. On the screen, the camera was focused on the exhibition hall. We watched as a man wearing a hat, heavy overcoat, and gloves walked directly into the room as though he knew exactly where he was going and what he wanted. In a few quick moves, he removed the Gauguin from the easel, wrapped the painting in a cloth he had taken from inside his coat, then put both beneath his arm and slowly walked out of frame. Seconds later, we could hear the back door slam shut.

I gripped the back of Hans' arm. I could feel him tense and worried he might try to do something crazy. I wasn't sure if Hans had a gun hidden in the office and might try to follow the man or call the police. But he did neither. Instead, Hans let out a laugh, then opened the office door.

"Are you okay?" I followed him out into the hallway. From here, we could see the empty easel in the exhibition room.

"I'm fine." He snapped.

He didn't sound fine.

"Shouldn't we call the police?"

"No. We should go to dinner. I'll explain later."

Chapter Six

Whether it was the cold or the fright of the burglary, I didn't know. But, as Hans and I stood outside the museum and I waited for him to lock the front door, I couldn't stop shaking. Even my teeth were chattering.

"You're freezing." Hans looked at me as he put the key in his pocket.

I nodded, my head like a bobblehead doll, and hugged myself to keep warm.

Hans straightened the scarf about my neck, then ran his fingers around the collar. "What is this, cotton?"

"I'm from Arizona. What do you think?" It was the heaviest coat I owned but not near warm enough for Munich's freezing temperatures.

"No wonder you're cold. Come, I can fix that. I have an apartment around the corner. My sister stays there when she's in town. She's about your size. You can borrow one of her coats."

"But, w…w…what about the burglary? The painting? Shouldn't we—"

"I told you, don't worry about it. I'll explain later."

I didn't like his answer, and I didn't like the idea of leaving a crime scene.

"No." I refused to budge and stepped back toward the door. My feet may have been frozen, but I wasn't going to take another step. "I'm not going anywhere, not until you tell me what's going on? Why don't you want to call the police?"

Hans grabbed my gloved hands and squeezed them between his own. "Look at me, Kat."

"What?" I looked at his eyes, then back at the museum. I wanted answers, and I wanted them now.

"The painting was a fake. Alright? I know it, and by now, the thief knows it too. The real Gauguin, the one you saw yesterday at the unveiling. It's locked in a vault beneath the museum. But if it makes you happy, we can stand here in the cold and argue about it while you freeze to death. Or, you can come back with me to my apartment where it's nice and warm, and I'll find you a warm coat. Then we can go to dinner, and I promise you, you can ask me anything you like. Deal?"

"Ugh!" It was too cold to argue. I weighed my options, frostbite versus maybe an arrest for leaving the scene of a crime. It didn't take a lot of consideration, not with Hans' confession that the painting was fake and my fingers so cold I couldn't feel the tips of them. "Deal," I said.

* * *

Hans' apartment was a two-bedroom, third-floor walk-up, a couple of blocks from the museum and about as barebones as it gets. Hardly the residence I would have expected for the founder of the Gerhardt Galerie. The furnishings were mismatched; a small brown sofa with two overstuffed chairs, a coffee table, end tables, and a couple of lamps. A five-piece vintage dining set occupied the dining room and looked like it might have been appropriated from a thrift store. In fact, everything in the apartment looked second-hand. The kitchen, not much bigger than a coat closet, included an under-the-counter refrigerator, a small stove top range, and a coffeemaker.

While Hans excused himself and disappeared into the bedroom to find one of his sister's coats—I snooped. Not that there was much to look through. No boxes or canvases were hidden in the closet or beneath the couch or the chairs. The walls were all painted a dull grey and bare, except for one wall on which a single fancy gold-framed painting hung.

I took my coat off, laid it on the back of one of the dining room chairs, and stepped closer to the painting. In the foreground, a drape had been pulled back to frame a scene, allowing the viewer to peek beyond the drape where the artist sat at an easel, painting a picture of a young woman holding

CHAPTER SIX

a book in front of a window. The delicate light from the window created an intimacy on the canvas, and I couldn't take my eyes off it.

"Is this real?" I hollered in the direction of the bedroom.

"The Vermeer?" Hans poked his head out the bedroom door. "Do you think I'd have an original Vermeer here and not in the museum?"

"Honestly? After the theft in the museum and what you told me about the Gauguin being a fake? No offense, but I don't know what to believe."

Hans shook his head and ducked back into the bedroom. No answer. With the coast clear, I crossed back into the living room, glanced down at the coffee table, shuffled through the newspapers and magazines, then stopped. A copy of *Journey International* had been stuffed between publications.

From the bedroom, I heard Hans. "Ahh, this should do."

I quickly put the stack back in the order I had found and replaced them on the table.

Hans returned from the bedroom with a coat in his hand. "Ready?"

"No. Not yet." I turned and walked to the window. I wasn't about to leave the apartment until I better understood what had happened at the museum. "I'm sorry, but I don't get it. Even if the Gauguin was a copy, why not call the police and report it? It was still a break-in."

Hans laid his sister's coat on the back of the couch. "I don't need a police report, Kat, not now. If word were to get out that the Gauguin had been stolen, and the media were to pick up the story, it would spoil the official unveiling and harm the museum's credibility. People might not show up, and those who did would wonder if they were looking at the real thing."

"What about me? You're not worried I'll report it?"

"Kat, no offense, but you work for a monthly travel pub. Whatever you write wouldn't see the light of day until after the unveiling. Trust me, the painting the thief stole was a nicely framed copy. You might say it was the museum's way of securing our collection."

"I don't get it. You have a museum full of masterpieces, and you don't have a twenty-four-hour guard?"

"Who do you think is going to steal a masterpiece? Another museum? Insurance companies pay pennies on the dollar, and thieves aren't about to negotiate with them. It's too risky. The real money is made on the black market. But if our burglar knew anything about art, he would have spotted it immediately."

"So, you know who stole it?"

Hans smirked. "Let's just say I'm not worried. And you shouldn't be either. The original Gauguin was there for the VIP viewing Thursday, and it will be again when we open for the official public viewing on Sunday."

"So what I saw was a fake."

"What you saw Thursday was the original. I doubt you could have seen a difference, and what you wanted tonight was an interview. Which I'm happy to give."

I swept the drapes back from the window and stared out at the view of the city. There was no point in discussing the theft further.

"Nice view, by the way." From here, I could see the red-tiled roof-topped buildings, covered with a lite dust of snow against the darkened sky, and the glow of the Glockenspiel atop the Rathaus. "You live here full-time?"

"Not full-time." Hans crossed the room and took the drape from my hand. "I use it when working at the museum, which lately is far too often. I own a small chateau in Oberammergau, where I have my art studio. I share this apartment with my sister, Erica. She's a professor at the university, and when she's in town, she takes the guestroom."

I didn't see any female touches to the apartment. There were no flowers on the table, no pictures of family or knickknacks, not so much as an embroidered pillow on the couch. It was hard to imagine that a woman spent much time here.

"She's not here to help celebrate the unveiling?" It seemed odd to me that she wouldn't be.

Hans stepped closer to me and let the curtain fall across the window. Any closer, he could have heard my heart beating. I could smell the earthy scent of his cologne.

"You ask a lot of questions, Kat. Is it the journalist in you? Or are you curious as to whether or not we're alone?"

I laughed nervously. "Are you coming on to me?"

CHAPTER SIX

"Would that be so wrong?" Hans slipped a curl behind my ear. His eyes held mine a moment longer than necessary, as though he were studying my face.

I put my hand on top of his. So, this was how he planned to divert my attention from the theft. Did he really think he might charm me into forgetting about the burglary?

"No," I said. "But it wouldn't be right either. The truth is, I find you very attractive, and the situation, I'll admit, is very tempting. But, for the record, I don't do dessert before dinner. And you did promise me dinner and an interview." I dropped my hand from his, confident that turning him down would make any game of cat and mouse more enjoyable.

Hans stepped back and raised his hands. "I think you've misinterpreted my intention, Kat. I'm an artist and find you attractive, but I didn't invite you back to my apartment to seduce you. I brought you back here because you were cold, and I thought my sister, who has a closet full of coats, might have one you could borrow. Believe me, if I intended to make love to you, it wouldn't be in an apartment I share with my sister. And, like you, I like dinner first."

Ugh! I dropped my head. I couldn't even look at him. How had I missed the signs? The man was doing me a favor. Just like he had been doing a favor for his nephew when we met earlier that day in the bookstore. Hans von Hausmann wasn't trying to seduce me. He was a nice guy.

"I am so sor—"

"Don't," Hans raised his hand. "You're smart, Kat, and I like that. And to answer your question, yes, my sister and her husband are in town. They brought my nephew with them for the unveiling." Hans crossed the room to the couch and turned to face me. "As you can see, the apartment's too small for four people. They took a room at the Mandarin Oriental. Great bar, by the way. It used to be the Opera House. You might check it out. It would make a nice feature for your magazine." Hans picked up his sister's coat from the back of the couch and held it up for me.

I tossed my coat on the couch while Hans helped me into his sister's. It was nicer than any coat I had ever worn. A hooded black mink belted at the waist with a fancy leather belt, a hundred times more expensive than my simple black trench. Hans put his hands on my shoulders and whispered in my ear. "And, by the way, the painting?" He nodded to the Vermeer on the wall. It's a copy. Unlike the coat on your back, which my sister likes to tell me is very real." Hans opened the door. "Shall we?"

Chapter Seven

Hans was extra careful as he steered me across the Marienplatz. With my trench coat neatly folded across one arm and his hand on my elbow for support, he pointed to black ice that would have caused me to slip, then casually offered me his arm. I took it willingly, anxious not to twist an ankle or fall into a puddle. After I had accused Hans of trying to seduce me, I sensed he wanted to put me at ease, and I wondered if the rumors about Hans von Hausmann might be, as he said, highly exaggerated. Thus far, he had been the perfect gentleman. And based upon what I had seen of his apartment with its minimalist furnishings, his interest in books, and his nephew's education, this was hardly some randy bachelor's pad. And yet…there had been that copy of *Journey International* on his coffee table. A publication he had told me he knew nothing about. Our first meeting earlier that day had been accidental, but something about me and the magazine had caused him to go out and buy a copy. And if I was right, this Mr. Nice-guy act was nothing more than to make sure I didn't learn anything more about him than he wanted me to know.

Well, two could play this game. And for the moment, I decided it best not to ask again about the break-in. I already knew from my initial briefing with Sophie that the stolen Gauguin wasn't the only fake Gauguin. The question was, just how many were there? And how might I learn more about the painting and Hans von Hausmann without raising suspicion?

I squeezed his arm, pulling him closer to me, and nodded toward the museum less than a block away. "You don't have much of a commute to work every day, do you? You must walk everywhere."

Hans responded politely. "Not always. I have a car, but I only use it when I go on holiday or to my chateau."

"Ahh, yes, the chateau," I teased, my nose in the air. "It sounds all so elegantly European." Sophie's briefing included detailed notes about the family's various residences. All of them, likely hiding places for Gerhardt's Hoard, prime targets for my investigation.

"I'm not so sure how elegant it is. It's more of a work in progress these days. Lots of reconstruction just to keep it habitable." Hans stopped and let loose of my arm.

Ahead of us, the Aygystuber am Dom looked like something out of a storybook. Outside, the restaurant door was framed with Christmas trees, while boughs of holly with tiny white lights hung on the windows dusted with snow and painted Yuletide greetings.

Hans opened the door and whispered in my ear as I entered. "Das ist Bayern. This is Bavaria. Welcome."

Inside the restaurant was warm and noisy. Buxom waitresses dressed in red and green Bavarian dirndls with white aprons carried liter-sized mugs of beer to crowded tables amid the heavy smell of roasted chicken, pork dumplings, and schnitzels.

Hans signaled a waiter. "Zwei Sitze bitte." Two seats, please.

The waiter led us to a long wooden table with four empty chairs at the end. We settled into the far two, leaving a space between ourselves and a group of men, boisterous diners with a dozen empty mugs on the table and at least half that many still full of suds yet to be inhaled.

"Do you come here often?" A noisy restaurant wasn't what I would have picked for an interview unless, of course, it was what Hans had planned.

"Too noisy?" Hans picked up the menu.

"For an interview, maybe."

"Don't worry." Hans leaned across the table. "It'll quiet down. Besides, the people here are all focused on food. Nobody's going to bother us. Beer?"

I nodded.

Hans ordered two beers. "If you like, I can order."

"How can I object?" It all looked good.

CHAPTER SEVEN

The waitress returned with our beers. Hans ordered a bit of everything on the menu: schnitzel, spaetzle, a dumpling-like noodle, Kartoffelsalat, rote wurst, a fiery red sausage, and a cucumber salad. More food than we could possibly eat. Then taking a swig of his beer, Hans leaned back in his chair. "So, what is it you'd like to know?"

"Alright. I confess I'm confused. Just who is Hans von Hausmann? Are you the man I met in the bookstore this morning, shopping for a book for his nephew? Gerhardt Galerie's handsome, erudite curator with a reputation as a lady's man, but who denies it? Or, as you've tried to tell me, a hermit artist forced from his chateau to support the financial needs of a family museum and his adoring fans?"

Hans snorted. My question surprised him. He grabbed a napkin and dabbed his chin.

"You make me out to be a far more complex man than I am. The truth is, I'm not all that interesting, and I'd prefer to keep it that way. If it were up to me, I'd sum my life up in a simple paragraph."

"And what might that be?" I put my fork down and took my pen and notepad from my bag.

"You do like to cut to the chase, don't you?" Hans put his elbows on the table and fisted one hand into the palm of the other. "Okay, here you go. I'm forty-five, single, and never married. And I'm not some celebrity-seeking curator, no matter what the papers say. In fact, I consider myself fairly studious. I graduated from the University of Bonn in three years with a master's in art history, but I'm more of a fine arts person. Until a few years ago, I worked as a curator for the Alte Pinakothek. After that, my sister and I opened the Gerhardt Galerie. If you'd like a list of our exhibitions, I'm sure Erika would be delighted to give you one. So, there you have it. There's not much more to tell. Not that a travel pub would be interested in anyway."

"No?"

"The museum's story, not me."

"Okay, then let's talk about the museum. How would you describe it?"

Hans explained that he and his sister owned little of what was displayed at the Galerie. The Gerhardt was more of a boutique with a traveling collection of paintings made available from private collectors who wanted to quietly show their works to discerning buyers. "Basically, we're nothing more than middlemen."

"Sounds like a good business model, but I have to ask. The name, The Gerhardt Galerie, it's not your name nor your sisters. Why use it?"

Hans took a swig of his beer. "It's a family name, my mother's maiden name."

"And one with a history, at least as far as the art world goes."

Hans' fingers tightened around his beer stein. "So, that's what you want to know? I wondered when you'd get around to asking that question. Is that why you're really here?"

"I've heard the rumors. I'm a journalist. I have to ask."

"Then you've also heard that my mother and her family were artists, collectors with a large gallery of their own. Otto Gerhardt was my mother's brother. He was very committed to the arts and a talented curator. Unfortunately, his exhibits caught the attention of the Nazis, who accused him of promoting degenerative art. Art that didn't fit Hitler's vision of what was suitable for the new Germany. My uncle's museum was raided, but instead of allowing the Nazis to destroy the art, my uncle suggested he help them to find a buyer. The money they raised was used to support the Third Reich. Whether my uncle acted on behalf of the art or saw an opportunity to save himself, I'll never know. But whatever happened, Herman Goring hired my uncle to work with the Nazis to identify art for the Fuhrer's Museum. My uncle wasn't alone in stealing from the homes of wealthy Jews and museums. There were many who did the same, but history's a harsh judge. Don't tell me you didn't know that. Everybody does. Just like I know your next question."

"Which is?" I tapped the tip of my pen to the pad.

"Do I know where my uncle hid all that art?"

"Do you?"

Hans picked up his beer and downed it. "That's a big question."

"Is it? Even after all these years? You either know or you don't. Seems it would be a simple yes or no question."

"Nothing in this world is that simple, Kat." Hans snapped his fingers

CHAPTER SEVEN

above his head, catching the attention of a beer maid as she passed our table. Quickly she stopped, her tray full, and placed another tall glass of suds in front of him.

I waited while he sipped the foam from the top.

"You know, I'd have to kill you if I were to tell you." Hans winked.

I laughed. Maybe it was the beer—Hans had three by now—but for the moment, I didn't think Hans viewed me as anything more than a curious American reporter who asked too many questions. Which was precisely what I hoped he would think.

"You're teasing, right? You wouldn't really kill me?"

"Probably not." Hans took a swig of his beer. "I like you, Kat, and I'm sure you would agree it would be a shame if you were to disappear just as we're getting to know one another."

I raised my mug. "I'm glad you see it that way."

"Then, for your sake and mine, we should agree that if I knew anything about my uncle's stash, I wouldn't tell you."

I touched my beer stein to his.

"Because if a cache like what you believe my uncle may have hidden did exist, it would be nothing but trouble. Whatever my uncle did, it ruined him. It ruined a lot of people. He died a lonely, miserable man haunted by the war and his past. He lost everything. The only art he ever had belonged to our family, and what little was left after the war, my mother inherited upon his death. And when she died, my sister and I sold what we had and used the money to establish the museum. There is no hoard, and there never was."

The waitress arrived with our dinner, and Hans ordered another beer. I decided to table the discussion about the museum and Gerhardt's Hoard for the time being and switched to a topic I thought Hans might find more suitable.

"Enough questions about you and the museum. Tell me about this German author you admire."

"Karl May?" Hans sliced into his schnitzel and took a bite.

"I had no idea a German author was writing about the American West."

"You're surprised I know about Cochise and Geronimo? Karl May brought us Winnetou and Old Shatterhand. You never heard of them?"

"No, but I plan to read the book you gave me."

"I hope so." Hans's cell phone rang. He glanced to check the caller, then apologized for taking the call. I took a bite of the schnitzel while I waited for Hans to finish his call. "You'll have to excuse me. I'm needed back at the museum."

"Another break-in?" I put my knife and fork down.

"No. It's my sister, Erika. I have to go, please, stay and finish." Hans got up and threw several Deutschmarks on the table. Enough to cover the meal. "I'm sorry, I was enjoying our conversation."

"So was I." I reached into my bag and pulled out my business card. "Maybe we could meet again?"

"I'd like that." Hans took my card, put it in his wallet, and handed me his. "The Gauguin opening is Sunday. I'll be busy most of the week, but if you're free, perhaps you could join me at my chateau in Oberammergau next weekend. It's not far from here, and there's a lot to see."

"I was planning on visiting the area for the magazine."

"Good, then it's a date?"

"Yes, it's a date," I said. I offered Hans my hand, and he leaned down and kissed my cheek.

"Auf Wiedersehen."

I could hardly wait to tell Sophie about my progress and how I had made up for missing my initial interview. As for Hans and whether he was as suspicious of me as I was of him, I'd have to be careful. It had been a long time since I had spent a weekend alone with a man, particularly one so attractive, and attraction when working undercover can make for strange bedfellows both above and below the covers.

* * *

Before leaving the States, Sophie had given me a special cell phone compatible with European cell services and designed, so I wouldn't have to go through an international operator to make a call, plus two numbers I could

CHAPTER SEVEN

use to reach her. The first was her cell, which I was to use only if it were an emergency, and the second was her office line at *Journey International*. Her instructions to me were straightforward. Should I need to relay information to her, I was to call the magazine and ask to be transferred to her line. If she wasn't in the office or it was after hours, I should press the button indicating I wanted to leave a message, and Sophie would call me back as soon as possible. As for the voicemail, I was advised to be creative. I should remember this was a business line, not necessarily secure, and anyone might listen in. Hence, Sophie instructed me to use mythical characters from German folklore when referring to Hans and Erika. Hans would be Krampus, Santa's evil twin, and Erika was Frau Perchta, a Christmas witch who children believed handed out rewards and punishments during the 12 Days of Christmas. The Gauguin would be 'The Present,' and should I strike gold and learn the whereabouts of Gerhardt's hidden treasures, I was to refer to it as 'Santa's Workshop.'

Since my message wasn't an emergency, I called the office, and when Sophie didn't answer, I left the following coded voicemail.

"Hi, Sophie. It's Kat. Greetings from Munich. I just wanted to call and tell you how much I love the German holiday markets and the festivities you told me about, particularly those with the evil Krampus and Frau Perchta, what characters they are. I don't think most Americans know about them. But I'm learning a lot, and they'll make a fantastic addition to the holiday feature I'm working on. By the way, I found *the present* you asked about. Can't wait to tell you all about it."

Chapter Eight

The first thing I noticed when I opened my eyes the following morning was the black mink coat Hans had lent me. I had hung it on one of the hotel's padded hangers on the back of the bathroom door, facing my bed, and it stared back at me like it belonged on some svelte, sophisticated minx. Like those nearly nude, life-sized mannequins I had seen in the Christmas windows, clad in expensive fur coats, throwing snowballs at each other. As a card-carrying member of PETA, I was uncomfortable wearing such a coat, and I wanted to return it as soon as possible. Hans had left so abruptly the night before that I hadn't a chance. But now, as I snuggled beneath the warmth of my bed's eiderdown comforter and stared at the coat, I thought, why wait? It was Saturday morning, the stores were open, and if I timed it right, I might be able to find a new coat and return this unfortunate mink to the museum before it opened. Which would give me another excuse to get back inside the Gerhardt Galerie and maybe even have a quick conversation with Hans.

I had passed several small boutiques from the hotel to the Marienplatz, all pricey and out of my league. But my guidebook recommended the Galeria Kaufhoff, a large department store, eight levels high, including a restaurant on the top floor with a view of the Marienplatz, and best of all, less than five minutes away.

After a quick shower, I dressed and debated whether or not to wear the mink while I shopped for a new coat or try to stuff the expensive fur into my backpack, which I immediately dismissed. I couldn't risk showing up at the Gerhardt Galerie and pulling a fur coat from my bag covered in peanut

CHAPTER EIGHT

dust. Five more minutes wear wasn't going to kill me, and indeed it would have been just that, were it not for a chocolatier's display on the first floor of the Galeria Kaufhoff.

I'm a sucker for chocolate, and the display was impossible to pass by without sampling. The chocolatier allowed me several taste tests, including some with liquors that, had I let myself, would have easily derailed my plan to make it to the museum in time for its opening at eleven. I bought a sampler box and several small gift packs to take home, including one I planned to bring back for Sophie as a peace offering for my poor start with the investigation.

From the chocolatier's display, I went immediately to the lady's coat department on the third floor. There I found a coat very similar to my black trench, but wool with a faux fur lining and much warmer and not nearly as expensive as I had imagined. I took the mink I was wearing, handed it to the clerk, and asked if she might cut the tags on the faux fur. She looked at me as though I had asked her to commit a cardinal sin. Then stroking the mink like it was a living thing, she lovingly placed it in a Galeria shopping bag.

With my mission complete, I left the Galleria in a hurry and crossed back to the Marienplatz as The Glockenspiel struck eleven. The protestor, who appeared to have become a permanent fixture in front of the Gerhardt Galerie, waved his sign with a picture of the Gauguin at me, yelled something in German, and attempted to stuff a flyer in my hand. With no time for interruptions, I shoved past him and hurried up the steps to the museum's main entrance.

It was still early, and when I entered, I realized I must have been the first caller of the day. Inga, the young woman who had prevented me from meeting Hans the day before, was seated behind the reception desk. Whether it was her heavy blue eye makeup, her short spiky blonde hair, or that I had interrupted her, she looked startled when she saw me at the counter.

I introduced myself. "Hi, my name's Kat Lawson. I was here yesterday for the private unveiling—"

"The American. Yes, I remember." Inga glanced down at her desk and the sign-in sheet from the day before. "What can I do for you?"

I placed The Galeria's shopping bag on the counter and nodded to the office door behind her. "I was hoping to speak with Herr Hausmann. I've something I need to return."

Inga stood up and reached for the bag. "I'm sorry, Herr Hausmann is unavailable. But if you like, I could give this to him later."

I pulled the bag toward me. "If you don't mind, I'd prefer to give it to Herr Hausmann myself. When do you expect him to be free?"

At that moment, the office door behind Inga opened, and Viktor Sokolov, the heavy-set Russian I had stood next to during the unveiling, barged out, pushed past me, and came to a stop in the center hall. Standing in the doorway, visibly shaken, and rubbing her wrist like she had been wounded, was a tall blonde about my height and size. And on the floor behind her lay what looked to be the remains of the forged Gauguin. Its frame was broken and splintered.

"Dummkopf!" The woman yelled at the Russian.

The Russian snarled back, said something I didn't understand, then bumped my shoulder as he went out the front doors.

The woman spat as the Russian retreated, then leaned back behind her and picked up a piece of the splintered gold frame.

"Erika!" Inga ran from behind the desk and put her arm around her employer.

Erika pushed the girl away and, seeing me, jutted her jaw in my direction. "Wer ist das?" Who is this?

"Das ist Kat Lawson." Then looking at me, Inga switched to English. "She's asking for Hans. She says she has something to return to him." Inga nodded to the bag on the counter.

Erika stepped forward and looked inside. "What is this? My coat? Why do you have my coat? Who are you?"

This wasn't how I expected to meet Hans' sister. I tried to explain that I was visiting from America and had dinner with Hans last night. He had lent me the coat, and I was here to return it. I deliberately left out the part about the burglary. Based upon Erika's reaction to Viktor and her emotional state,

CHAPTER EIGHT

I didn't think now was the time to bring it up.

"I don't believe you. Hans never mentioned anything about an American to me. I'm his sister. I know all his lady friends. Why would he give *you* my coat? Do you have any idea how expensive it is?" Erika grabbed the bag off the counter and started back toward the office.

"Wait," I said. "Is Hans here? I'm sure he can explain."

"Explain what?" Erika snapped.

Before I could answer, the double doors burst open, and a blast of cold air ushered in a man dressed in boots and a long camel coat.

"Friedrick, mein schatz." Ericka screamed, dropped the Galeria bag on the floor, and ran to him, throwing her arms around his neck. As they embraced, I spotted a shoulder holster and the butt of a gun beneath his open coat.

I glanced back toward the office. Inside, the office appeared in disarray, the desk messy, and the Gauguin on the floor in its broken frame. Had Friedrick arrived a few minutes earlier, I feared I might have witnessed a shoot-out.

Erika touched the man's face, whispered something to him, then looked back at me. "Ms. Lawson, I'm afraid you've come at a bad time. I need to speak with my husband. I think you should go."

Erika picked up the bag with the mink inside and hugged it to her chest.

"Yes, I can see that. I'm sorry."

Erika looked sharply at her husband. "This woman says she's a friend of Hans. She claims he lent her my coat. Do you know anything about her?"

Friedrick looked at me with a firm shake of his head. "Nein."

"Good, then I think we're done here, Ms. Lawson. Thank you for returning the coat. I'll tell Hans for you. Now, if you'll excuse me, we're very busy, and as you can see, Hans is unavailable. I think you should go."

Chapter Nine

Whatever I had just witnessed inside the Galerie between Viktor and Erika wasn't good, and any opportunity for a relationship with her felt like it had just blown up. I needed to salvage what I could, and quickly. I picked up my phone and called Kirsten. My hope was that she was close enough to Hans and Erika and could help to smooth things over. If I were to uncover anything about Gerhardt's hidden treasures, I couldn't leave things as they were. Fortunately, Kirsten agreed to meet me at a konditorei, a sweet shop I had passed earlier that morning while on my way to the Galeria Kaufhoff.

When I arrived, the café was busy, and I found the only free table in the back, next to a long glass display case full of bakery goods; decadent chocolates with cherry toppings, apple strudels, and cheese-filled turnovers dusted with powdered sugar—each one a work of art. I hadn't eaten breakfast, and other than the few chocolate liqueurs I had sampled at the Galeria that morning, I was starving.

While I waited for Kirsten, I ordered a cup of coffee and tried to untangle impossibly long words on the menu. Words like Schwartzwalder Kirsch torte, Baumkuchen, and quarkbällchen. None of which I understood, but mixed with the smell of cinnamon, hot chocolate, and the sound of steam escaping the café's giant brass samovar, caused my stomach to growl. Fortunately, I didn't have to wait long before I heard the hollow ring of cowbells on the back of the café door. I looked up as Kirsten entered, her cheeks rosy from the cold.

"Grüß Gott." Kirsten greeted the barista, then spotting me in the back of

CHAPTER NINE

the café, hurried towards my table.

"Guten Morgan." I greeted her brightly, thankful for her friendly face.

"Ah, du sprichst Deutch. You speak German. Sehr gut. Very good." Kirsten leaned down and kissed me on the cheek.

"Thanks. I'm doing my best to pick up a few words."

Kirsten signaled to the waitress, who arrived with a pitcher of coffee and filled the empty cup in front of her. Then pointing to the display case, Kirsten ordered what looked like two deep-fried doughnuts, but without the hole, filled with jam and dusted with powdered sugar.

While we waited for the waitress to return with our order, Kirsten took her flask from her purse and splashed her coffee with a healthy dose of schnapps. "Would you like some?"

"I'll pass, thanks." I poured cream into my coffee. This was the second time since meeting Kirsten that I noticed she liked to sweeten her coffee with schnapps, and I wondered if her taste for the fruit-flavored liquor was more of a habit than because of the cold. "It's a little early for me."

"Not for me. I'm celebrating. Did you see this morning's paper?" Kirsten took a copy of today's newspaper from her bag and placed it on the table. The front page had a picture of Hans standing next to the Gauguin. The story beneath it included Kirsten's byline.

"Nice. Front page, and above the fold. I'm impressed." Feature articles seldom garnered such a prime position. "That's got to make the museum happy."

"It helps that it was a slow news day, and it never hurts to be good friends with the editor."

"Peter?" I asked.

"Too bad you can't read German." Kirsten spun the paper around so that I could see it. "It's a great article, even if I didn't write all of it myself."

"Erika helped?"

"Like always, but I don't care as long as I get the credit."

"Speaking of which…" I paused and stirred my coffee. I didn't want to appear overly anxious, but the story's position in the morning paper provided the obvious segway. "Have you talked with anyone at the museum today?"

"Of course. Erika called me on her way in this morning. She loves it."

The waitress arrived with our food. Kirsten took a bit, then dabbed her lips with her napkin. She obviously knew nothing of Erika's altercation at the museum with Viktor.

"About that," I said. "I may have stepped into something and could use your help."

"Does this have anything to do with your dinner with Hans last night?"

I put my cup down. "How did you know we had dinner?"

Kirsten rolled her eyes. "You told me you would meet Hans at the museum after it closed. What else would you do?"

"Right." *What else would we do?* I had a few ideas. But I didn't dare let my mind wander. Whether it was the excitement of the break-in, the cold weather, or that I could feel myself warming to the curator's charms, I didn't dare. Not yet, anyway.

Instead, I explained how I had met Hans at the museum as planned and left out the part about the break-in. Until I better understood what was going on with Hans and the fake Gauguin, I thought it best to keep what little I knew about the theft to myself.

"Afterward, we left for dinner. It was freezing out, and I couldn't stop shaking. Hans noticed my coat wasn't nearly heavy enough and suggested we stop by his apartment to pick up one of his sister's coats."

Kirsten smirked. "The mink or the Russian Sable?"

I raised my hands. I had no idea. *Mink. Sable. To me, they were all the same.* "It had a black belt. I don't know."

"That'd be the mink. Nice coat."

"Yes, it was. Which was why I wanted to return it this morning." I explained how I had witnessed the argument between Erika and Viktor at the museum and how upset Erika was. "Even worse, when she realized I had her coat, she lost it. I don't know what she thinks, but I'm worried." I paused and stirred my coffee. "Look, I know this doesn't concern you, but I can't afford to blow any relationship while I'm here in Germany. This is my first assignment with the magazine, and Erika strikes me as someone I'd rather have on my side than not. I'm sure you understand."

CHAPTER NINE

Kirsten put her cup down. "I'm sorry. I had no idea about any of this. But if it helps, Erika hates Viktor. He's been hanging around the museum since they agreed to let him exhibit the Matise, and now that it's sold, they can't get rid of him. And right now, with the Gauguin unveiling, Erika's patience is paper-thin. If Viktor came by this morning, it's no wonder Erika was in a bad mood. Coat or no coat, it's easy to get on Erika's bad side. But, if you like, I can put in a good word."

"Would you?"

"Of course. You said you'd put in a good word for me with your publisher, right? Why shouldn't I do the same for you with Erika?" Kirsten took another sip of her coffee. "Besides, I owe Erika and Fritz a favor."

Kirsten explained that Erika and her husband Friedrick lived in Tegernsee, a small spa town on a lake near Munich. Together, they were the caretakers of a natural history and craft museum.

"Erika's always looking for press. Between the museums and her position with the university, she's got her hands full. And Friedrick's not much more than a pretty face. He takes care of the mail and handles security."

I hadn't noticed the pretty face. But if Friedrick's job was security, that explained the gun I had seen beneath his coat.

"So, what's his story?" The report Sophie had given me on Hans and his sister was nothing more than the basic facts, names and birthdates, residences, education, and a few pictures.

"My opinion? This will sound cruel, but I think it's true—Erika wanted to have a baby. She wasn't exactly young when she met Friedrick, and she's not particularly pretty. She's okay, I mean, money can buy looks, and with the right clothes and makeup, she stacks up to the competition pretty well. But, by the time she met Fritz, her clock was ticking, so she got married. He's old-world aristocracy. His family didn't have much but a name, and Fritz ended up working security for the Alte Pinakothek, where Hans worked. It was Hans who introduced them. In Erika's mind, Fritz was perfect. He had class. He was tall, handsome, and most importantly, fertile."

"And Fritz? What did he get out of it?"

"What didn't he get? Erika's got money, and property, and together they have status. The full package. Something neither of them would have without the other. If you like, I could suggest to Erika that you'd be interested in doing a feature for your magazine on the museum. It'd go a long way to help smooth things over with her."

"That would be great." Kirsten's idea was perfect. It would allow me to interview Erika without raising suspicion.

"Good, I'll call and see if I can set something up." Kirsten finished her donut. "So, how's the holiday story coming?"

"Fine," I lied. Beyond a few brief notes, I had done nothing, but Kirsten didn't need to know that. "It's easy when you don't have an editor breathing down your neck. None of this needs to be turned around right away. So, I can take my time and enjoy myself."

Kirsten put her cup down and looked toward the front of the store. Something or someone had caught her attention.

"Well, would you look at that?" Kirsten tilted her head toward the front counter. "Guess who just walked in?"

"Is that—"

"Inga. And with what you just told me about what happened at the museum this morning, I guess it's no accident she's here. In fact, I'll bet she's following you."

"Why?"

"I can think of a couple of reasons. One, you showed up at the museum this morning with Erika's coat, and Erika asked Inga to keep an eye on you. Or..." Kirsten finished the last of her coffee. "Inga's curious about you yourself. For a while, she had a thing for Hans. You ask me, the girl's looking for a man to take care of her. Just look at the way she's dressed. A little too much eye candy, don't you think?"

I hadn't thought much about Inga or how she had been dressed, but looking at her now, Kirsten did have a point. Inga was dressed in a red and yellow striped cap, a short puffy red jacket, and—despite the cold—a short plaid miniskirt with long socks and tall black patent leather Doc Martens boots.

"Was Hans responsive?"

"No. Hans may be a womanizer, but Inga's not his type. A little too much

CHAPTER NINE

bling for his tastes. Erika finally had to tell Inga her brother was off-limits. Either leave him alone, or Erika would fire her. But for all I know, Inga still has a crush on him."

I took a sip of my coffee. "And what about you?"

"Me?" Kirsten seemed surprised I would ask such a question.

"Why not? You're attractive."

"But, I'm not stupid. I had Hans and Erika figured out right away. They helped me get my start with the newspaper. And ever since, they stepped up. If I needed something, whatever it was, information, tickets to concerts, events? They took care of me. I wasn't about to mess up a good thing. Besides, Hans is a one-and-done type of guy, and you may have noticed my dance card is full these days. I may play around, but not like that." Kirsten stood up and reached for the check. "Look, it's getting late. I need to go. I'm meeting Peter for lunch, and I don't like disappointing him."

I put my hand on top of hers. "Let me get the check. I feel like I owe you."

"Vielen Dank. Thank you," she said.

I smiled and took the check. "Bitte."

"So, what are you doing this weekend?" Kirsten took her hat and gloves from her bag and started to put them on.

"Hans invited me to Oberammergau."

"Really?" Kirsten paused.

"Have you ever been?"

"I was there with a bunch of Hans' and Erika's friends for the housewarming." Kirsten stuffed her blonde hair beneath her cap. "It was a while back. I had just started working with the museum. But you'll like the chateau. It's beautiful, and I'm sure he'll love showing it to you." Kirsten stretched her fingers into her gloves, then slapped her hands together. "I'm off. Will I see you again?"

"I hope so. I should be around 'til the end of the month. Maybe we can have dinner sometime."

"I'd like that. I'll call and let you know about the interview with Erika." Kirsten kissed me on the cheeks again and bid me goodbye.

"Auf wiedersehen," I said.

Chapter Ten

Later that afternoon, I returned to my hotel room and put in a call to Sophie. It was still early Friday morning in New York, but I suspected Sophie would be in her office with her nose in a book despite the early hour. Near as I could tell, the woman didn't have much of a private life, and I wasn't surprised when she answered on the first ring.

"Sophie Brill, here." Sophie's brisk New York accent was all matter of fact. No friendly chit-chat. No, how are you? Just straight to business.

I responded in kind; my speech clipped.

"Sophie, hi, It's me. Kat."

I paced the room with the phone pressed to my ear. I had a vision of Sophie sitting in her office behind her desk, stacked with books, as she had been when we first met. Sophie had final approval on who the FBI would send in as her eyes and ears, and I had flown to New York for our initial meeting. This was to be no easy interview. Her office was cluttered. Books and folders were everywhere, on her desk, floor, and lining the walls. And yet, upon seeing me, this frail, graying art historian, who didn't look like she could have been more than eighty pounds, jumped up and moved a stack of artbooks that must have weighed at least half as much as she did and commanded me to sit—which I did. When it came to art, and the repatriation of those works lost during the war, Sophie possessed an iron will and would accept nothing less from those with whom she worked.

"Well, it's about time, Kat Lawson. Where have you been? I got your voicemail about Krampus and The Present. Why didn't you call my cell?"

"I'm sorry, I—"

CHAPTER TEN

"Sorry? That's not an answer, Kat. I don't need excuses. I need results." In the background, I could hear the squeak of Sophie's chair, followed by the click-clack of her heels as she crossed her office floor and slammed the door shut. "I have reports to make and a team of investigators I'm working with here and in Europe waiting for them. When something happens, I need to know."

I winced, pulled the phone from my ear, and shook it in my fisted hand. Dammit. This woman wasn't easy. But I didn't have a lot of options. I would have to learn to survive Sophie's verbal abuse if I wanted this job. I put the phone back to my ear.

"Got it," I said.

"Good. Then we won't need to have this conversation again, will we? When you've got breaking news, you call. You understand?"

"Loud and clear."

"Now, about Krampus, am I to understand that you've made contact with Herr Hausmann?"

"I have. And I've good news. Hans and I had dinner together last night, and—"

"Hans?" Sophie snorted. "So, you're on a first-name basis now?"

"We are." I recapped how I had run into Herr Hausmann at a bookstore where he was shopping for a gift for his nephew. "We bonded over the author Karl May. He wrote novels about the American West, and—"

"I know who Karl May is, Kat. You don't need to educate me. What I need to know is what happened with Hans?"

"When Hans realized I was from Arizona, he invited me to the museum for a private showing." Sophie chuckled, and I paused. "You knew that would happen, didn't you? Arizona's one of the reasons you chose me, right?"

"I did my homework on both of you. I suppose you could say I'm a pretty good matchmaker. I knew Herr Hausmann was a fan of the old west. And, I didn't imagine it would take long for him to figure out where you're from, and I'm sure he liked what he saw."

I felt like a pawn on a chessboard that Sophie was manipulating, but I let it go.

51

"He invited me to the museum, and when we were there—"

"There was a break-in. Yes, I know."

"H-h-how—" My voice caught in my throat. "How did you know?"

"We've had eyes on Viktor Sokolov. I get reports."

"So, it was the Russian then?"

"Don't get ahead of yourself, Kat. Tell me what happened. I need to know what Herr Hausmann said to you and what happened after the theft."

"That's what's so strange. Nothing happened. Hans told me the painting was a fake and that the real Gauguin was in the vault beneath the museum. He acted like it was no big deal. Maybe he expected it. I don't know. But he didn't want to wait around, and more importantly, he didn't want to report it."

Sophie typed as we spoke. "And what did you do?"

"I didn't know what to do. I refused to go to dinner until Hans called the police, but—"

"He convinced you otherwise." Sophie hmphed. "Interesting. And then this morning, you went back to the museum. Why? What was that all about?

I sat down on the bed. "How did you know I went back to the museum this morning?"

"I told you, we have eyes on Viktor."

"Who?" I asked. "Who's here watching Viktor?"

"That, you're better off not knowing. All you need to know is that we have a tail on

Viktor. Hans is your target, not Viktor Sokolov. Now tell me, why did you go back to the museum this morning?"

There was no point in arguing. Sophie had made it very clear I was on a need-to-know basis, and until she wanted me to know more, I was in the dark. My job was to be her eyes and ears in the field, supply what information she needed about Hans and Erika, and hope for the best.

"It was snowing when Hans and I left the museum. I was cold. The coat I brought wasn't nearly warm enough, and Hans suggested we stop by the apartment he shares with his sister and I could borrow one of her coats. But the coat he gave me was a mink, and I wanted to return it. So, early

CHAPTER TEN

this morning, I decided I'd buy myself a new coat and return Erika's to the museum. I thought it might be a good excuse to see Hans again."

Sophie stopped typing. "And did you see Hans?"

"No. Hans wasn't there, or at least he wasn't available. Inga, the receptionist, tried to take Erika's coat from me, but I wasn't about to leave it. Not a mink, anyway. And while we were talking, Viktor came out of the front office, and Erika was right behind him. I recognized her from the photo you included in the dossier you gave me before I left the States. Judging from the look on her face, she and Viktor had been arguing, and it looked like it had gotten physical. Erika was rubbing her wrist, and the Russian was all red-faced."

"Then what happened."

"Not much. Erika said something in German. Viktor said something back, then brushed by me and went out the door. A few minutes later, Erika's husband Friedrick showed up...with a gun."

Sophie continued to type as she talked. "Kat, I'm going to remind you. Your job is to stay close to Hans. Leave Viktor alone, you hear me? The man's bad news."

"You're not the first to tell me that." I explained that when I missed meeting Hans at the museum the day of the press conference, I had met a reporter who worked for *The Munich Zeitung*. "Her name's Kirsten Muller. She says she's close to both Hans and Erika. I'm not sure what all she knows, but she definitely doesn't like Viktor."

"What did she tell you?"

"Viktor wasn't expected at the unveiling. His name wasn't on the guest list, and Kirsten suspects that Inga may have gotten him in."

"And Inga, is she young and pretty?"

"Very," I said.

"Then she should be careful. Young girls have a way of disappearing around Viktor Sokolov." I could hear more papers rattling around in the background. "So, did Kirsten volunteer anything about Hans and Erika's Uncle Gerhardt or his cache of stolen artwork?"

"She thinks the story's all rumor. It could be the company line. She admitted she does a lot of PR for the museum, and I suspect it's without the paper's knowledge. The woman's got expensive taste, and somebody's paying for her clothes. She carries around a two-thousand-dollar Louis Vuitton handbag. No journalists I know makes that type of money."

"So she's on the take and wouldn't say anything even if she knew."

"Probably, but on the other hand, Kirsten has no idea why I'm here, and I think she might be helpful. I called her back this morning after the mishap at the museum and told her I thought I had gotten on the wrong side of Erika, and Kirsten offered to help. She said if I wanted, she could set up an interview with Erika in Tegernsee, where she and her husband Friedrick manage a small natural history museum. Said they could use the publicity."

"Nice work."

"Yes, well, it comes with an ask. Kirsten wanted me to mention her to you in case you're looking for a stringer, someone to cover the occasional story in Europe. She says she could use the work."

"Stay close to her, Kat. Tell her we spoke, and I took her number. She could be a good source. I can always use a stringer in Europe for legitimate travel features. She might be useful down the line. Meanwhile, ask her if she can get a couple of photos of you for the article. It would add a nice personal touch to the holiday feature you're working on."

"I'll mention it to her."

Sophie's chair squeaked again, and I knew we were finished speaking about Kirsten.

"So, talk to me more about your dinner with Hans. Did he mention his uncle to you?"

"He did. And he was very forthcoming. He admitted his uncle was one of Hitler's art historians but then went on and posed a couple of possibilities that caused me to pause. He said; *if* the story about Otto Gerhardt smuggling stolen art from the Nazis was true, there was no evidence. Nobody's ever seen such a cache. And, *if* his uncle had stolen art from the Nazis, it was because he was trying to save it before they destroyed it. And here's the clincher, he said, if Otto Gerhardt had stolen anything from the Nazis, they would have murdered him. So why didn't they?"

CHAPTER TEN

"That's a few too many *ifs*, Kat."

"Maybe so, but I'm not certain Hans isn't telling the truth. He admitted his uncle had sent what remained of their family's private collection to Bavaria. He said he arranged for a lot of the art to be hidden in castles like Neuschwanstein. He made it sound like Gerhardt was doing exactly what the Nazis were doing, moving as many masterpieces as possible out of harm's way before it was destroyed by the allied bombs."

"And after the war, did Hans tell you how Otto Gerhardt forged papers to collect not only the family's collection of art from the Allies but thousands of paintings and valuables that the Nazis had stolen and hidden in the salt mines as well?"

"No." I felt blind-sighted. Hans hadn't said a word about how his uncle had retrieved his family's art collection. "He didn't say anything about that."

"And did Hans tell you where he and Erika got the money to start the Gerhardt Galerie?"

"He said they sold one of the paintings from the family collection and the rest of the art they sold off to finance their lifestyle."

"He's lying, Kat, and I hope you didn't believe him. Hans and Erika may have legitimately sold a painting from their family's collection. And they may have even paid the German tax on the sale back then. But the art world knows Hans and Erika are sitting on hundreds, maybe thousands of pieces of stolen art their uncle collected while working for the Nazis."

"But how do you know for sure?"

"The Germans kept meticulous records. We have lists of art recovered by the allies, some of the art on those lists we believe was turned over to Otto Gerhardt by mistake. From time to time, those in the art world would hear that something we thought had been missing was for sale. Word on the street would be that a certain masterpiece was available, and then nothing. Either the seller got nervous because they were afraid of being discovered and pulled the painting back or sold it quietly to some private gallery, most likely a South American drug cartel or Russian oligarch. Either way, the work disappeared. It could be generations before we see or hear of it again. It's one of the reasons we think Viktor was hanging around the museum.

We think Viktor suspects Hans and Erika are sitting on their uncle's stash, and he's waiting to make a move."

"Then you'll be happy to know I'm seeing Hans again this weekend. He's invited me to his chateau in Oberammergau."

"The family home, I'm impressed. I've long suspected there might be something hidden there."

"According to Hans, the chateau is a work in progress and has been for some time. But with a little luck, it'll give me a chance to snoop around. Maybe find something."

"Be careful, Kat. I'm warning you. Hans has a lot to lose. Things could get ugly if he suspects you're on to him."

"I don't think you need to worry. I'm pretty sure Hans thinks I'm nothing but a travel writer looking to write a good story."

"Make sure it looks that way. Fax me some notes every day. Give me an update on what's happening, okay?"

"No problem."

"And remember, Viktor Sokolov's a dangerous man. Stay out of his way. It's important he thinks you're nothing but a feature writer working for a travel pub."

Chapter Eleven

Sophie's warning didn't go unheeded. And, with six days before I was due to visit Hans at his chateau in Oberammergau, I planned to do everything I could to look like a busy travel writer. I made a list of museums to visit, including Nymphenburg Castle. I even signed up for a cooking class and made an appointment to visit one of Munich's world-famous spas. Aside from doing research for a travel feature, I wanted to look extra good before I left for Oberammergau to see Hans again. But the following morning, my cell phone rang before I opened my eyes.

"Guten morgen, Kat. Wie gehts? How are you?"

"Kirsten?"

"I have good news. Erika's agreed to an interview. She wants to meet with you tomorrow at noon. She apologized if she appeared rude yesterday. She hopes you won't hold it against her."

"Tomorrow?" I blinked at my bedside clock. It wasn't yet eight a.m.

"The museum's closed on Mondays, so it works for her, and she's arranged for Fritz to give you a private tour. Afterward, she'll make herself available for an interview." I blindly padded the nightstand for my notepad. I wanted to jot Erika's number down and go back to sleep. "Kat?" Kirsten sounded irritated. "Are you awake?"

I yawned and covered my mouth.

"Barely," I said.

"I'm sorry to call so early. But getting an interview with Erika is difficult, and I wanted to check with you before you plan your week."

I rubbed my eyes.

"And now that you're awake, I thought—"

"What?" I groaned.

"I thought it'd be fun to show you Nymphenburg Castle. It's a fairytale this time of year. And if you like, I can take photos."

"You don't have to work?"

"It's Sunday, Kat. I have the day off. We can take the train. It's a short ride, and if we get there early, I can get us in before the crowd. I have connections. But you'll have to hurry. Meet me in the lobby at eight-forty-five. It'll be fun."

I would have hung up and rolled over if I didn't need Kirsten more than I needed sleep. But so far, Kirsten had proved an asset, and I wasn't about to let go of a good thing.

"Fine, I'll be there." I yawned and sat up. So much for sleeping in.

* * *

Kirsten greeted me in the lobby with a steaming hot cup of coffee-to-go and was nonstop chatter about Hans and Erika and how excited she was that Erika had agreed to an interview. If I hadn't been convinced that what Kirsten knew might be important, I might have tuned her out, my brain still foggy from the time change. I took a sip of my coffee and followed her out the hotel's front doors and across the Marienplatz while she prattled on about Erika.

"Erika's sorry about yesterday. But off the record, Erika's got a temper. She's never been easy, but lately—whatever's going on—you do not want to get in her way!" Kirsten pushed ahead toward the subway entrance, talking as fast as she walked. "She and Hans are barely speaking, which is something because they're usually close."

"They haven't been getting along?"

"You think he was there when you stopped by? No way. They're never in the office together anymore. Oh, they've had their tiffs before, but right now, Erika's no fun to be around and super stressed. And when it comes to Viktor, I'm surprised she didn't punch him right in front of you."

CHAPTER ELEVEN

"Why, what did she tell you?"

"About Viktor? Not much, just that she wasn't expecting him, and he surprised her. After the museum sold *The Seated Woman* for Viktor, Erika thought she'd be done with him, but evidently not. If I were him, though, I'd be careful. The woman's got a hell of a left hook. And don't think she wouldn't use it. I've seen her take after Fritz. Between you and me, I think Fritz is afraid of her."

"Sounds like Erika has a lot on her plate."

"She does, and Inga's not much help. Erika would have fired her if things weren't so busy right now. The only reason anything runs smoothly at all is because of Erika. She's the brains behind things."

"And Hans?"

"He's the popular celebrity curator whose photos you see in all the magazines with a beautiful woman on his arm. And believe me, that doesn't happen by accident. Erika arranges for everything. She makes certain Hans is present for all the big fundraisers, that they donate to the right charities, and are seen as the elite doing good."

"And she doesn't do any of that herself?"

"As little as possible. Erika hates the limelight. But behind the scenes, everything happens because Erika believes it's good for their image and, ultimately, the museum. She's very organized. And, when I told her who you were and that you'd be interested in doing a feature story about the museum in Tegernsee for the magazine, she couldn't have been more apologetic. She wanted to make sure you understood you had caught her at a bad time and that she's looking forward to the interview." Kirsten looked at her watch. "Come. If we hurry, we can catch the next train to Nymphenburg Palace. It leaves in five minutes."

***

I couldn't believe the grandeur of Schloss Nymphenburg. It was much bigger than I expected, and looking at it, I felt like I was about to walk back in time. The Palace, a 17th-century baroque mansion, sat facing a five-hundred-acre park on what had once been the Bavarian Royal family's private hunting grounds. Everything around me, the frozen lakes, the trees with their boughs full of white powdered snow, was like a winter wonderland.

Kirsten knew the Palace. She claimed she was a distant relative of King Ludwig I, who she said was her great-great-great uncle. She wasn't sure exactly how many greats, only that she had been coming to the Palace since she was a small child and referred to King Ludwig 1 as her Great Uncle Ludwig.

I had no idea whether there was any truth to Kirsten's relationship with the Palace's former resident, but Kirsten seemed to have a certain amount of *pull*. Rather than join a long line of ticket holders, who shivered in the cold, waiting for the Palace doors to open, Kirsten linked her arm through mine and, after a brief and very animated conversation with a guard, we were waved ahead of the crowd, like VIPS.

"Welcome to Steinerner Saal, the grand hall." With her hands above her head, Kirsten stood on the marble floor in the entry beneath an enormous crystal chandelier that hung from the pavilion's central dome. The dome must have been at least three stories high, and a gold-frescoed picture of Helios in his chariot was painted above it. Kirsten gestured to either side of the pavilion. "To my right is the King's wing. And to my left, the Queen's. I can show you each, but trust me, with so much to see, you'd best allow me to show you the highlights now, and you can come back later and see whatever you like."

We agreed on a shorter tour. Kirsten led me through what had once been the private chambers of royalty, through secret doors and hidden hallways that opened onto opulently furnished rooms with elegantly carved furnishings and bedrooms with elevated platform beds and velvet spreads beneath ornate canopies. Kirsten snapped pictures of both the king's and queen's chambers, then grabbed my hand.

"Come, you have to see the Galerie of Beauties. It's what earned the castle its name."

Kirsten pulled me ahead, the halls still empty of visitors, as we rushed from the queen's chamber to another high-ceilinged room lined with portraits.

CHAPTER ELEVEN

"And here," Kirsten dropped my hand and gestured to the gallery's walls, "is where the king kept his stable of beauties, portraits of beautiful young women he brought to court to entertain him. And who, despite his Queen's objections, he housed here in the south pavilion. Thus, earning the Palace its name, the Nymph's Castle."

I counted thirty-six gold-framed paintings on the walls, women whose made-up faces stared blankly out from the canvases.

"Must have made for a very cozy court," I said.

"They were the cover girls of their time. Here, let me get a picture of you." Kirsten positioned me in front of one dark-haired beauty, then backed up and, looking from behind the lens, teased, "Come on, Kat, give me a pose. Something with a little attitude."

"No. I'm not doing this."

"Oh, come on. It'll be a great souvenir. Just for fun." Kirsten looked up at the ceiling and tossed her hair. "You know what I mean, something campy."

I relented and mugged it up for the camera while Kirsten snapped candid shots. In college, I had done a little modeling, but I was never comfortable in front of the camera. All the same, I knew enough to glam it up a bit and gave Kirsten a couple of kittenish poses, then scowled at the camera. "Enough already. Let's go."

* * *

It was past ten p.m. by the time I returned to the hotel. I hurried to my room and jotted down a few notes on the hotel's stationery about the places Kirsten and I had visited that day, then went back downstairs to the hotel's business office and asked to use the fax machine. Per Sophie's instructions, my fax was to include nothing but highlights about what I had seen and planned to see as it pertained to the magazine. But, because I was anxious to chat with her about my upcoming interview with Erika, I added a short note to the last page informing her I had an opportunity for an exciting sidebar piece and hoped she might be able to talk about it. I then raced back upstairs. It was just after four p.m. in New York, and I figured I would have no problem reaching Sophie. But when she didn't answer, and the call went to voice mail, I had no choice but to leave a coded message.

"Hi, Sophie, it's Kat. I'm off to Tegernsee tomorrow. I know it wasn't on the schedule, but I got word about a new natural history museum inside an old Benedictine Abbey, and I couldn't resist. I hear they have an exhibition of traditional handicrafts. With all the research I've been doing on German folklore and the holidays, I hope to learn a little more about the origins of the evil Frau Perchta. Wish me luck. Talk soon—Auf Wiederhoren."

Chapter Twelve

I could have gone by train to Tegernsee, it would have taken about as much time, but I wanted the freedom to explore the lakeside town and some of its sights. Fodor's Travel Guide said the property along the lake shores was not only the most beautiful but most expensive in all of Germany, and without a car, I wouldn't be able to see it. But I had no idea when I rented a Fiat with Italian plates that the drive would be so harrowing.

There are few speed limits on German autobahns and practically none on rural roadways. A few Germans have lobbied for them but without much success. Tourists and nervous drivers, beware. Some German drivers view the autobahn and rural roadways as a racetrack. And daredevils have been known to speed up behind slower-moving vehicles, ride their bumper, then just as quickly disappear.

Of course, I knew none of this until I got on the road and moved to the far left lane like I might if I were driving in the States. I couldn't have gone but a mile when a black muscled Mercedes swooped down on me at a high rate of speed. In a matter of seconds, its gold grill was on my bumper, like melted cheese on toast. Any closer and my pursuer would have been in my back seat.

I gripped the steering wheel, afraid to take my eyes off the road ahead for fear of crashing into the mountainside. From behind me, I could feel the heat of the black beast's engine on my neck. I couldn't shake him. Right. Left. The muscled car stuck to me, blocking any chance of my escape. I pressed my foot to the floorboard, willing the car up the mountain road, its engine screaming, the Mercedes tight on my fender.

A slim guard rail marked the difference between the road and a sheer cliff. The Mercedes blasted his horn. One good bump and the Fiat, with me inside, would plunge down a thousand-foot mountainside to an icy death. Up ahead, I spotted an exit. I pulled to the right without signaling and fishtailed onto the exit ramp. The black Mercedes missed the turn, and I watched in my rearview mirror as it disappeared in a blur up the mountain.

I skidded to a stop in the parking lot and collapsed my head against the wheel, my fingers so tightly clenched I didn't think I would ever be able to let go. When my heart stopped racing, I got out and walked around the car to examine the rear bumper.

There were scrapings along the back of the car, but nothing to prove the black Mercedes had tried to push me off the mountainside. For a brief moment, I wondered if I had been followed, then dismissed the idea. I was being paranoid. More than likely, I was driving too slowly in the fast lane, and someone wanted to teach me a lesson. Either that or some irate German motorist had spotted my rental car's Italian plates and had a score to settle. Whatever the cause, I decided to drive more defensively and kept my eyes on the road ahead and my rearview mirror, ready to move to the far righthand side at first sight of an approaching car.

* * *

Tegernesee was postcard perfect. My guidebook described the area as a tourist haven, settled on the lake beneath snow-covered Alps, a hiker's and boater's paradise with ski runs that crisscrossed the slopes above the town in the winter and hiking trails in the summer. Lakeside, the shore was dotted with mansions, expansive properties with private docks, and gated walls that allowed for the type of privacy afforded only to the ultra-rich. If Erika and her husband had been looking for a quiet place to lie low, this was it. I couldn't imagine a more idyllic place to hide in plain sight.

I found the museum, a yellow stucco building with shuttered windows, directly across from the local brewery and parked out front. I was barely up the museum's stairs when the door opened.

CHAPTER TWELVE

"Grüß Gott." I recognized my greeter as Erika's husband. He was dressed in a grey fitted jacket with black velvet trim and silver buttons—traditional Bavarian dress for the area. I wondered if, like before, he had a gun hidden beneath his coat.

"I apologize. I don't speak German."

"No problem, Ms. Lawson. I speak English. I am Herr Schönburg."

"Please, call me Kat."

"And you may call me Fritz." He offered me his hand. "I'm Erika's husband, and she asked if I would show you around. I'm afraid she is busy at the moment. She'll speak with you later."

"That's very kind of you. I appreciate you taking the time, and I brought along a small gift as a thank you." From my backpack, I took out a box of the chocolate liqueurs I had bought earlier at the Galeria Kaufhof and the latest copy of *Journal International*. "I hope you and your wife enjoy chocolate, and I thought perhaps you might like of copy of the magazine."

"Danke. I'll see she gets it." Fritz took the chocolates and the magazine from my hand and nodded to the front door. "Please, come in."

I followed Fritz inside and was immediately taken by the openness of the gallery. While the front room was small, the light streaming through the windows brought a delicate warmth to the entry with its yellow wooden floor and cobalt blue walls. Fritz excused himself and walked several feet ahead of me into the room, where he pushed open a small jib door flush with the wall and barely visible. He placed the chocolates and the magazine immediately inside the door, on what appeared to be a table or small desk. Leaning against the opposite wall, I noticed several wooden frames partially covered with a drop cloth. Fritz closed the door before I could see more.

"Now, if you'll follow me, I'll be happy to give you a tour."

I trailed behind Fritz, taken in as much by the view of the lake and mountains from the windows as I was by the paintings and photographs on the walls. "Have you been here long?"

"Several years. My family had a close connection to the area and its history. Before the war, they owned a small ski chalet on the mountain there." Fritz stopped at the window and nodded to the slopes. "

"Is it still there?"

"No. No more. But after Erika and I married, we built a home on the lake." Fritz tapped the window and pointed across the lake to a large, two-story neoclassical house surrounded by what looked like ten walls. "Das ist Mein Herrenhaus or, as you would say, my mansion. It's why we opened the museum. We wanted to spend more time here."

"It's beautiful." It also looked well-fortified and big enough to hide a secret cache of stolen artwork the world might never find.

Felix continued down the hall and stopped at a map depicting a glacier dating back to the ice age. The first settlement in the area didn't happen until the 8th century when monks founded a Benedictine monastery. With Felix explaining the significance of each display, we toured a maze of smaller rooms with paintings, handmade artifacts, and tools from the middle-ages, then stopped again when we came to a three-dimensional diagram of the abbey.

"Here, this you must see. Before the war, the museum was a parsonage, and during the war, because the abbey housed the wounded, both were spared from heavy bombing, and what you see today is much like how it looked years ago."

"Ms. Lawson?" From behind me, I heard Erika's heavy accent.

"Ach mein Schatz." Fritz kissed his wife on the cheek, then introduced us. "Ms. Lawson, this is my wife, Frau Schönburg."

It wasn't lost on me that Fritz had introduced his wife as Frau Schönburg. No doubt, an effort to keep us using first names and put me in my place. Erika was dressed in a similarly styled Bavarian grey coat, like her husband's, with black velvet trim and silver buttons, but with a matching grey skirt.

"I'm sorry, I was busy when you arrived and couldn't show you around myself, but Fritz knows as much about the history of the area as I do. I hope you enjoyed your tour." Erika extended her hand and offered me a firm shake. Everything about her felt forced, from her thin icy smile to the cold grip of her hand on mine. "Come. We can chat in my office."

Fritz took both my hands in his, bowed his head, and wished me a good day. "Auf wiedersehen, Ms. Lawson."

CHAPTER TWELVE

I followed Erika back to her office, another brightly lit room with a large, paned glass window and a view of the lake. On her desk was a stack of mail along with the box of chocolates and the copy of *Journey International* I had brought with me. She glanced at the chocolates and magazine, thanked me, then gestured to a handsomely carved antique chair in front of the desk.

"Please, have a seat."

I waited while Erika sat down and took note of the room. On the wall, directly behind her, were two heavily gilded-framed works of art, cubist in style. Very different from the art I had seen in the museum and not what I would have expected to find in a natural history museum.

"Are those Picasso?"

Erika put her hands on her desk and paused. "So you do know something about art."

"Some." I wasn't about to tell Erika I had done a deep dive into art looted by the Nazis before I left for Germany. I smiled and hoped she'd let it go.

But she persisted. "Obviously, you know enough that you recognize a master when you see it."

"Picasso's one of the few I remember from an art history class I had in college."

"You've got good taste." Erika got up from her chair. In front of the window, a sideboard hosted a bar of crystal decanters and several etched glasses. "Would you like a drink? Wine? Coffee? Or perhaps something stronger?"

"No, thank you. I'm fine."

Erika poured herself a brandy, returned to her desk, and sat down. "I'm a fan of Picasso. He was one of my favorite artists. Very versatile and quite prolific. Did you know he produced more than 150,000 works before his death in 1975? But you're not here to talk about Picasso, are you? Erika picked up the copy of *Journey International,* began to thumb through it, then stopped on the masthead page with a list of the editorial staff and contact information. "Strange. I don't see your name listed here. Why is that?"

I was thankful Sophie had prepped me for such questions. Stick to the truth as much as possible. A lie is always easiest to build off the facts.

"You're looking at last month's edition. I'm new to the magazine. This is my first assignment." I explained how I had been working for a local newspaper in Phoenix and had been laid off. "Newspapers these days. Everybody's merging with everybody. There's no job security. I thought it might be the right time to try something new."

"And this is your first trip to Europe?"

"No, I was in Hungary last year. After getting laid off, I needed a little time for myself and wanted to travel. When I heard about an opening with *Journeyl International*, I went for it."

Erika closed the magazine. My answer appeared to have satisfied her.

"I apologize for being rude when you came by the Galerie the other day. I was distracted. The man you saw leave was a colleague. We had a difference of opinion. Unfortunate situation. I'm sorry you had to witness that."

"You don't need to apologize. You weren't expecting me. And I was there to see Hans."

"And to return my coat." Erika lifted her glass as a way of thanks and took a sip. "Which was very kind of you. And if I seem surprised you knew my brother, it's because Hans doesn't have much time to fraternize these days. He's very busy with the museum. And I know most of his lady friends. I've introduced them."

"Yes, well, I can assure you, ours was a very accidental meeting." I reached into my backpack for my notepad.

"You see, my brother is an artist and a very creative man—it runs in the family. Artists aren't always the best judge of character. When it comes to women, he can be easily distracted, and I've often felt the need to protect him...and us as well." Erika dropped her chin and stared at me. "I'm sure you understand. A family such as mine has a history. And, unfortunately, it's not always been...shall we say, tidy. These days, I'm very careful to guard what's left of my family's name. You wouldn't be the first woman to try to distract Hans or a reporter with an ulterior motive."

If Erika expected me to flinch, I wasn't about to give her the satisfaction. To do so would have indicated I had an ulterior motive. Instead, I answered as truthfully as I dared.

CHAPTER TWELVE

"Ms. Schonburg, I'd have to be deaf not to have heard the rumors about your uncle. But I can assure you, I have no interest in your family's history, nor am I out to trap your brother into a messy affair. That's not my style nor the purpose of my trip to Germany."

"Perhaps not. But you wouldn't be the first reporter to come looking. Rumors of Otto Gerhardt's Hoard have a way of bringing out all kinds of hacks."

I tapped my notepad with the tip of my pen. The sooner I convinced Erika I was no threat to her, her brother, or her family's secret, the more successful my mission would be.

"I'm not a hack, Ms. Schonburg. You and I don't know one another, but let me assure you, as far as your brother goes, I'm no treasure hunter and have no interest in him romantically. My plate's quite full in that department." I paused to make sure Erika knew her remark was unappreciated and unnecessary. "As for the rumor of your uncle's past, that's not the purpose of my visit here today. I'm a travel writer. I'm only here because Kirsten thought the museum might make an interesting story. But, if you're not interested—" I dropped my notepad inside my backpack and started to get up.

"Wait. Allow me to start again, and please call me Erika. If Kirsten thinks you're fine, I must, too. The truth is, Hans and I haven't spoken a lot lately. We've been too busy. But I appreciate your visit and taking the time to write something about this museum for your magazine. We're small, and we could use the publicity."

"It's my pleasure." I took my notepad from my backpack and dropped it on the floor.

I may have convinced Erika I had no ulterior motives, but she kept her guard up. If I asked anything personal about where she had grown up or her interest in art, she would remind me of the importance of Tergensee's history and launch into a long tirade about the five Bavarian glaciers that fed into the mountain lakes and the prospects that they may one day disappear. It was enough to make my eyes glaze over.

But when something rustled behind the wall next to her desk, her eyes shifted, and for the first time, I noticed a small jib door, like what I had seen in the lobby. A closet, perhaps or maybe a secret passageway like Kirsten had shown me inside Nymphenburg Castle. I clicked off the possibilities in my head. A secret hallway? A hiding place for stolen art, Gerhardt's hoard, or part of it? A private hallway might explain why I hadn't seen Erika pass by Fritz and me with the mail in her hands as we toured the small museum and how the chocolates and the magazine I had brought for Erika had ended up on her desk.

Erika stood up. "I think that's enough for the day. If you have any other questions, there should be a brochure in the lobby. Fritz can see you get an English language translation. But for now, I'm afraid I have to cut this short. You'll have to excuse me."

I hadn't expected our interview to end so quickly, but I had what I came for, a short piece for the magazine about the Tergernsee Tal Museum and a chilly but working relationship with Erika. I picked up my backpack and thanked her for the interview. I got as far as her office door when she stopped me.

"Ms. Lawson. I forgot to ask, do you intend to see Hans again before you leave?"

I paused. Did Erika still think I might be a threat to her family's secret? Had I not defused that bomb with our interview? Or was she that much of a mother hen to her younger brother? I weighed my response.

"He invited me to visit him in Oberammergau this weekend. He thought I should see the area."

Erika jerked her head, a small, subtle move I might not have noticed were I not looking for some sign of surprise. Then catching herself, she added, "How lovely. The area's quite beautiful. I'm sure you'll enjoy yourself."

"I'm looking forward to it. Auf Wiedersehen."

Chapter Thirteen

After leaving the museum, I drove around the lake and stopped for a late lunch. A Bavarian café, an A-framed structure, its wood deck dusted with powdered snow, and walls decorated with a fresco hunting scene advertised wurst and wiener schnitzel. Inside, the café wasn't crowded. A fire was lit, and several wooden tables sat empty in front of the window with a view of the lake with the mountains in the background. I found a chair and ordered a schnitzel, pomme frites, and a glass of white wine.

I had come to Germany to uncover a past, a secret cache of stolen art, and all I had seen were picture-perfect quaint holiday scenes, mountains covered with snow, the Marienplatz with its twinkling white lights, giant Christmas tree, and the sound of sleigh bells. But for all the scenic beauty, the partially frozen lake in front of me, and the snow-capped Alps dotted with skiers, I sensed a gray undertone. A paradox of rosy-cheeked people who kissed and greeted each other grüß Gott while they hurried on as though anxious to escape the shadowed memory of a past that lay just below the surface they dare not talk about.

When Sophie hired me, she told me about paintings and priceless items the Nazis had hidden in caves and castles to save them from the Allied bombings. She described those pieces of artwork ripped from the walls of museums and stolen at gunpoint from the homes of wealthy Jews as *the last prisoners of war*—the biggest art heist in history.

It was here that Sophie's dossier began. Page after page of research and notes she had collected outlining the last days of the war and her own experience as a holocaust survivor. How Nazi SS officers had entered her home with Otto Gerhardt, who selected from her father's collection those pieces he wanted and made her father an offer he couldn't refuse. His life and that of his family in exchange for a few Deutsche marks and the art on their walls. But ultimately, it was too late. Even after a deal was made, Sophie, her sisters, and her mother were sent to Dachau and her father to a work camp. Sophie's mother and sisters died in the camp. Sophie survived and later reunited with her father and moved to the United States.

And Otto Gerhardt had been on Sophie's radar ever since.

After the war, the Allies established repositories in Munich and Wiesbaden for artwork the Nazis had hidden. Art that was clearly identifiable, like Veit Stoss' wooden altar from St. Mary's Church in Krakow, was returned. While other works, whose provenance was more difficult to establish, were cataloged, boxed, and sent on to secondary depositories, where they were stored until they could be claimed—legally or otherwise.

The rumor that Otto Gerhardt had made off with thousands of stolen masterpieces may have been shocking to some, but under German law, it was entirely legal and was no surprise to those in the art world. The Germans were excellent record keepers. Art shown to have been bought and paid for was legally the buyer's property. And any claim that works from a private collection had fallen into the Nazi's hands under duress was impossible to prove. So, Otto Gerhardt showed up at one of the secondary depositories and demanded what he believed to be rightfully his, the Allies transferred crates of boxed masterpieces into his truck, no questions asked. And Otto Gerhardt wasn't alone in his confiscation. Nazi bureaucrats who had avoided prosecution at the war's end were believed to have paintings by Cezanne, Picasso, Matisse, and other great artists in their private collections, some of which were stacked in Swiss vaults with little hope it would ever be seen again.

When Otto Gerhardt died, his sister inherited her brother's estate. And later, upon her death, Erika and Hans received what they also believed was legitimately theirs. Under German law, the rules of Adverse Possession applied, assuring everything Otto Gerhardt owned or had stolen was legally

CHAPTER THIRTEEN

passed on to his heirs.

I finished my meal and, over a second glass of wine, took out a map and marked my location in Tegernsee. The museum, with all its hidden doors, was a likely hiding place, but for a thousand priceless pieces of art, much too small. If Gerhardt's Hoard was as big as Sophie suspected, it was more likely somewhere without public access and with enough space to be easily hidden. I stared across the lake at the mansion Erika and Fritz had built and wondered if it might be there.

* * *

I folded the map and hurried back to the car. In another hour, the sun would set, and I didn't want to be on the road after dark. Plus, if I called Sophie now, it was still early enough in New York, I could catch her before her day began and give her an update on my visit to Tegernsee and my visit with Erika. I put the key in the ignition and waited for the car to heat up while I placed the international call. When Sophie didn't answer, my call went to voice mail, and I left another coded message about my visit with Frau Perchta.

"Hi, Sophie, it's me, Kat. I've been doing a little more research into holiday traditions here, and I think you'll like how the story's coming. I visited Tegernsee, and—wow! So much to tell. Call me."

Five minutes later, my cell rang, and I pulled off to the side of the road.

"Kat, it's Sophie. Are you alone?"

"Yes, why?"

"I need to give you a heads-up."

"What's going on?"

"We have reason to think you may have a little competition."

"What kind of competition?"

"The international kind. The kind we don't want."

"Who? The Germans?"

"No, the Russians."

"Viktor Sokolov?" Sophie had warned me, but I couldn't imagine how I had piqued his interest. "It's him, isn't it?"

"We have reason to believe Viktor Sokolov's not only looking for Gerhardt's Hoard but that he may have zeroed in on you?"

"Me? Why?" I folded my arms across my chest and hugged myself. "How do you know?"

"The tail we have on Viktor overheard him talking with Inga—"

"Hans' assistant?"

"Inga's Viktor's plant. She's working for him. Viktor told her he suspects Hans and Erika may be hiding something, and he's suspicious of anyone trying to get close to them. Which means you, Kat. Our agent overheard Viktor say that the Americans are looking for Gerhardt's hidden treasures. You need to keep a lookout."

Now might be the time to explain the black, gold-grilled Mercedes nearly driving me off the autobahn. But I wasn't about to jeopardize the operation because some crazy driver had frightened me. I had no proof it was Viktor. It could have been anyone. And even greater than my fear of being found out, I liked what I was doing. After losing my job at the paper, I was lost and needed to be part of something. It felt good to be a member of a team again. It had been a long time, and I wanted to prove that I could do this job to Sophie and myself. If Sophie thought my cover had been blown and Viktor was on to me, I'd be back on a plane to Phoenix before nightfall.

"I'll keep my eyes open." The car started to steam up, and I wiped the windshield with my sleeve. "Did you get my message about Frau Perchta?"

"I did. So how did it go with Erika at the museum?"

"It was okay."

"Just okay?" Sophie laughed. "You mean to tell me that your west-coast charm that worked so well with Hans met with some resistance?"

"A little," I said. "If Kirsten hadn't convinced Erika that meeting with me might be good for the museum, there's no way she would have given me the time of day. As it is, Erika didn't tell me anything more than I could have read in a brochure. In fact, she insisted I take a copy."

"I'm sorry to hear that."

"Don't be. I didn't come away empty-handed."

CHAPTER THIRTEEN

"Oh?"

"I got a good look at the museum. Erika's got two Picassos hanging on the wall in her office. I have no idea if the paintings are part of Gerhardt's Hoard, but she's obviously not concerned about it. Like you said, it's not illegal. However, seeing the paintings did cause me to wonder if there might be more from where those came." I explained the barely visible closet doors that I thought might lead to a hidden hallway and the large, well-fortified lake house. "If Gerhardt's Hoard is real, they've got plenty of places to hide the art. "

Humph. "And you don't think Erika suspects you?"

"She was surprised when I told her I would visit Hans in Oberammergau this weekend. She doesn't like anyone she hasn't vetted getting close to her brother. But other than asking questions about the magazine, no. I don't think she suspects anything."

"And Hans? You're sure he's not on to you?"

"You know how men are. The only thing Hans wants is a pretty face and a little female companionship that doesn't have anything to do with the Galerie. With me, he's got both."

I couldn't let Sophie think I had any doubts. There was never a time when I had worked as an undercover reporter that I didn't have some fear I'd be found out. But the excitement of living a lie, the high of knowing that my cover might be blown at any moment, was addictive. I didn't know how to live without it and didn't want to. Not now that I had an opportunity to uncover a story that would get me back in the game.

"Don't get full of yourself, Kat. These people have been at this a lot longer than you, and they have much more to lose."

"I'm kidding, Sophie. Don't worry. Hans hasn't got a clue."

"Keep it that way, Kat. You don't want to have Erika, Hans, and the Russians on your tail."

Chapter Fourteen

By the time I got back to Munich, it was dark, and light snow had begun to fall. Nobody does Christmas like the Germans. Between the sounds of string quartets playing Christmas carols in the Marienplatz, the sweet smell of gingerbread, and the sight of the giant Christmas tree in front of the Neues Rathaus, it was like nothing I had ever seen. Growing up in Phoenix, snow was a novelty item we bought in a can and sprayed at the base of our three Saguaro cacti we decorated to look like the Three Wise Men with white cotton beards and Christmas lights every year. Munich was magic.

I loved the soft, wet feel of snowflakes on my face and stopped in the middle of the Marienplatz to enjoy a glass of warmed gluhwein, spiced wine, and Lebkucken, a traditional holiday gingerbread cookie. Not exactly a healthy dinner, but after a late lunch, I wasn't hungry for a big meal. The sights and sounds were a feast in themselves. I wandered the stands trimmed with evergreen boughs, piled high with row upon row of toys, stuffed animals, and nutcrackers that looked like wooden soldiers. I was debating whether or not to buy one when a heavyset man in a dark coat and fur cap darted out between the stands.

Viktor Sokolov!

I recognized him immediately, and behind him was Inga. She wore the same red and yellow striped knit cap and the tall, patent leather boots she had worn the day I saw her at the bakery. I ducked back beneath one of the evergreen boughs, pulled the hood of my coat over my head, and decided to follow.

CHAPTER FOURTEEN

Viktor took Inga by the hand, crossed the Marienplatz, and stopped in front of the Rathaus. I paused behind the Fischbrunnen Fountain, grabbed my camera from inside my backpack, and pointed it toward the Glockenspiel above their heads. I clicked off a couple of shots and watched Inga, like a defiant child, pull her hand away from Viktor. The Russian was twice her size, took her chin in his hand, forced her to look at him, then reached into his jacket and handed her something. Inga looked at it and shook her head. From the pinched look on her face, she wasn't happy. Viktor walked away, and I snapped another shot of her standing alone in front of the Rathaus, like a lost soul.

If Sophie was right, and the FBI had eyes on the Russian, where were they? I didn't see anyone following him. I stuffed my camera in my bag and tagged behind him for several blocks, stopping long enough to look into windows to avoid being noticed. Then just as Viktor turned a corner onto a busy boulevard, a couple of jolly revelers—good-sized beer-bellied men—knocked past him and approached me. The two had obviously had too much to drink and, spotting me, tried to engage me in a conversation.

"Guten Abend." The larger of the two men, unsteady on his feet, waved his hand in front of my face and nearly fell on me in his drunken stupor.

"I'm sorry," I said. I tried to push past him, but he took one right for every step I took left. Like a silly dance, I couldn't get around the man. "If you'll excuse me, I'm in a hurry."

"Ah, du bist Amerikaner. What's your rush? Would you like a drink?"

"No, thank you." I spun around, ducked beneath the bigger man's arm, and ran smack into the center of the second drunk, who stood directly in front of me like a linebacker. Using the heel of my hand to his chest, I pushed him aside, an effective move I'd learned in a self-defense class. But Viktor had disappeared by the time I was free of the drunker's block.

Damnit. I missed my opportunity.

The two drunks wrapped their arms about each other's shoulders and started to stagger off, but not before one bowed and the other waved goodbye to me. "Auf Wiedersehen."

I backtracked to the Marienplatz in hopes of finding Inga. But by then, the crowds had thinned, and it was getting late. Convinced she had gone home, I headed back to the hotel. A brisk walk in the snow but no more than a couple of blocks. I turned the corner and was within sight of the hotel's doorman when I paused to let several cars pass, their tires whipping wet snow onto the sidewalk. I waited for the intersection to clear, then crossed the street and was about to step up onto the curb when—

WHACK!

I tumbled onto the walk, then everything went dark. I don't know how long I was out, but I woke to find the hotel's doorman standing over me.

"Bist du in Ordnugn? Are you okay?"

"W-w-what happened?" The world was fuzzy. I rubbed the side of my head. I could scarcely remember where I was. The doorman helped me to my feet, and I brushed the snow from my coat, then felt for the shoulder strap of my backpack and panicked. "My bag!"

"It's gone, Miss. Someone stole it." The doorman pointed in the direction of where my assailant had fled. "I'm sorry. Let's get you back to the hotel. We'll call the police."

Chapter Fifteen

"Do you know where you are?"

I was sitting in a chair in the hotel's lobby. A police investigator had arrived to question me, but my memory was blurred. The last thing I remembered was crossing the street in front of the hotel, then feeling as though I had been pushed forward and waking with my face planted in the snow.

"I'm sorry, it all happened so fast." I patted my pockets. "Where's my bag, my backpack?" My passport, my wallet, my phone…everything was in it.

"Your bag was stolen, Miss. I'm here to take a report. Did you see anything?"

"No, I don't remember anything." It hurt to shake my head.

"There was a woman behind her. "The doorman interrupted, speaking in English for my benefit. "I saw her as Ms. Lawson crossed the street.

"Can you describe her?:

"She was young and wearing a long black coat. When Ms. Lawson got to the curb, the woman shoved her, then grabbed Ms. Lawson's bag and ran away."

The investigator looked at me. "You don't remember anyone following you?"

"No, not at all." My memory was blank. All I could think about was what I had lost.

"Wait." The doorman interrupted. "I did notice one thing. The coat the girl was wearing was hooded. But when she shoved Ms. Lawson, the hood fell back. She was blonde and wearing tall black boots with buckles."

"Sound familiar?" The investigator asked.

"No." I scratched my head. But, even as spaced out as I was, I knew from the doorman's description my attacker had to have been Inga. But I wasn't going to say anything until I talked with Sophie.

"That's it then." The investigator stood up and shoved his clipboard beneath my nose. "You'll need to sign here. I advise you, Ms. Lawson, to report to the American Consulate tomorrow morning. You'll need to arrange to have the proper papers issued to you in the absence of your passport."

I thanked the doorman for his help, went upstairs to my room, and locked the door. I considered calling Sophie, but her cell number was lost with my phone, and I wasn't about to contact information for the magazine's number and leave a message on her voicemail. The last thing I wanted to tell Sophie was that I had been mugged. Sophie would undoubtedly tell me she had warned me to be careful and that I had foolishly exposed myself and threatened the operation's success. I wasn't up for another of her lectures. My head was already banging from where I had hit it.

Instead, I checked in the mirror for damage to my head. A lump had already formed above my eye, and the lid was swelling. I decided ice would be the best treatment and got some from the machine in the hall. I wrapped a few cubes in a washcloth and held them against my head while I took inventory of what I had lost. Fortunately, before I went out, I had the sense to lock a few extra bucks, a bank card, and a credit card in the room safe, along with my spiral-bound journal containing notes from Sophie about my mission.

Convinced that whatever I had lost in my purse wouldn't reveal anything more about me other than who I pretended to be, I settled myself on the bed and began to scribble my thoughts about the day in my journal; the black Mercedes that had nearly run me off the autobahn, my visit with Erika, the museum, and the doorman's description of my attacker. *It had to be Inga.*

I closed my journal and felt for the knot on my forehead. The ice had helped, but I'd be lucky if I didn't have a shiner in the morning. I set the clock for six-thirty and crawled under the eiderdown. I wanted to be up and

CHAPTER FIFTEEN

out early.

*　*　*

I decided to walk from the hotel to the Consulate the following morning. It was cool but sunny when I got to the guard gate. I presented the only ID I had, a single credit card with my photo that I had left in the safe the night before. The guard took one look at my ID, grunted, and then as though he had expected me, led me inside, where I was summarily handed off to a second guard, along with my ID.

"Ms. Lawson?" The guard held my ID up to my face. Instinctively, I felt the bump on my head while he compared my face to the picture on my ID. Then satisfied, I was who I claimed to be, the guard handed me back my card. "If you'll follow me, please."

Without further conversation, I followed the guard down a long hallway. The only sound was that of our footsteps on the highly polished floor. We passed several closed doors until we reached what appeared to be our destination, at which point, the guard unlocked the door and nodded for me to enter. The room was small, no more than twelve by twelve, and sterile looking, with a single barred window that looked out onto the street. The only furniture was a small wooden table in the center of the room and two chairs. A thin manila envelope had been placed on the table, and on top of it was a cell phone.

With his back to the door, the guard informed me that he had been instructed to show me to the room and that I was to wait for further instructions. "In a few moments, the cell phone on the desk will ring. Answer it, and you'll be told what to do. In the meantime, don't open the envelope." Then with a curt nod, the guard bid me a good day and shut the door.

I stared at the small silver flip phone on the desk and willed it to ring. When it didn't, I walked to the window and peered out between the bars. The scene was cold, the trees bare, and the street wet with black snow from the traffic. I recapped in my mind what happened last night. *Was this somehow related?*

When the phone rang, I grabbed it from the table and held it to my ear. "Hello?"

"What's going on, Kat?"

"Sophie?" I wasn't so much surprised to hear Sophie's voice on the other end of the line as I was amazed at how quickly she had gotten word of my attack. It was four a.m. New York time, and she sounded as alert as she might have been at nine a.m.

"I'm looking at a report on my desk from the Munich police department."

"I'm sorry, I was going to call, but I was mugged, and—"

"I know what happened, Kat. I can read. Did you think I wouldn't find out? I was alerted as soon as the police report was filed. Your cell was registered with the FBI. They called and told me…at four a.m. What I don't understand is why on earth you were following Viktor? I warned you to stay away from him."

"How did you know I was following Viktor?"

"How do you think? I told you we had eyes on the Russian. Those two drunken Germans who stopped you before you caught up with Viktor? You're lucky they did. If Viktor thought you were following him, he might have slit your throat."

I put my hand to my neck. "They're working for you?"

"They're working for the Germans. And not that I should share this with you, but the man you shoved? You nearly broke his sternum. He didn't think you'd be that strong."

"Yea, well, my trainer used to say that, too." If there was one redeeming quality from last night's surprise attack, it was knowing that those secret agents assigned to tail Viktor now understood I wasn't just a pretty face the FBI had sent in to get close to Hans.

"You didn't mention a trainer, Kat, or anything about self-defense training when you interviewed for this job."

"Did it matter?"

"It helps if I know your skill sets, Kat." I hated that my life had become an open book for Sophie.

"Fine. If you must know, I took a few self-defense classes while working

CHAPTER FIFTEEN

for the paper."

"And?"

"It didn't end well, okay?"

"So, this was a dating relationship?"

"More like a fling."

"A what?"

"Don't judge me. There was chemistry. He was attractive, and we hung out for a while."

"And it ended badly."

"Let's just say things got out of hand. He didn't understand the word no. Not until I reminded him of what a good student I was and knocked him flat on his back."

"I see." Sophie chuckled. I knew she was weighing her options regarding my future with the magazine and, more importantly, the FBI. I could hear her chair squeak as she settled in front of her computer.

"When it comes to undercover work, I don't believe in coincidences. I can't afford to. If Viktor had any doubts about you before, he doesn't now. You've been made, Kat. The fact your purse was stolen. Why else do you think that would happen? Viktor and Inga are on to you. I'm sorry, but I can't—"

"Stop." If I didn't stop Sophie in another second, I knew she would cancel my contract and tell me to go home. "Look, I know you think Viktor and Inga suspect me. But they don't have any real proof. Viktor's paranoid. The man's a thug. He's probably got enemies everywhere. And Inga? She does what he tells her to do. From what I saw last night, the girl's terrified of him. And if you think Viktor set Inga up to steal my bag, you're probably right. But there was nothing in my bag a reporter wouldn't have. Nothing that would tie me to the FBI or any investigation. If I leave now, they'll suspect something. But if I stay and continue to do my job as a reporter, I'm just a journalist who got mugged on her way back to the hotel last night."

"Kat, you're getting into some pretty risky territory. This wasn't what I intended. You'd be better off going home and—"

"You can't fire me, Sophie. I'm too close. Hans trusts me, and Erika's no reason to think I'm anybody. Just some reporter her brother's interested in. Don't give up on me. I can do this."

There was a long pause.

"Sophie?"

"Okay, here's what is going to happen. Keep the cell phone you're talking on. It's a clone of a phone that was stolen. All the numbers you entered were automatically uploaded to our satellite, so you don't need to worry about re-entering them. They're all there."

"Thanks—"

"I'm not done yet, Kat. How are you fixed for cash?"

"I'm okay. I had a credit card, some small bills in the hotel safe, and my bank card."

"Forget your bank card. It won't be any good to you now. The minute I heard your bag had been stolen, I had the FBI put a stop on all your cards. There's an envelope on the table. Open it."

I cradled the phone to my ear and looked inside.

"There's a temporary passport. A couple hundred dollars in cash and an Amex credit card in your name. I was going to tell you to use the card to book a flight home. But we may be in the clear if you're convinced you had nothing in your bag to connect you to the FBI. However, you need to understand, Kat, this isn't the same job you signed up for. If you've been compromised, your level of risk is much higher now, and we may not be able to protect you. The closer you get to Hans at this point, the higher the stakes, and if he suspects you—"

"Don't worry—"

"Listen to me. Your life may depend upon it. The Amex card is tied to an FBI instant message center. Use it, and we can track you. It's the best we can do. It'll signal us you need help."

"Got it," I touched the knot above my eye. My sensible side told me to forget everything, take the Amex card and book the next flight home. But after last night, I wasn't about to walk away. I may have convinced Sophie I didn't think Viktor or Inga was on to me, but I had a gnawing feeling I was being watched. And if I were, I was one step closer to the biggest story of

CHAPTER FIFTEEN

my life, and I wasn't about to let go.

"I hope you understand what you're doing. These are dangerous people, Kat. If Hans and his sister think you're looking for their secret cache and that you might expose them, there's no telling what might happen. It may not be illegal in Germany to own stolen art, but they don't want the fallout that would result from the world knowing who they really are."

"And what are they, Sophie? Ex-Nazis sitting on stolen art, part of some black-market smuggling operations that sells art to private collectors who don't care to know where it came from? Or just a couple of Germans who happened to be the niece and nephew of a man who looted art for the Fuhrer's Museum, who *may or may not* have made off with some of the world's masterpieces. Guilty by association, but certainly not with any proof. At least not yet."

"Be careful, Kat. You're not the only one looking for Gerhardt's Hoard. And if you find their hiding place and Viktor learns of it, he'll kill you to stop you from exposing it before the Russians can get to it. Whatever you do, I'm warning you. Don't. Trust. Anyone."

Chapter Sixteen

"Welcome back, Ms. Lawson." It was late afternoon when I returned to the hotel, and a new doorman greeted me. I wasn't surprised he knew my name. After last night I was sure every member of the staff was aware of the purse-snatching incident. Nobody wants bad press, particularly from a travel writer on assignment. "You have a package at the desk. Would you like some help?"

"No. Thank you. I'll be fine." My arms were full. After leaving the consultant, I spent the afternoon shopping and picked up some warmer weather things. I hugged my bags and went directly to the front desk.

"I understand I have a package?"

"Yes, you do. A young woman brought this in this morning and asked that it be delivered to you soon as possible." The clerk pulled a tag attached to an extra-large brown paper sack and shoved it across the counter.

I glanced inside. My backpack had been stuffed in the bottom, and my keys, wallet, and camera were on top. "Did she leave her name?"

" I am sorry. It was busy when she arrived. But if it helps, she was young and had red hair." The phone behind the counter rang, and the clerk excused himself.

If the redhead had been someone from the police department, she would have identified herself to the clerk and left a business card or an official list of items found. And since the clerk hadn't mentioned either, my gut feeling was that whoever had returned my backpack had less to do with the police than it did my mugger. I took the sack from the counter and returned to my room with the rest of my shopping bags. Once inside, I locked the

CHAPTER SIXTEEN

door behind me, put the bag with my backpack on the bed, and drew the blinds. The sun had just begun to set, and I wasn't about to take any chances someone might be watching.

Returning to the bed, I took my wallet and camera from the bag. My wallet hadn't been touched. Money. Credit cards. Driver's license. Even my library card. And my camera, a simple point-and-shoot, was still loaded with film. I pulled my backpack from the bottom of the bag and dumped its remaining contents onto the bed. My passport, reporter's notepad, pencils, pens, and pieces of my cell phone fell out. Someone had smashed my phone to smithereens. I flipped through my notepad. There was nothing in my notes that would have indicated I was anything but an American travel reporter on assignment. Nothing to show I was a spy. I sat down and ran my hands over the bits and pieces of the crushed cell phone. And then, I found something I didn't expect to find—a bright pink press-on fingernail with rhinestones.

I had seen the likes of such long pink talons before. Like a cat's claw, Inga had curled her long-manicured fingers around Hans' elbow as she scurried him away at the Galerie's unveiling. There was no possible explanation for why such a fake nail would be in my bag. It had to be Inga's, the rhinestones alone matched those on her pink cell phone. The girl appeared to be obsessed with bling. I thought back to the last time I had seen her with Viktor beneath the glockenspiel. Viktor looked angry, and Inga was frightened. Was I the source of the conflict? Had Viktor convinced Inga to steal my backpack, and had she later had a change of heart?

Buzz...buzz...

My new cell phone vibrated from within my coat pocket. I glanced at the caller ID. Hans Hausmann. I wasn't surprised by the call. I had expected Hans would call to firm up details about my visit to Oberammergau, but my trip wasn't for five more days, and the timing felt odd. I put the phone to my ear.

"Hi."

"Hallo, Kat. Wie gehts? How are you?" Hans' voice sounded friendly, almost flirtatious.

"I'm fine. And you?" I decided it was best not to tell him about the mugging.

"Alles is gut. Verstehen? You understand?"

"Enough to know my German's not good enough to carry on this conversation auf Deutsch. English, bitte?"

Hans chuckled. "I suspect you have a better ear for languages than you know. Perhaps if you were to stick around, I might teach you."

"Very tempting, Herr Hausmann. But I doubt you'd have enough time."

"I always have time for people that I find interesting." Hans cleared his throat. "My sister tells me you visited her in Tegernsee yesterday."

So that was the purpose of his call. Erika had called her brother, not because she was suspicious of me, but to compare notes with him about me. I had given her no reason to doubt my credentials or my mission. And if Erika wasn't worried about me, I was one step closer to getting Hans to trust me.

"I hope she was pleased. Kirsten set up the interview."

"That sounds like Kirsten. The woman's a busybody, always got her hand out, looking for a favor, but in this case, it appears to have been a good deed. My sister's museum can use the PR, and she told me how embarrassed she was about how she acted when you came by the Galerie. I'm sorry if she was rude. Erika can be difficult. She's not nearly as charming as I can be."

I laughed. "Is that so?"

"Tell me, how did you like Tegernsee?"

"It was pretty. The mountains. The snow. The lake. Like a picture postcard, in fact."

"And did you find what you were looking for?"

"I'm sorry. Looking for?" Suddenly what felt like a flirtatious conversation took an unexpected turn, and I wondered if the purpose of this call was to test me.

"History," Hans said. "I assumed you were interested in the area's history."

"Yes, Erika's husband gave me a tour of the museum. It was fascinating. And your sister, you'll be happy to know, was very—"

"Icy. Yes, I know. I hope she didn't scare you off. It's the reason for my call. I wanted to make sure we're still on for Saturday."

"Of course, I've been looking forward to it." Sophie would be so proud of

CHAPTER SIXTEEN

me. Whether it was her yenta-matchmaker instincts that had convinced her that I'd be a good match for Hans or my undercover reporting skills, which admittedly on an international level needed honing, Hans was becoming an easy mark. One I looked forward to getting to know better.

"Good. There is a train from München to Oberammergau. It's better for you not to drive, particularly if you're not used to the autobahn. German drivers can be aggressive. It's a short trip. If you leave by noon, you should get there around one-thirty. I'll pick you up at the train stop. There is much to do there, and things I would like to show you. Things I think you might like to see and some that will surprise you."

Chapter Seventeen

By Saturday morning, the bump on my forehead was no better. No matter how I tried to hide it, there was still a swelling the size of a small robin's egg above my eye. The only possible way to camouflage it was to wear my black-brimmed hat low on my brow and a pair of overly large dark glasses. I caught my reflection in the hotel's mirror as I left for the train station; dressed in my black belted coat with a leather satchel over my shoulder, I looked like a spy.

If Hans asked about my bruised brow, I planned to tell him I'd fallen on the ice. After Sophie's warning that I trust no one, I wasn't about to mention the mugging. I was already nervous about meeting Hans at his chalet. I didn't need any more thoughts about what had happened in front of the hotel. I may have convinced Sophie I'd be fine, but now, as the train started pulling away from the station, I began to wonder who I was fooling? If Hans had any idea of my real intent, this was a trip from which I might never return. I took a deep breath, rested my head against the back of the train seat, and watched out the window as the scenery began to change. Within minutes we had left the city center and started to chug through sleepy little Bavarian hamlets nestled between the snowy mountain passes covered with blankets of fog so thick I couldn't see the mountain tops. I closed my eyes and tried to focus on the purpose of my mission.

My plan was to get close to Hans, draw him out about his uncle, and get him to talk about Gerhardt's hidden hoard, or lack of it, without raising suspicion, and I didn't have a lot of time to do it. While Hans had invited me to Oberammergau to see the sights, I would have been a fool not to know

CHAPTER SEVENTEEN

where a weekend alone at his chateau might lead. Sex can be a slippery slope, and men like Hans were used to getting what they wanted and just as quick to dispose of what they didn't. I couldn't allow this weekend to become a one-and-done type of affair. And while the thought of a casual dalliance was tempting, I needed to make sure whatever happened between us didn't happen before I got close enough to Hans to learn the truth about Gerhardt's Hoard. If not, and Hans were to discover the real reason for my mission to the chateau, he might not only seduce me, he might kill me.

* * *

I was surprised when the train pulled into Oberammergau to see Hans dressed in traditional Bavarian costume, bundhosen—goat-skinned pants with suspenders—heavy wool socks, a Tyrolean green jacket, and a feather-adorned hat. I scarcely recognized him. He had grown a beard since I last saw him, giving him a very outdoorsy, woodsman look. The lines around his eyes were softer, more like laugh lines than stress. As I stepped off the train, I couldn't resist a smile. Here in the fresh mountain air, so cool it burned my lungs, Hans looked free from the burdens of his city life.

"Grüß Gott." Hans reached for my bag and greeted me heartily with a big hug, arms around my shoulders, and a squeeze so tight that my hat fell into the snow.

I stooped for my hat, but Hans was faster, picked it up, and handed it to me. Then noticed the bump above my eye.

"Was ist das?"

I pushed the hair from my face. "It's nothing. I fell in the snow. I still haven't learned how slippery it can be."

Hans put his arm around my shoulder, pulled me close, and whispered in my ear. "Then I shall have to hold you very tight so that you do not fall again. Come, I've much to show you."

Part of me wanted to melt into his arms. Mentally I knew the game I had to play, but I hadn't counted on how it might feel with him so close, with his arms around me in the cold alpine air. I felt as though the deck had been stacked against me. I had to focus. *Keep it friendly, Kat.*

I leaned into his chest and scratched his beard. "This is new."

"I never shave when I'm away from the museum." Hans took my hand from his face and held it in his own. Then nodded ahead. "Look, I have a surprise. Come see."

Climbing out of a large black SUV was a small boy who looked no more than six or seven years old and dressed like Hans in leather bundhosen and a heavy wool cardigan. He came running towards us.

"Ist das das amerikanische Cowgirl?"

Hans stepped ahead of me, knelt, and threw his arms open. "Ja. Das ist dadsamerikanishche Cowgirl." Then standing, he added, "Kat, this is my nephew, Baret. He's the one I was buying the book for about your American West when we met. Baret, this is Kat Lawson."

Baret extended his hand. "Guten tag."

"Good day to you, too," I said. Then looking at Hans added, "You told him I'm a cowgirl?"

"I told him you're from Arizona."

"Do you know Cochise or Geronimo?" The boy looked at me, his blue eyes wide.

I tousled his sandy-colored hair. "They were a little before my time. But yes. I have heard of them. Just like you have."

"My sister sent Baret down for the weekend. Something came up, and she asked if I might take him. I hope you don't mind?"

"Not at all," I said. "It'll be fun."

I dropped my head to hide my smile while Hans and Baret ran ahead to the car. So much for thinking things might heat up around the chateau. I took a deep breath of the fresh mountain air and silently thanked Erika. A chaperone would make my job so much easier.

We drove back through the town. Everywhere, the streets were neatly plowed with berms of crisp white snow and busy with shoppers bundled against the chill, dwarfed beneath the towering white Alps. Oberammergau, with its onion-domed church and small stores, their windows decorated with Christmas boughs and cottages with green shutters and frescoed scenes

CHAPTER SEVENTEEN

of saints and former residents, was as picturesque as a Christmas card.

Hans insisted we get out and walk, and Baret skipped ahead. It was chilly. The snow was hard-packed and crunchy beneath our feet. Hans offered me a sip of schnapps from a flask he had hidden inside his jacket, then took my arm, and we window-shopped like tourists.

"Onkel, komm and sieh!"Baret hollered for his uncle to come, then came running back and grabbed him by the hand, dragging him down the street to a window display of Christmas elves playing Pokemon games and dealing cards. Hans leaned down and whispered in the boy's ear, and a look of delight crossed his young face. Whoever Hans Hausmann was, whatever terrible things Sophie thought he may have done or was capable of, the man standing in front of me was a caring, attentive uncle.

We stopped for lunch. Tempted by the smell and sight of a large rotating spit grill with racks of slow-roasted chicken in a window, we couldn't resist. Inside tables were set with blue and white checkered tablecloths and pewter plates on the walls. I ordered a glass of white wine. Hans had a beer. Baret a Spezi, a non-alcoholic soft drink made with orange soda, and we split a roasted chicken with Pommes Frites and a cucumber salad.

Hans leaned back in his chair when we finished and patted his stomach. "Ich bin satt. I've had enough." Then looking at his nephew, he added, "Bist du satt, Baret? Are you full?"

Baret wiggled in the chair and pointed to a display of gingerbread cookies next to the front counter. I couldn't resist the urge and suggested I buy several.

"For the road," I said.

"Gut. And then we must go." Hans stood up and paid the bill. "I promised Baret we would go back to the chalet and go ice skating. Do you skate?"

"You have a lake?"

Hans didn't answer. Instead, he tipped his head in the direction of his SUV. "You'll see."

* * *

Hans said his chalet was nestled in the shadow of the Zugspitze, the highest mountain in Germany. Nine-thousand, seven hundred and eighty feet tall. Easily the most rugged, snow-capped, and sheer-faced of the mountain ranges I had seen.

"Buckle up. It's a short ride, a few hairpin turns, but if you're not used to it —"

"Es ist gruselig!" Baret giggled from the back seat.

Hans patted my knee. "He says it's scary. But you needn't worry. We're not going all the way to the top. Just a few hundred meters."

I snapped my seat belt. Ahead was nothing but a narrow, snowy mountain road covered with a swirling mist of grey fog that allowed for only the occasional view of the jagged terrain surrounding us.

I gripped the grab handle and held tight. "How did you ever find this place?"

"I didn't." Hans downshifted, and the car slowed as we navigated a hairpin turn. The view from my window was a thousand-foot drop. "My mother did. After the war."

"Früher war es eine Burg." Baret giggled.

"English, Baret. Miss Lawson doesn't speak German. You need to practice."

"It was a castle," Baret said.

"That was a long time ago," Hans corrected. "We think it might have been a 14th-century fortress, but whatever was left of it was demolished during the war."

"And your mother rebuilt it?"

"The foundation was good, and it was quiet. It's what she wanted after the war. She built on top of it. It's from her that I get my talent. She was a great artist."

"So, you grew up here?" The area seemed remote for a cultured man like Hans, who appeared so at home in the city.

"On and off. I went away for college, but after my mother died, I returned and decided to stay. I found some of her plans, her early drawings for what she wanted to do here, and decided I'd finish what she started. I've had some help, but most of the work I've done myself. There's still more to do, but it's

CHAPTER SEVENTEEN

livable."

"But don't go downstairs." Baret put his hands on the back of my seat and leaned forward. "There's a dungeon. It's where they tortured witches."

Hans patted Baret's hand. "I think I've read you too many German fairytales. You know those aren't real."

"But Mutter says—."

"Well, your mutter is wrong. There's no dungeon beneath the castle. And that's enough talk about witches. We don't want to scare Kat, now do we?" Hans stopped the car, reached into the glove box, and took out a remote.

Directly in front of us was a large wrought iron gate held on either side by a rock watchtower that looked centuries old.

Hans pushed the remote, and the gates swung slowly open. "Willkommen. Das ist Schloss Hausmann, my chateau."

There's no other way to say it. My jaw dropped as we drove forward into a circular drive. Kirsten said I would like the chateau, but this was beyond what I had imagined. In front of us, a classic two-story, nineteenth-century manor house stood with a grey slate tile roof and two chimneys. I noticed smoke coming from one. A pair of medieval-looking hand-carved double doors graced the entry with three tall narrow windows on either side.

"I thought you lived alone." I pointed to the smoke coming from the chimney while Baret ran ahead.

Hans got my bag from the trunk. "I do. But I have a couple of day laborers, Ozan and Cahill. They're guest workers, what we call Gastarbeiter. They help me from time to time. They're around this weekend. I asked them to freshen up the guest quarters before you came. It needed a few touchups. And I asked Ozan to light a fire to take the chill off." Hans held out his hand to me. "Come. I'll show you around."

Chapter Eighteen

There were six stone steps leading up to the front balcony. Baret sprinted up the steps to the top, then put his hands to the sides of his mouth and yodeled.

"Yodel-ay-ee-oooo." From the mountains, his child-like voice echoed back.

Hans put my bag down, chased up the steps, and did the same. A chorus of yodels from every direction bounced from one snowy mountaintop to the next. It was impossible to know from where the sound would volley or how many refrains there might be.

I joined them on the steps and hollered. "Helloooooooo!" I counted five reverberations, each sounding further and further away, then clapped my hands. In the distance, I could see the rooftops of Oberammergau and Garmisch-Partenkirchen nestled in a blanket of white snow, while behind us, the face of the Zugspitze, Germany's highest peak, loomed above the chateau.

"Kommen Sie." Hans clapped his hands, then pointed to our feet. "Stiefel aus. Boots off." Hans opened the front door, stomped the snow from his feet, then took his boots off and threw them inside to a mat by the door.

I followed Hans inside with my boots in my hands and stopped. "Is that—"

"My security alarm." Hans took my boots and tossed them on the mat.

Beneath a tall circular staircase, posed for an attack, stood a silver-armored medieval knight. He must have been at least six and a half feet tall, and behind him, on what looked like a freshly painted white stucco wall, was an arsenal of medieval weaponry; a breastplate, spears, daggers, crossbows, and a circular array of knives.

CHAPTER EIGHTEEN

"In the middle-ages, kings tried to intimidate their enemies by displaying their weaponry for all to see upon entering. So far, it's worked." Hans winked, said something to Baret in German, and pointed to the staircase. The boy disappeared upstairs, and Hans gestured for me to follow.

"He needs to change if we're going to skate. It's getting late. The sun will set soon, but first, come. There is something I think you might like to see."

The living room or the great room was down two stone steps to the right of the entry and framed by a stone archway. I stopped on the steps to take it all in. The room was huge, with dark wooden floors and six floor-to-ceiling windows, three on either side of the room. One set of windows looked out the front of the house toward the entry gate, and the second onto a snowy parklike setting behind. The ceiling must have been at least twelve feet high and supported by giant wood beams, along with a massive stone fireplace, which gave the room a rustic feel. Scattered rugs covered the floor, and modern and abstract artworks were on the walls. To my left, in front of the windows that looked out onto the backyard, was a bar area, and beyond it, a hallway that I assumed led to the kitchen. The main seating area was in the center of the room, beneath a large iron chandelier. A leather sofa, glass table, and several overstuffed chairs faced the fireplace, and to my right, a smaller seating area with two small, cushioned chairs faced a wall of bookshelves crammed with volumes of leatherbound books.

"Here, I want you to see this." Hans pointed to the bookcase. "My collection of Karl May." Hans pulled a book from the shelf, opened it, and traced the author's signature with his finger. It was obviously a collector's edition. "He died in 1921, but for Germans, he was our introduction to your wild west. Every summer, we celebrate Old Shatterhand and Winnetou with costumes and trick riding. You should include something about it in your magazine." Hans put the book back on the shelf. "And look, I even have his Henry rifle, exactly like the one in the book." Hans picked up the antique firearm, one of three, from a gun stand next to the bookcase and pointed it toward the front window.

I stepped back. "I hope that's not loaded."

"Don't worry, I don't use this for hunting." Hans put the rifle back in the stand. "It was a housewarming gift. It's more like the art on the walls, just something to look at."

Above the gun stand was a painting of an old-world hunting scene. "Like that?" I asked.

"Nice, isn't it? It's by Józef Brandt, a Polish painter. It's called *The Hunting Scene*. It was thought to be lost in the war, but I was lucky enough to find a collector who'd sell it to me like these rifles."

"Is it real?" I leaned forward to get a better view of the painting.

"It is. And you know how I know?"

"No, I've no idea."

Hans took the painting off the wall. "Here, look at the back, not the front. The verso. Any good painter could copy a work of art, the paint, the type of paint, the color, even the artist's stroke. But the stamps on the back, the labels, the wax seals, and the nails used to attach the canvas to the frame verify a painting's provenance. And that story is often as interesting as the painting itself." Hans hung the painting back on the wall. "But here, if you want to hold a real piece of history in your hands. Try this; it's a repeating rifle, the first of its kind. Used during your Civil War." Hans handed me one of the rifles from the rack and stepped back.

It wasn't the first time I had held a rifle. I braced the butt on my thigh, slapped the barrel to break the bridge, checked to make sure it was empty, then hit the bridge back in place and pointed the rifle in the direction of the fireplace.

"I'm impressed."

"Don't be. It's just one of the things I picked up growing up in the desert. You may know about art, but I know a thing or two about rifles. Kids used to come to school with long barrel rifles mounted in the rear window of their trucks. But I've never seen a piece like this." I lowered the rifle and ran my hand across the smooth finished barrel and the highly polished wood butt. "Looks like it belongs in a museum."

"It was, in fact."

I handed the rifle back to Hans. "Kind of an unusual housewarming gift. Where I come from, if you give someone a set of knives, you include a penny

CHAPTER EIGHTEEN

for each knife to ensure the friendship's not cut. I'm not sure what you give with a rifle."

"Perhaps if I had insisted on a penny, that friendship might still be intact." Hans took the rifle from me and placed it next to two others on the stand.

"Onkel Hans." Baret entered the room. He had changed into long pants and held a pair of ice skates in one hand. "Bist du bereit?"

"Do you skate?" Hans looked at me quizzically.

"Ice skate?" My voice cracked.

Hans smiled, being with his nephew all afternoon had given him a sense of whimsy, dimples formed on either side of his bearded cheeks.

"Not in years. And—" I looked at my feet and raised the palms of my hands. "It's not like I travel with skates."

"This is not a problem. Come." Hans motioned for me to follow. "Grab your boots; it will be dark soon."

Quick as I could I slipped on my boots and tagged behind Hans and Baret through the kitchen and out the back door through a mudroom, where Hans picked up a pair of ice skates. Then with one hand on Baret's shoulder and his skates under the other, I followed them as we traipsed through the snow to a small snow shed a hundred yards from the house, next to a pond.

"I've skates inside and heavy socks if you need them. Find whatever fits and join us on the ice." Hans shoved the shed's wooden door open and pulled on a chain to turn on a light.

The shed was full of snow gear, old-fashioned wooden snowshoes, skies, poles, and hanging on the wall, a half dozen skates. I sorted through several, one newer-looking pair with pink laces, and wondered about their origin, then tossed them aside until I found a pair that fit.

"I hope you're not expecting much." I braced myself against the shed and hollered to Hans on the ice.

"Come, you'll be fine." Hans held out his hand.

I staggered toward the pond, one foot in front of the other, struggling to keep my ankles straight, arms stretched out like airplane wings, trying to keep my balance. When I reached the pond and put one foot onto the ice, I swayed like a drunk and felt like my feet were about to slip out from beneath me. I must have looked ridiculous.

Hans skated up behind me and put his hands on my hips. "I've got you, relax."

I straightened up, and with Hans holding me, we skated together while Baret dashed ahead. Then taking my hand, Hans pulled me next to him, and with his arm around me, we skated side by side with the cool mountain air in our faces. By the time we circled the pond twice, I was beginning to feel like I knew what I was doing. Like riding a bike, it all came back to me.

The day went better than I expected. Baret's presence made it easy for me to ask questions about the chateau and its history. Hans chatted about how he and his sister had moved with their mother from Dresden after their father had been killed in the war and what it was like growing up here. And after skating, we had a quiet dinner in the kitchen, a traditional German supper, Hans said. Cold cuts, cheeses, and bread, followed by a steaming cup of hot chocolate in front of the fireplace in the great room. Hans and Baret roughhoused a bit, wrestling like puppy dogs before settling down to a card game, while I sat on the couch in front of the fire and thumbed through several art books I found on the bookshelves. At nine p.m., the grandfather clock chimed, and Baret stood up and announced it was time for him to go to bed. He shook my hand, bid us goodnight, and excused himself.

"He's very well-mannered," I said. I would have expected Hans might have needed to persuade him, but Baret appeared to be acting on his own accord.

"My sister is very strict with him. If it were up to me, I'd be less so." Hans got up from the couch and went to the bar. He looked relaxed, his hair mussed, his wool shirt askew from roughhousing with his nephew. "Would you like a brandy?"

"Yes," I said.

Hans paused and glanced in the direction of the staircase. "Gute Nacht, Baret."

I suspected Baret had snuck down the stairs and was spying on us.

"Gute Nacht, Onkel Hans."

When Hans heard the door close upstairs, he smiled and poured two brandies into crystal snifters.

CHAPTER EIGHTEEN

"Does he visit often?"

"Not as often as I'd like. Unfortunately, my sister and I don't always see eye-to-eye on things. Baret being one." Hans offered me the snifter and sat down on the couch. "Did you have a good time today?"

"I did." I swirled the bandy, then tilted the snifter to my nose. The smell was warm and spicy and tickled my nose. "Very much."

"It's not often I get a day like today to just enjoy myself." Hans took a sip of brandy. "Thank you for coming."

"I'm the one that should thank you. You're an excellent tour guide." I curled my legs beneath me and cupped the glass in my hands. "But I have to say, I'm surprised."

"How so?"

"Big celebrity curator like yourself, I never would have expected to see a softer side. The way you are with Baret, you're a natural. If I didn't know better, I would have thought you were his father and probably had a brood of boys just like him at home."

"Life doesn't always give us what we want. Fortunately, I have Baret. How about you? How is it an attractive woman like yourself is alone?" Hans took my right hand and laced his fingers through my own. "Or is there someone?" Hans nodded to the simple gold band on my right ring finger.

I pulled my hand from his and cupped them both around the snifter. In my head, I could hear Sophie telling me, stick to the facts, Kat. A lie was always easiest to build from the truth.

"There was," I said. "Actually, I've had two husbands. The first, when I was still in college." I held up my hand and wiggled my right ring finger. "The ring was from then. He was a pilot. Shot down in Vietnam. MIA. Never came home. And the second, he was a con artist."

"Really? I'm surprised. You seem too smart to be anyone's fool."

I looked down at my drink and swirled the snifter. "Like you say, life doesn't always give us what we want."

Hans ran the tips of his fingers up my arm. "And what is it you really want, Kat?" I could smell the brandy on his breath, and my heart began to race. "Tell me." Then turning my chin to his, he kissed me gently.

"Onkel Hans?"

Hans jerked his head away. "Baret?"

The boy stood beneath the living room's arched entry. Dressed in his pajamas and slippers, he rubbed his eyes and mumbled something that, in any language, meant he couldn't sleep.

Hans kissed me lightly on the forehead above my bruised brow. "To be continued?"

"Another time," I said. "It's getting late, and I think your nephew needs you more than I do tonight."

Chapter Nineteen

I couldn't sleep. The bed was comfortable with a soft feather eiderdown, and the room was dark and quiet, but my mind was like a ping-pong ball, bouncing from thought to thought about Hans von Hausmann. Just who was he? The charming man I'd met in the bookstore, who doted on his nephew? The erudite art historian with a celebrated reputation as a womanizer? Or, was this all a cover, and Hans von Hausmann was, as Sophie believed, warden to those last prisoners of war.

I knew Hans had gone to bed, so I waited until the sounds of the house had settled, then quietly got up. It was time I did a little investigating. If Hans was hiding anything, the chateau would be the perfect place. It was not only remote but also the house Hans had grown up in and inherited from his mother. Hans admitted after finding his mother's original plans that he had remodeled a lot of the chateau and that there were still unfinished areas of the house.

At the end of the hallway, past the bedroom doors, a large plastic sheet hung from the ceiling to the floor, covering the entrance to a staircase. Hans said the stairs led to an unfinished area in the attic. No point in showing me—just a lot of workman's tools. Tools Cahill and Ozan needed to use to finish off the chateau. But I wondered, might there be another reason? Perhaps a likely hiding place to stash his uncle's hoard?

I took my robe from the foot of the bed and stepped barefoot onto the floor. I paused to ensure I hadn't been heard, then tiptoed to the bedroom door. With my hand on the handle, I twisted the knob, slowly inched the door open, and listened. Nothing. All was quiet. Thinking I was safe, I slipped silently down the hall to the staircase and behind the plastic sheeting, then stopped at the foot of the stairs. Moonlight from an upstairs attic window beamed just enough light down the stairway. I grabbed the handrail and took each step like I was navigating a minefield. When I got to the top, I closed my eyes and exhaled, thankful I hadn't been heard.

The landing at the top of the stairs was narrow. The window that had lit my way was directly in front of me. To my left was the unfinished attic with tools and workbenches, exactly as Hans had said. Even in the low light, I could see no evidence of any cache, certainly not hundreds of canvasses hidden beneath the chateau's eves. But to my right was a wooden door, and a metal latch with a heavy padlock bolted to it.

I knew I would be pushing my luck to try and pick the lock and hope not to be heard. But I couldn't tell Sophie I had visited the chateau and come up empty. If I were to prove the existence or nonexistence of Gerhardt's Hoard, I had to try. I needed to know whatever lay behind the door, and I knew I could pick the lock with ease. I had interviewed enough burglars who had bragged about how easy it was to pick a lock. One had even shown me how. And with a bit of luck, I thought I could do it. All I needed was a bobby pin. And I had plenty. Before I went to bed, I scrunched my hair and pinned it to my head so my hair would have a little lift in the morning. It was a trick I learned a long time ago, and it beat traveling with hot rollers. With my hands shaking, I pulled one of the bobby pins from my hair and bent the prongs 90 degrees. Then slipping the pin into the keyhole, I held the handle tightly in one hand and jimmied the lock with the other. Within seconds, it fell open in my hand.

I replaced the open lock on the latch and pushed open the door. Hans had lied to me. This part of the attic had been finished off. Moonlight spilled through two large glass windows in the chateau's slanted ceiling, illuminating an art studio. In the center of the room was an easel covered with a canvas tarp. Next to it was a table, and on it was a palette smeared with paint and jars with brushes and stained paint cloths. A large portrait, *The Seated Lady* by Matisse, was hanging on the wall directly beneath the attic windows as though she were welcoming me. Unless this was a copy, it

CHAPTER NINETEEN

had to be the same painting that had hung in the Gerhardt Galerie. I moved forward to see it better and discovered several more canvases beneath her, leaning against the wall. One was a life-sized portrait of Erika and Fritz with Baret, and next to it, an unfinished copy of Gauguin's *Fruits on the Table*. I picked up the unfinished copy. Was Hans the artist? Had I stumbled upon his studio? I stared at the Gauguin. The painting was exactly like what I had seen in the museum. How many copies were there? And why? I looked back at *The Seated Lady*. Tacked to the wall beside her were photos of other masterpieces and crude pencil sketches with paint samples.

"Ahem...have you found what you came looking for?"

My heart stopped. There was no explaining my presence in the attic, not at this hour. I reached for the palette knife on the table.

Too late. Hans stepped forward and caught my wrist. "Don't even think about it."

"Let go of me! You're hurting me."

We struggled with the knife.

"Not until you tell me why you're here." Hans pinned my arms behind my back. "Who are you working for? The Russians? Did Viktor Sokolov send you? Or is it the Americans?"

"I don't know what you're talking about." I tried to pull away, but Hans' grip was too tight.

"I think you do." Hans wrested the knife away from me. "Look, I'm not going to hurt you." Hans let go of my wrists, slapped the blade on the table, and put his hands up. "But I need to know who sent you?"

"Nobody sent me." I rubbed my wrists and stared at the knife. There was no way I could get to it, not without a repeat of my fruitless efforts. And then what? Where could I go? Where would I run?

"Nobody? So you're in the habit of sleepwalking and picking locks, are you?" Hans pulled the padlock from his robe's pocket and dangled it in front of me. "Look familiar?"

"I couldn't sleep. I got curious and decided to get up and look around."

"You're lying. I could taste the lie on your lips when I kissed you tonight. You're not here for any travel feature or even a friendly romp in the hay.

Although if I'm right, you wouldn't have objected."

"You're crazy. I'm here to do a story. I work for a travel publication—"

"Save it, Kat. It's not going to work." Hans shut the door behind him. "Erika called and gave me a heads-up about you right after you left Tegernsee. She was suspicious from the moment she met you. It's her nature. But this time, it appears she had reason. She recognized your publisher's name. Sophie Brill, right? It was on the masthead of the copy of *Journey International* you gave her. Erika remembered Miss Brill from a convention they had attended years ago while Erika was still at University. Sophie was the keynote speaker. I'm sure you'll find the title of her speech fascinating. 'The Last Prisoners of War, Germany's Hidden Treasures.' I know Erika did."

There was nothing I could say. I had been wrong about Erika. She was on to me from the minute she saw Sophie's name in the masthead. And now, Hans was on to me, too.

"What did you tell her?"

"I told her she was overthinking things. Not a surprise after Viktor, but I'd check it out. Just because a journalist shows up working for a former art historian turned travel publisher doesn't mean you're a spy."

"And she believed you?"

"You're here, aren't you? If Erika didn't trust me, she would have sicked Fritz on you, and you never would have made it back from Tegernsee."

"And yet, she sent her son to chaperone."

"That wasn't her decision. You see, after I got off the phone with Erika, I did a little research of my own and called *Journey International's* office in New York. I spoke with Miss Selma, the office manager. Did you know Selma is a German name? Her first name's Brigette. Charming woman, very chatty. She answers the phone and relays messages to Sophie. She doesn't know much about you, only that Sophie recently hired you, and you've been leaving messages for her. Almost daily. People like Brigette need more than a paycheck to make them feel important. Single woman, working alone for a travel pub, never been anywhere. Doesn't take much more than a friendly ear, a few words in her native tongue to learn what she knows, or to get her to listen in on a few prerecorded messages like those you left." Hans

CHAPTER NINETEEN

picked up the palate knife and tapped the blade against the palm of his hand. "Krampus, Kat? That's how you refer to me? And my sister Erika as Frau Perchta? Very clever."

"So, what are you going to do? Kill me?"

Hans pulled a stool from beneath the table and nodded for me to sit. "I have something else in mind. Perhaps I'll paint you. Would you like that?" Then grabbing the back of my neck, Hans pulled me close and tilted my head up to his. "You've good features, Kat. Nice eyes. Soft skin." Slowly, he relaxed his grip and traced the line of my jaw, his thumb coming to rest on my mouth. "And very kissable lips."

"Stop." I grabbed his hand and pushed it away. "I think we've already established that's not what you want."

"Not entirely, but yes, you're right. What I want is your help. But first, there are some things you need to understand, and when you do, I think you and I can help each other."

I massaged the back of my neck. If Hans had wanted to kill me, he could have done it by now.

"Alright. Help me understand. Just what it is you want me to know?"

"Like I told you, I wasn't surprised the night the Gauguin was stolen. I'd been expecting it. It's why I left the copy on the easel out in the open. I practically gift-wrapped it for him."

"Then you know who stole it."

"I've got a pretty good idea. The first is the Gauguin's legitimate owner, Kraus Kemper. He's certainly angry enough and has reason to be. A year ago, he approached my sister. Herr Kemper was a friend of a student in Erika's art history class at the university. He was curious about a painting he had found among his father's possessions after he died. His father had been a farmer and had found the Gauguin abandoned on a train twenty years ago. He liked the painting and hung it above his cow in his barn. Can you imagine a painting by Gauguin hanging in a barn? When Herr Kemper's father died, his son thought the painting might be worth something, and his friend suggested Herr Kemper bring it to my sister for evaluation. Erika recognized the Gauguin right away and knew its history. *Fruits on the Table* had been stolen from a private gallery in London. The gallery had subsequently closed due to the death of the proprietors, and the art, because there was no living family, was donated to a London Museum. And Erika—"

"Saw an opportunity and snatched the painting for herself." It wasn't hard to imagine Erika taking advantage of the situation.

"My sister's no saint, but when she realized the painting was an original Gauguin, she couldn't help herself. We needed the Gauguin to get rid of Viktor Sokolov."

"Really?" It was difficult to keep the sarcasm from my voice. "You have a gallery full of paintings, and probably a lot more from where they came from, and you still needed the Gauguin?"

Hans sighed. "Let me explain. Right after Erika and I opened the Galerie, Viktor Sokolov showed up. He presented himself as a Russian art dealer and said he had a painting and needed a place to display it. He offered us a small percentage of the sale in exchange. When we realized what he had, we couldn't believe it. A painting like *The Seated Lady,* missing for so many years, would guarantee a draw for the Galerie. But ultimately, the price was too high. Viktor kept hanging around, and Erika didn't like it. She thought he was spying on us and steering business away from us for his own personal interests. And when Klaus showed up with a Gauguin, Erika saw an opportunity. She knew one of Viktor's American clients was looking for a Gauguin. We had worked with the client before, but rather than work with him again, Erika wanted to set Viktor up."

"So, Erika stole the Gauguin, and you copied it?" I pointed to the unfinished Gauguin on the floor. "You're not just an art historian. You're a painter as well. The paintings in this studio, did you paint them all?"

"I did. I'm good, but I've never been original enough to do anything more than copy the greats. I figured copying one more painting wouldn't matter. Erika told Klaus she doubted the painting was real, but she needed time to examine it. She asked if he would leave the painting with her, and Klaus agreed. When he returned to pick it up, Erika gave him a copy. She told him her initial reaction had been correct. That the painting, while very nice, was a fake."

CHAPTER NINETEEN

"Which explains the protests outside the museum."

"If anyone has a legal claim on the Gauguin, it should be Klaus. But what was he going to do? We had the painting and forged its provenance. Everything looks legitimate. Klaus had nothing but a story about a painting his father found and hung in a barn. He tried to threaten Erika, but Fritz kept a close eye out, and beyond Klaus' protest, he's not much of a worry. Besides, with the Gauguin in our possession, we now had what we needed to ruin Viktor."

I shook my head. "So, you sold Viktor the copy?"

"Not sold. Traded. Erika exchanged the Gauguin for the Matisse. *The Seated Lady* was worth more, but Viktor needed money. He was desperate. He's been trafficking young Russian girls, and the costs had caught up with him. With the Gauguin, Viktor could sell the painting to his American client and disappear. So, we waited. Confident that Viktor would be caught for selling a forgery or human trafficking. Either way, he'd be out of our hair."

"Only he wasn't. The Americans didn't arrest him."

"Which was why I thought you either were working with him or the Americans."

"I'm not working with Viktor. The first time I saw him was the day of the unveiling, and after that, when I came by the museum to return Erika's coat. He was coming out of your office, and Erika looked upset."

"Your timing wasn't the best. Viktor threatened Erika. He said we had sold him a forgery. Erika lied and told him the Gauguin hanging in the museum was a forgery and that we had given him the real painting. It's a trick art thieves use all the time. A stolen painting resurfaces, the finder copies it, maybe several times, then sells the copy back to the museum and keeps the original for himself or sells it quietly to a private gallery." Hans picked up the Gauguin and stared at it. "But Viktor wasn't convinced. He believed Erika had the original Gauguin and the Matisse he had traded for it, and now he wanted both of them back. Plus, everything my uncle had stolen during the war. He told Erika he knew Gerhardt's Hoard existed. If she didn't tell him where it was, he'd kidnap Baret, and she would never see her son again."

"So that's why Baret's here with you. You're protecting him."

Hans leaned the Gauguin back against the wall. "Erika tried to tell Viktor we didn't have anything. My uncle had saved a couple of paintings from the family's collection, but he and my mother had sold them to start over after the war and put the money in a Swiss bank. Everything else was destroyed in the firestorms that followed the Allied bombings. There was nothing left. But Viktor didn't believe her. Then, Erika remembered I was working on a copy of Raphael's *Portrait of a Young Man*. The painting's been missing for years, but she told Viktor it was one of the paintings our uncle had refused to sell, and she offered it to him."

"This?" I picked up a small photo of the portrait off the table.

"Yes, it's my latest project. I've been working on it for some time. Look." Hans took the tarp covering the easel from the canvas. "Erika told Viktor that *Portrait of a Young Man* was equally as exciting as Matisse's *Seated Lady*. She promised to get it for him, but said it would take some time. Viktor agreed to give her until the end of the week. Either that, he said, or he'd kidnap Baret, and she'd never see him again. But when Erika told me what she had promised to do, I said no."

"No?" I couldn't believe Hans would allow any harm to come to his nephew.

"I had another idea. Erika wasn't wild about it. It's caused a rift in our relationship, but it's something I should have done a long time ago." Hans replaced the tarp on the painting. "And I could use your help."

"With what exactly? I'm not sure I understand." Nor was I sure I could trust him.

"You will. But for now, go back to Munich. Do what you need to do for the magazine, and come back here next weekend."

"Why?"

"I'll explain everything when you return." Hans put his hands on my shoulders, then tipped my chin to face. "Trust me, Kat. You won't be disappointed."

"But what about Erika?"

"My sister won't be a problem. I've convinced her you're exactly who you say you are."

"And Gerhardt's Hoard?"

CHAPTER NINETEEN

"For now, you don't need to know anything more than what I've already told you."

Chapter Twenty

I woke the following morning to the sound of laughter coming from the kitchen and the faint smell of bacon wafting up the stairs. I pulled the eiderdown up around my shoulders and tried to imagine the scene with Hans and Baret in the kitchen and what the day might bring. After last night, I knew Hans was ready to talk. And if I was right, I would know where Gerhardt's Hoard was hidden by next weekend. Hans wouldn't say or do anything with his nephew here. But for now, I was close to getting everything Sophie wanted. I just needed to be patient. Today, I'd put on a good front. I'd be Kat Lawson, travel journalist on assignment. But next weekend, I'd be Kat Lawson, undercover agent, about to uncover a story that would shock the art world. The idea excited me.

Halfway down the stairs, I realized Hans, Baret, and I weren't alone in the chateau. Hans had company. Angry voices trailed from the entry. I stopped and cowered behind the bend of the stairwell, where I could see and hear what was happening. Two men dressed in paint-stained dungarees stood inside the front door, and whatever they were talking about, the conversation was heated. Hans looked frustrated. He ran his fingers through his hair, reached into his pocket, and pulled out a handful of bills. One of the men grabbed the money. There was a bit of grumbling between the two as they counted the bills, then shuffled out the door. I waited until I heard Hans close the door, then continued down the stairs.

"Company so early?" I squinted and nodded to the front door. It wasn't yet eight o'clock.

Catching the concern on my face, Hans smiled and clapped his hands.

CHAPTER TWENTY

"Nothing to worry about. A couple of disgruntled workers, that's all. You like pancakes?"

I followed Hans into the kitchen. The curtains over the sink were open, and the light coming through the windows was so bright there was no need for artificial light. The kitchen was like a showroom with black and white floor tiles, white painted brick walls with glass-finished cabinets, and copper pots that hung above a center island that doubled as a cooktop with extra room for dining. I paused in the entry and took in the room. Baret was seated at the counter with a glass of orange juice. Next to him, Hans had set two more place settings with coffee and a small bowl of blueberries and whipped cream on each placemat. On the stove, Hans had taken a large copper skillet from the rack above, and a large blue bowl with pancake preparations was on the counter.

I took a seat next to Baret. "Do you like pancakes?"

"Ja. Mit Blaubeeren."

"English, Baret." Hans stood at the stove and gestured with the spatula, shaking it gently, a reminder to use English in my presence. "You need to practice."

"Yes, ma'am. With blueberries. Do you?"

"They're my favorite," I said.

I poured myself a glass of orange juice from a pitcher on the counter, then sat back to take in the serenity of the kitchen. The morning light through the windows, the smell of freshly cooked bacon, and Hans at the stove preparing pancakes. Everything in the kitchen was picture perfect, nothing out of place.

Except? "What's that?" I pointed to a door. Next to the arched entry leading to the great room was a white-washed wooden door, and like the attic door last night, latched with a padlock.

Baret looked down at his pancakes, then at his uncle, as though asking permission. "That's the dungeon!"

Hans put a finger to his lips. "We're not supposed to talk about that. We don't want our guests to go down there. Remember?"

Hans transferred a plate-sized pancake from the pan to his nephew's plate and sprinkled it with a handful of blueberries. Baret began to make a smiley face on the pancake.

"A dungeon. Really?" I took a berry from Baret's plate and swallowed it.

"It's not what you think." Hans raised a brow. "It's a wine cellar. The lock keeps Cahill and Ozan from helping themselves to my collection when I'm not here. That's all it is, I promise."

By ten a.m., we had finished eating, the dishes were washed, and we were out the door and on the way to the train stop in Oberammergau. Hans asked Baret to wait in the car and walked me to the train platform.

"You're good with our agreement? You'll come back next week?" Hans rested his hand on my shoulder while I looked in my bag for my return train ticket to Munich.

"Yes. I'm looking forward to it. But this time, I plan to drive. I want to take in the sights. Believe it or not, I do have a story to write."

"Suit yourself. I should be back by Friday afternoon, but if you get here before I do, you'll need a key and the gate code." Hans reached into his pocket, produced a small tan envelope with the gate code printed outside, and pressed it into my hand. "The key's inside. Ozan and Cahill will have finished up the work I've asked them to do, and the chateau should be empty."

"And you? Where are you off to?"

"I have a business trip to Switzerland. If Viktor's watching, it's what he expects me to do. The Swiss hid much of what was stolen during the war in their vaults. They weren't the pacifists the world thinks. They were the bankers. There's probably more stolen art in Switzerland than anywhere else. When I return, Viktor will expect me to have Raphael's *Portrait of a Young Man* with me, and I will have arranged to give him the copy you saw in my studio last night."

The copy? I closed my eyes and shook my head. "It never stops, does it?"

"Not until I say it does. But I promise you it will."

"And what about Baret? What are you going to do with him?"

"Baret's coming with me. I'll leave him with his father's family in Bern until Viktor's no longer a problem. Which, trust me, he won't be." Hans bussed me on the cheek. "Alles ist gut? Ja?"

CHAPTER TWENTY

"Ja," I nodded. Hans sounded so convincing. I wanted to believe him. "All is good."

"Then I will see you Friday. Auf Wiedersehen." I hugged Hans goodbye and watched as he trudged back to the car, his shoulders were hunched, and I wondered, was he still playing me? Did I dare trust him?

* * *

I called Sophie's cell from the train. When she didn't answer, I left an urgent message. It was Sunday morning, not yet five a.m. in New York, but I figured between learning that Sophie had a spy inside her offices and that I was close to uncovering Gerhardt's Hoard, it was worth an emergency, early morning wake-up call. But just to be safe, I left the message in code.

"Sophie, hi, it's me, Kat. I didn't want to leave a message on your answering machine at the office, so I'm leaving this on your cell. The office line isn't secure. I've news about Krampus, and I'm close to finding Santa's workshop. We need to talk. ASAP. Call me when you get this."

For the remainder of the ride, I held the phone in my hand, hoping it might ring as the train chugged through the mountain pass en route to Munich. It was nearly three o'clock in the afternoon by the time I entered the hotel lobby, almost nine a.m. in New York, and still no call. I couldn't imagine why, but I had an uncomfortable feeling something was wrong.

Chapter Twenty-One

"Ms. Lawson?" The hotel's front desk clerk called to me as I entered. "You have a guest."

"Excuse me?" The clerk pointed to a frizzy-haired old woman sitting by herself beneath a reading light. She was dressed in a tweed coat, wearing a pair of sloppy-looking galoshes with a suitcase at her feet, and reading the Suddeusche Zeitung. I approached her cautiously. "Are you looking for me?"

The woman looked up over her readers. Despite the gray wig and obvious disguise, I recognized Sophie's blue eyes.

She stood slowly, placed her hand on my shoulder, and whispered in my ear. "Whatever you do, don't say my name. We're being watched."

I hugged her like an old friend. "Well, what a surprise, Gertrude. What are you doing here?" I figured if I faked a name, anyone who might be watching would be thrown off.

In response, Sophie answered in a voice a little louder than necessary. "My plane to Frankfurt was delayed. I don't suppose I could convince you to join me for coffee and maybe some of that German Schwartzwald cake? I'm famished."

I picked up Sophie's bag. "Let me freshen up a bit."

Then, like a welcomed friend, I linked my arm through hers and ushered her toward the elevator. Once the doors closed, Sophie dropped my arm.

"We need to talk." I knew something was wrong from the hollow tone of Sophie's voice. I waited to respond until we got to my room.

"What's going on?" I crossed the room and closed the blinds. Sophie

CHAPTER TWENTY-ONE

obviously hadn't gotten my voicemail. "What's with the disguise?"

"I don't want anyone to know I'm in the country." Sophie slipped the wig from her head and tossed it on the bed. "I caught my receptionist playing back my voicemails. I'm sorry, but there's nothing more you can do here." Sophie reached into her bag and took out a passport and an airline ticket. "You need to leave. And the sooner, the better."

"Leave?" I laughed. "You can forget that. I'm not about to go home. Not now." I snatched the ticket from Sophie and threw it on the bed. "You're right. Hans does know who I am, and if you had listened to the voicemail I left on your cell, you would know he knows about you, too."

"How do you know this?" Sophie pulled at her gloves, one finger at a time, and stuffed them in her bag.

"You first," I said. "Seems to me that I should know who else is on this team. It's starting to feel lonely out here all by myself."

"I can't give you names, Kat. That's not how it works, but I will tell you, the protestor outside the Galerie—"

"You mean Klaus Kemper, the man whose father found the Gauguin."

"That's not Klaus Kemper, Kat, the man in front of Galerie's an agent. After Herr Kemper approached the German authorities about what he suspected to be a fraudulent copy of Gauguin's *Fruits on the Table*, they agreed to investigate. The agent assumed Kemper's identity—nobody would have known who he was standing outside the museum, dressed like he was in a heavy parka and hat—and ever since, we've been able to get eyes and ears on the museum."

"That still doesn't explain how you knew Erika and Hans were on to me."

"We tapped the phone lines and got an audio tape of Erika talking to Hans. She called Hans right after you left the museum in Tegernsee."

"I know. Hans told me Erika recognized your name from *Journey International's* masthead. She was worried, but he told her not to be."

"It's my fault, Kat. I met Erika Schönburg ten years ago at an international conference for art historians in London. I was teaching at the time and had worked off and on as a consultant for the FBI on special projects. Erika had just finished her Ph.D. and was using her married name. I had no idea who she was or that our paths would ever cross again. Then later, when I retired and launched the magazine, the FBI approached me about using the publication as a cover for some of their agents."

"It doesn't matter, Sophie. I'm not leaving. It's not me, or the Americans Hans is worried about finding Gerhardt's Hoard. It's the Russians. Viktor's threatened to kidnap Hans' nephew Baret unless Hans and Erika show him where their uncle's art is hidden."

"So Hans admitted to you that he's hiding his uncle's collection?"

"Not in so many words. Baret was with us all weekend. But Hans invited me back to his chateau next Friday. He says he has a story for me that will make my editor very happy. So, you can forget about me leaving. I'm not going anywhere without the story, and certainly not until I know Baret's safe."

"I tried to warn you about getting emotionally involved, Kat."

"Yeah, well, it's a little late for that."

"Kat. Take the ticket. Go home. It's not safe for you here anymore."

"I'm not leaving. You didn't fly here to fire me. You could have done that on the phone. I'm your only hope of finding Gerhardt's Hoard, and you know it. If I don't get to it first, the Russians will."

"It's not your problem, Kat."

"Maybe not. But Gerhardt's Hoard isn't just another secret cache of stolen artwork. For you, it's personal. It's why you're here. What is it?"

Sophie got up and walked to the window. Her eyes focused on the snow falling outside. When she started to speak, her voice was soft.

"I grew up in a small city south of Stuttgart. My father had been a doctor and an art collector. Our home was lovely. But one day, Otto Gerhardt came to our apartment with his Nazi goons. I'll never forget the sounds of their heavy boots as they marched into our home, traipsing mud across the floors and ripping artwork from our walls. Herr Gerhardt tried to tell my father he was doing us a favor, offering to buy what we had, but for a fraction of what it was worth. My father refused, and Herr Gerhardt took everything. My mother and I were forced into a truck and driven to a train, where we were carted like cattle into a boxcar. I don't know how many days we stood

CHAPTER TWENTY-ONE

huddled next to each other because there was no room to sit. Only a slop bucket to relieve yourself. No food. No water. At night, the wind would howl like a wild animal as we passed through the Alps." Sophie wrapped her arms around herself as she spoke. Her small frame looked like a child's as she retold the story. "Some nights, I can still hear my mother's voice. She died before we got to Buchenwald. I was pulled off the train and marched to a section of the camp with children. We were forced to do things I never imagined. I don't know how I survived or why. Only that I did. I saw things no child should ever see."

I knew Sophie was a survivor. I had no idea what had happened or how much pain she had hidden over the years, but I could hear the quake in her voice, and I knew the time was like yesterday, a memory she would never forget.

"I swore one day I would find Otto Gerhardt. He was never punished for what he did. After the war, he maintained he was a victim of Nazi persecution. He said he was one-quarter Jewish. That he had lost his job as an art curator and forced to work for the Nazis. And now that we're this close to finding his cache, I won't let it go. Not until it's been exposed."

"If I leave now, Sophie, you'll never get this close again. You know that."

"The stakes are high, Kat. Trusting Hans could be dangerous. He may want you to return next weekend, not because he plans to give you a story, but because he wants to shut you up. You know too much."

"Well, he hasn't shut me up yet. And he certainly had the chance this weekend."

Sophie stared at me. "Maybe because his nephew was around, and he didn't want the messy job of disposing of your body with the boy there."

My throat tightened.

"It's a risk I'm willing to take. And I promise you, you won't be disappointed." It wasn't lost on me that the words I uttered were the exact same words Hans had used the last time we were together. In my mind, the man that hadn't killed me in his studio wasn't the erudite museum curator or the womanizer the press had made him out to be—but a man at odds with his history, a reclusive artist who craved a simpler life, as much as I wanted his story.

"You could be walking into a trap, Kat. Think about it. These are dangerous people."

I took Sophie's hand. "Please, let me see this through."

"Then do me a favor."

"What do you need?"

Sophie dropped my hand and took a small photograph from inside her coat pocket. "This is a picture of a Rembrandt sketch, one of several the artist made. It used to hang on a wall with several others like it in the home I grew up in. It's. *The Lying Lion*. It's my favorite."

"You think it's among those works Hans and Erika are hiding?"

"I know that Otto Gerhardt took it. And if you find it, I want you to bring it back to me. But you need to keep this secret. If the FBI knew what I wanted, they would consider it a crime, and I'd be prosecuted. Maybe it is, but I'm sixty-five years old, Kat. I haven't seen anything from my family's home in more than fifty years. If Gerhardt's Hoard is found, I'll have to wait for the courts to settle any claims against it, and I may never live to see that."

"I'll do what I can."

"I appreciate it." Sophie picked her bag up and handed me my passport. "Be careful, Kat."

"Where are you going?" In another few seconds, I knew Sophie would be out the door. I didn't know where or when I'd see her again.

"That's none of your business. The less you know, the safer we'll all be. In the meantime, you'd be wise to keep busy. And remember, you're a reporter covering the holiday traditions in Germany. Make it look that way. Finish up here in Munich, then take a couple of days and visit the Christkindlmarkt in Nuremberg. You'll want to include it in your story. If you need me, call my cell."

"Will I see you again?"

"Let's hope so." Sophie pulled on her gloves. "If what you believe about Hans is true, and he comes clean about Gerhardt's Hoard, then you'll have a story for me. And if all goes well, you can share it with me in person next week. Call me, and we'll celebrate."

CHAPTER TWENTY-ONE

"And if I'm wrong?"
"Don't be."

Chapter Twenty-Two

I took Sophie's suggestion to finish up my seasonal tour stops in Munich and, the following morning, penciled in my weekly calendar with a few more places I wanted to visit before leaving for Nuremberg on Thursday. Top of my list was a cooking class. I was up for a bit of food therapy and called that morning to ensure I could get into a pastry-making class. After a rollercoaster weekend with Hans—everything from meeting his nephew to finding me in his studio and thinking he was about to kill me—I planned to drown my angst and frustrated libido with forbidden sweets while learning to make a colorful Christmas Stollen like I had seen in the windows of all the Konditori shops. There is nothing like a plate full of sweet carbs to satisfy a lusty loss. I should know. I'm a veteran.

But, as I crossed the Marienplatz, taking a shortcut to avoid being out in the cold any longer than necessary, and passed the Galerie, I noticed Inga alone on the front steps. She was dressed in another of her short miniskirts and those heavy Doc Marten black boots and had balanced on her knee a box of printer paper. She appeared to be fishing in her bag for the key. I considered this an opportunity for a moment alone and hurried up the steps.

"Hey, can I help you?" I grabbed the box just as it was about to tumble from Inga's knee.

"Danke," Inga looked nervously at me, then glanced quickly over my shoulder at the Marienplatz.

"Not a problem." I waited patiently with the box in my hands while Inga fumbled in the bottom of her bag for her key. "Glad to help."

Then finding the key, Inga pulled it from her purse along with a red wig

CHAPTER TWENTY-TWO

that fell to her feet.

"Ahh!" Inga gasped and, in one quick, very fluid motion, grabbed the wig and stuffed it back into her bag while her eyes darted from mine, then back again to the Marienplatz. Whether it was fear I saw in her pale blue eyes or shock that I had seen the wig, I knew in that instant that Inga had been the red-headed girl who had returned my bag to the hotel, and suspected that she had not been a willing partner in any crime at all. But a victim.

"I think we should talk," I said.

Inga opened the door "Schnell. Come quickly." Inga stood back as I squeezed past her with the box in my hands. "If you're here to see Erika or Hans, they're not here. The museum doesn't open for another hour."

"I'm not here to see them. I'm here to talk to you." I nodded to the box. "Is there somewhere you'd like me to put this?"

"Dort." Inga tilted her head toward the office, then shut the outside door behind me and locked it.

The only time I had been inside the office was at night when Hans had pulled me behind the door and dowsed the light because of the burglary. I couldn't see a thing beyond the grey-blue light of the security monitor. My eyes had frozen on it as I watched the thief make off with the Gauguin. But now, I could see more clearly in the light of day. A barred window allowed light to stream into the room. A coat rack stood in the corner next to a file cabinet, and a richly carved mahogany desk was in the center of the room. A montage of art and family photos covered the walls. Pictures of Hans and Erika as children in front of the chateau. One of them with their mother hiking. Another of their mother dressed in Bavarian costume with two men, one of whom I figured must have been her husband, and the other her brother—Otto Gerhardt—taken some time before the war. Clues of their ancestry were everywhere.

I put the box down and sat behind the desk where Erika or Hans might have sat if they were there. It was a presumptive move on my part, but I wanted Inga to know I was in charge and my presence was no accident.

"Are we alone?" I asked.

"Ja." Inga nodded. "The museum won't open for another hour. I usually come in early to answer messages and straighten up."

"This won't take long. Tell me, was it you who stole my bag and then returned it? The bellhop at the hotel said it was a girl with red hair wearing a long black belted coat." I pointed to the coat rack in the corner. "Probably like that one there. Isn't that Erika's? I'm sure it'd be a bit long on you, but it'd be enough of a disguise, like that red wig in your bag."

Inga sat down in the chair directly opposite me and closed her eyes. I gave her a moment. "It wasn't my idea."

"Returning the bag or stealing it?" I asked.

"Viktor made me do it." Inga looked down at her hands.

"Why?"

"Viktor, he is crazy. He thinks everyone is bad. The Americans are after him, the Germans he doesn't trust. Then you showed up for the Gauguin unveiling, and you are late. Your name, it's not on the list Erika has me send out. But you signed the ledger, and when Viktor checks it, he wants me to find out who you are. He makes me follow you and steal your bag."

Inga's eyes started to tear.

I grabbed a tissue from a dispenser on the desk and handed it to her. She thanked me and blew her nose.

"And then you returned it. Which was nice of you, by the way. Which tells me something."

"What?" Inga blew her nose and crumpled the tissue in her hands.

"You're not a thief. And if I'm right, you brought the bag back to my hotel because you're looking for someone to help you. You're scared and don't know what to do."

Inga sniffed. "I thought if I returned it, we might talk. But you were leaving the hotel when I came in. We passed each other in the doorway, and I was afraid if I stopped you, Viktor might see me. So, I left your bag with the desk clerk. I was going to leave a note, but he was busy, and I got nervous and left."

"And the wig? Why the wig?"

"Why do you think? If Viktor knew I had tried to see you, he would have killed me. Or even worse, he would send me to Prague with his other girls

CHAPTER TWENTY-TWO

to entertain his business associates. I'm not a whore."

"I didn't say you were." I had interviewed prostitutes before, and most of them, like Inga, had been blackmailed into a trade from which there was no return and had little option for a better life. "Why don't you tell me what you're doing here and how you think I can help?"

Inga explained she had met Viktor while working in Hamburg at a museum coffee shop. She had been born in Warsaw right before my mother and father moved to Hamburg. "We were Aussiedler, outsiders, and my father worked as a laborer, my mother a housekeeper. We didn't have much. My father died before my sixteenth birthday, and my mother took up with a boyfriend. I wanted to go to university, but girls like me don't go to university. That's when I met Viktor. He would come into the shop and ask how I was doing. He was nice to me, and I was struggling. He offered to help. He said he was an art historian and worked with museums around the world to help build their collections and that I might be able to help him."

I sat back in the chair. It didn't take much for a man like Viktor to make a young girl like Inga feel important.

"That must have felt good," I said.

"It did. Viktor was a way out. He said he could get me a job at a museum in Munch. Very nice place, he says. The people, they need an office girl, someone who speaks German and English. I've always been good with languages, and the job is easy. Light typing and answering phones. It was better than going home and listening to my mother and her new boyfriend fight. Viktor finds me an apartment with a view of the Isar River, and I am living in Munich. At first, I think everything is good. Viktor brings me gifts and takes me to fancy restaurants, the theater, and places I never go to before. Then I realize he wants me to do more than just work at the museum."

I expected Inga to tell me Viktor had set her up so he could visit her whenever he wanted. But Inga explained she quickly learned it was more than sex Viktor wanted.

"He wanted me to spy on Hans and Erika. He said their uncle had stolen art from the Nazis and that if I helped him to find it, I'd be rich. All I had to do was listen, watch what was going on, and report back to him."

"And did you?"

"I didn't have a choice." Tears started to form again from beneath Inga's lids.

I handed her a second tissue. "I'm not here to judge, Inga."

"Viktor threatened to murder my mother if I didn't help him. And if I went to the police or said anything to Hans or Erika about him, I'd disappear." Inga wiped her eyes with the back of her hand.

"I promise you, that's not going to happen."

"If Viktor ever found out we were talking—"

"He's not going to."

Inga looked at the clock on the wall. It wasn't yet ten-thirty.

"I'll be out of here before the museum opens. Nobody needs to know I was here today. Whatever you tell me, it stays between us. Okay?"

Inga nodded.

"And if I can help you, I promise I'll do whatever I can. But I need to know what's going on and what you know."

Inga wiped her nose. "That's just it. I don't know anything. And Viktor thinks I'm not trying hard enough."

"So, you haven't seen anything—"

"No! Nothing." Inga dabbed the mascara beneath her eyes.

"Okay, let's start with what you do know. It may be more than you think. Tell me, what it is you do here?"

"Like I said, answering the phone. Typing. Sometimes I send out press releases and help to organize events. Guest lists. Catering. That type of thing."

"And you've not seen anything that looks suspicious?"

"Like what? I don't even know what I'm looking for." Inga shrugged her shoulders. "Erika keeps me busy in the office, and when I'm not busy here, she has me clean. I don't have time to wander around."

"And you've not seen any secret hiding places, maybe in the walls or the vault where there might be old canvases?"

"There's nothing in the vault, and it's not very big. It's more like a crawl space beneath the museum. Sometimes a new canvas will arrive, and Hans

CHAPTER TWENTY-TWO

and Erika might hold it for a day or two while arranging for a private showing. There's a small room off the main gallery for smaller events, but the room's locked, and I'm not allowed in when there's a viewing. People come, and when they do, Erika sends me out to get something for them to eat. A day or two later, the room's empty, and Erika will ask me to go in and clean up. That's all I know."

I scratched my head. If Hans and Erika were babysitting their uncle's hidden hoard and using it to finance their lifestyle, the museum was a logical viewing sight. A prospective buyer could come and go without raising any suspicion. But if what Inga told me was true, then the Gerhardt Galerie wasn't big enough to be a secret hiding place for Gerhardt's Hoard.

"How about Erika's home or the museum in Tegernsee? Have you been there?"

"I'm an employee. They don't invite me home for the holidays."

"And Hans' chateau in Oberammergau? I saw a pair of ice skates with pink laces. Are they yours?"

"No. I don't go near Hans. He's nice, I think. But Erika would fire me if I did."

"But you must have seen something. You've been here since the museum opened."

"That's what Viktor keeps saying. I told him it was going to take time. That I needed to build their trust. Viktor said we didn't have time and that I didn't know what I was doing. Then about a month before the Gauguin unveiling, Viktor just took off."

"Did he tell you where he was going?"

"Viktor doesn't tell me those things." Inga wadded the tissue and threw it in her bag. "But he came back the day before the unveiling. Erika hadn't put Viktor's name on the list, and he wanted me to sneak him in. I let him in the back door. When Erika realized he was there, she got angry with me. I told her I didn't know how he got in, and she must have believed me because she didn't fire me. Then later, after the unveiling, Viktor insisted I give him the names of everybody who had signed in that day. I made a copy of the list. He knew everybody on it except for you."

"Which was why Viktor convinced you to steal my bag."

"I had never done anything like that before. Viktor said he had to know who you were. It was important to him. He thought maybe you were an American and needed me to find out. Something about the Americans worried him. I got the feeling he thought they might be after him."

"Considering Viktor Sokolov's track record, I'm not surprised."

"Can you help me?"

"Maybe," I said. "But first, I need to know, did Viktor know I was going to Tegernsee?"

I felt I already knew the answer. Inga must have known Erika had agreed to meet with me. But Inga's response would convince me that I could trust her.

"I heard Erika talking with Kirsten about a meeting with some American reporter, and when Erika left for Tegernsee the next day, I figured it was to meet you."

"So, you told Viktor I'd be there?"

Inga nodded. She wouldn't look me in the eye.

"And does Viktor drive a black Mercedes sedan with a gold grill?"

"Yes."

I had my answer. Inga had told me the truth. It was no random driver that I'd angered on the autobahn. It was Viktor's gold-grilled Mercedes that had nearly driven me off the road.

"Then I think we can help each other." I handed Inga my business card and asked for her number in return. I didn't know how I might be able to help her, but I wasn't going to go home until I had.

Chapter Twenty-Three

I left the museum the same way Viktor had the night of the theft—out the back door. I was late for the start of my pastry class and figured I had probably lost a prime seat at the counter, but if I hurried, I might be able to talk my way into the back of the room where at least I might observe. I trudged down the alley, working my way between parked cars, using my gloved hands against the brick walls to balance myself on the slippery hard-packed snow. I had just about reached the Marienplatz when my phone rang.

"Kat, hi, it's Kirsten. How was the weekend?"

"Where are you?" I stopped and caught my breath. The cold air burned my lungs.

"It's Monday. I've got the day off. Do you want to meet for coffee? I've got pictures for you for the magazine. Can't wait to show you."

Ahead of me, tourists gathered on the plaza in front of the Neues Rathaus. It was exactly eleven a.m. The clarion bells from within the giant glockenspiel had begun to ring.

Kirsten recognized the sound. "You're in the Marienplatz. I'm not far away. There's a konditorei directly across from the Neues Rathaus. Meet me there. They've got the best apfelstrudel in the city. You'll love it."

"Sounds perfect. I'll meet you there."

The konditorei wasn't hard to find. All I needed to do was follow the crowd and the warm smells that wafted from within the shop onto the plaza as tourists, one after the other, came out with their coffee and sweets. I ducked behind one anxious patron who hurriedly ordered a coffee with a sticky bun to go and found a small table next to a window where I waited for Kirsten to arrive. We spotted each other at the exact same moment.

Kirsten hurried in from the cold.

"Grüß Gott." Kirsten stooped to kiss me, noticed the bump on my head, and stepped back. "Was is das? What is this?"

I touched my brow. "Nothing. I fell on the snow."

I wasn't about to share anything with Kirsten about my mugging or that I knew Inga and Viktor were responsible. I didn't want to give her a reason to think I might be more than the travel journalist I had led her to believe I was. The less she knew, the better.

"I am so sorry. Does it hurt?"

"No. Looks worse than it is. I promise you, it's nothing."

Kirsten tossed her gloves in her bag and sat down. "Erika called. She thought the interview went very well. Which for Erika is unusual. Thank you, by the way."

"Why?" I stirred my coffee. "I should be thanking you."

"You forget, anything I can do for them is good for me." Kirsten grabbed a menu off the table, then signaled the waiter and ordered two apfelkuken and a coffee.

"You missed your calling, Kirsten. You would have been a good PR agent."

"Why should I choose? I've got the best of both worlds. Nice job with the paper, and Hans and Erika are good friends. I help them when I can, and they help me. That's what friends do, right?" Kirsten reached into her overly large Hermes bag, took out a manila folder, and laid it on the table in front of me, "Speaking of which, these are the photos I took from our tour the other day. I hope your editor likes them."

I opened the folder. A stack of four-colored glossies, much better than any I could have taken with my point-and-shoot. Kirsten had a good eye. Sophie would be happy. "I'll see she gets them."

"But there's one you may not want to show her. Here, look." Kirsten took a single photo from inside her purse and placed it on the table between us. The picture was one Kirsten had taken of me in front of King Ludwig's Galerie of Beauties. I had mugged it up for the camera and looked deranged.

CHAPTER TWENTY-THREE

"It's just for fun."

I laughed. "What are you trying to do, blackmail me?"

The waiter arrived with our order, and I slipped the photos Kirsten had given me for Sophie inside my bag for safekeeping. Kirsten picked up the picture of me in front of the Gallerie of Beauties and held it up one last time.

"You sure you don't want this one, too?"

"No." I waved my hand in front of my face. "Get rid of it."

Kirsten waited for the waiter to leave, then leaned across the table. "Tell me. How was your weekend? Did Hans behave himself?"

I nearly choked. "Excuse me?"

"You know, was it romantic?" Kirsten raised her brows. "Everything you expected?"

I'm not in the habit of sharing details about my romantic life, or lack thereof. But Kirsten's question, campy as it was, deserved a reply. She had, after all, set up the interview with Erika. The least I could do was play along.

"His nephew was there." I rolled my eyes.

"Ouch." Kirsten blew on her coffee. "So, are you disappointed?"

"Not entirely. We had fun. Just not the type of fun you're implying. I suspect Erika didn't like the idea of me visiting her brother and arranged for Beret to chaperone."

"Don't take it personally. Erika doesn't take kindly to strangers or those she thinks beneath her."

"Beneath her? What are you saying?"

"Erika's a snob. And you're an American."

"And that's a problem?"

"Not for me, but for Erika, yes. She's never gotten over Germany losing the war."

"Oh, come on. It's been forty-plus years. It looks to me like she's doing very well. A house in Tegernsee, and a job at the university. Not to mention the Galerie."

Kirsten put her cup down. "Erika's old world. She's never gotten over everything her family lost in the war. Money. Property. Status. And she blames everyone. Hitler. The allies. As far as she's concerned, her world was destroyed, and she can't get over it. Trust me, she made it very clear from the start who she thinks she and Hans are, and nobody else matters."

"Including you?"

"In Erika's mind? I'm the equivalent of a cheap forgery. The illegitimate child of an illegitimate child. The descendant of one of Ludwig's painted Beauties. I'm as authentic to her as my bleached hair."

"I hope you don't believe that."

"It doesn't matter if I do or not. Erika rewards me for my efforts, and I appreciate it. A lot." Kirsten picked up her Hermes bag. "She gave me this for my birthday. And my coat?" Kirsten stroked the fur collar around her neck. "It was a Christmas gift from last year. It's not sable, but it's nice enough."

Kirsten pointed to my apfelkuken. I had been so busy with my questions I had yet to take a bite.

"You haven't touched your cake. I hope you're not disappointed with me. Some journalists might think doing PR for the museum while working on the paper's wrong, but I don't make much money as a journalist. I'm just trying to survive. And what the paper doesn't know won't hurt them, right?"

"Hey, whatever it takes." Kirsten's dual roles would have gotten a reporter fired in the States, but it made her a valuable source for my purposes. I took a forkful of the apfelkuken.

"You like?" Kirsten waited while the sweet, warm apple with cinnamon melted in my mouth.

"Yes, very good."

"And us, we're good too, right?"

"Of course."

"And the photos? You promise you'll give them to your publisher."

"As soon as I can."

Kirsten's cell rang. She checked the screen and raised a brow. "Give me a minute. It's my editor, Peter."

I had no idea what Kirsten was saying, but between the eye roll and what sounded like a forced giggle, I suspected Peter and I were like Erika and Hans, useful until something better came along.

Kirsten clapped her hand over the phone's mouthpiece. "Peter wants to go

CHAPTER TWENTY-THREE

skating tonight at Nymphenburger Schlosskanal. You should see the canal behind the castle at night with all the lights. You want to go?"

I mouthed the word no, and Kirsten stuck her lower lip out and made a pouty face. "You're no fun." Then returning to the phone, she chatted for another minute and then hung up. "I wish you would come along. He's such a bore."

"Sorry. I've got work to do."

Kirsten stood up and stuffed her hair beneath the brim of her hat. "Will I see you again?"

"I hope so. I'm off to Nuremberg later this week for the Christkindlmarkt, then back to Oberammergau."

"You're going to see Hans?"

"He invited me."

"Does Erika know?"

"I doubt it'd make a difference."

Kirsten rolled her eyes. "I hope you know what you're doing."

"I'm having fun." I held my palm up, and we slapped hands. "I'll call when I get back from Nuremberg. We'll have dinner."

"Auf Wiedersehen."

Chapter Twenty-Four

By midweek, I had a pretty good handle on Munich's highlights. I visited the Alte Pinakothek Museum and toured three of Munich's most prominent churches, St. Peter's, Frauenkirche, St. Michaels, and the Viktualienmarkt. Despite the cold, I marked the colorful outdoor market as a must-see for foodies and holiday shopping. If Viktor or Erika were watching, I wanted there to be no doubt about my duties as a travel writer. Thursday morning, I ordered a quick breakfast from room service, coffee, and Brötchen, a hard-crusted roll with butter, then hurried to the train stop beneath the Marienplatz for the ride to Nuremberg. I was pleased with the ease with which I could read the train's schedule. Already I could identify several impossibly long German words and picked up several phrases. And as I boarded the commuter train to the Munich Hauptbahnhof, where I would change trains to Nuremberg, I began to feel less like a tourist and more like a seasoned traveler.

The Hauptbahnhof was crowded with mid-morning passengers, all bundled in heavy coats and hats as they huddled against the chill on the platform while waiting for arriving coaches. When the train to Nuremberg pulled into the station, I squeezed between those getting off and on and headed for the first available window seat. As I stuffed my backpack into the overhead storage compartment, I was bumped from behind, and my guidebook fell to the floor.

"Entschuldigung." The man who had bumped me apologized and picked up my book, never bothering to make eye contact.

"Danke Schön.," I took the book from him and smiled, expecting he might

CHAPTER TWENTY-FOUR

do the same. Instead, he tipped his hat, slipped into the seat directly across from where I intended to sit, and unfolded his newspaper.

"Excuse me." With my hand on the seat rest behind the stranger's head, I apologized as I stepped awkwardly over his knees to take the seat opposite him. The space between us was so close that my long legs ended up straddling his. Awkward. But evidently, not enough to solicit any kind of response. I thought odd, if not rude, until I realized the stranger wasn't reading the newspaper but using it as a shield to look over my shoulder.

I have a good memory for faces, and even though the stranger had avoided making eye contact, from what little I could see of his face beneath the brim of his hat and from above the top of the paper, he looked familiar. Something about the shape of his brow and cheekbones caused me to think I had seen him before. Then I remembered. The protestor. The man sitting across from me was the same man I had seen in front of the museum carrying a placard denouncing the Gauguin unveiling. The same broad-shouldered linebacker who had prevented me from following Viktor Sokolov the night I was mugged. The undercover German spy Sophie had told me had been assigned to follow Viktor.

Instinctively, I wanted to look behind me to see if the German spy's presence on the train was because the Russian had followed me, but I resisted. Unable to see behind me, I did the only thing I could think to do. I stumbled over the stranger's lap and excused myself to use the water closet at the front of the car. Whether my seatmate knew I recognized him or not, it didn't matter. The bigger question was, why was he here? Was he following Viktor, and if so, was Viktor following me?

I paused in front of the water closet and glanced at the car's rear. It was crowded with passengers, but beyond where I had been seated, toward the back, I recognized the Cossack's big fur hat. Like my seatmate, Viktor was reading a newspaper and appeared not to notice me. I ducked into the WC, and with my cell phone clutched to my chest, slid slowly to a sitting position with my back against the door. I considered calling Sophie. But what could she do? If Viktor had followed me, it was either because he wanted further proof that I was a travel journalist on assignment or—a more chilling thought—because he suspected my friendship with Hans might lead me to Gerhardt's Hoard. Which ultimately could only mean one thing, Viktor Sokolov intended to eliminate the competition.

If ever I needed a lifeline, now was the time. But who could I call?

I didn't dare call Sophie. She had to know the German undercover agent was following Viktor. But she may not have known Viktor was following me or that all three of us were on the same train to Nuremberg. If I called Sophie and told her Viktor was on my tail, I feared she might alert the German police. And, if they boarded the train and attempted to arrest Viktor, maybe charge him with the attempted kidnapping of a foreign journalist, the entire operation would be a bust. What I needed was 48 hours—just two days—time enough to meet with Hans and, if I was right, find Gerhardt's Hoard. In the meantime, I had to think of a way to throw Viktor off my trail.

Sandor. I could call Sandor.

If there was anyone in all of Europe who had nothing to do with Hans, Erika, or Gerhardt's Hoard, it was Sandor and his wife Aanika. I had planned to call Sandor when I got on the train and tell him I was headed north to Nuremberg. Only now, instead of telling him I was coming their way to visit the Christkindlmarkt and shop for my future godchild, I had a slightly bigger favor to ask.

I stood up and looked in the bathroom mirror. The bump on my head was slightly better, but I still had dark circles beneath my eyes. I splashed cold water on my face, towel dried it with a paper towel, then determined I needed to act, dialed Sandor's number.

"Sandor?" I pressed the cell phone to my ear.

"Kat? Is this you?" Sandor's voice felt like a breath of fresh air.

From behind him, I could hear Aanika. "Is that Kat? Tell her we found the kinderwagen." Aanika took the phone. "I can't wait to show you. It's a shame you can't come to Nuremberg. The shopping is fabulous—"

"I'm here," I said. "Or almost anyway. I need you to pick me up at the train station."

Chapter Twenty-Five

If I thought my sudden call to Sandor might be a surprise, Sandor had an even bigger surprise waiting for me when I arrived. I didn't tell Sandor why I was coming to Nuremberg. I didn't want to expose Sandor and Aanika to any trouble. As far as Sandor was concerned, I was working on a story for a travel pub for next year's holiday edition, and it only made sense I'd visit Nuremberg and the Christkindlmarkt. Sandor had no idea the real reason for my mission, and I wanted to keep it that way. I wasn't about to tell him I was being followed by a Russian goon that made his living trafficking stolen art and young women or that I feared Viktor might now be tracking me. Whatever I did, I needed to keep a low profile. But when I walked out of the train depot and saw Sandor across the street, standing in front of a bright yellow Maserati, I realized my mistake.

Sandor doesn't do low-key.

"Kat!" Sandor hollered to me, both hands high above his head, his arms spread wide. "Over here!"

Sandor was parked in a passenger zone opposite the train station. Despite the rush of people anxious to make their train, the sight of a big Hungarian standing in front of a vintage car with his hands in the air and a jovial smile on his face had managed to stop traffic. Or at least, make enough of a scene that I was sure Viktor and the German spy following him had seen us.

It would have been impossible not to. Particularly when Aanika came running up to me, squealing hello and looking like she was sporting a beachball beneath her heavy coat. So much for hoping to blend in and lose Viktor in the crowd.

Aanika wrapped her arms around my neck, hugged me, then pushed me away with her hands on my shoulders and held me at arm's length.

"What's this?" She pointed to the bruise above my eye.

"Nothing," I said. "I slipped on the ice, that's all." Anxious not to draw attention to myself, I nodded to the Maserati. "What happened to the truck?" A horse-drawn carriage would have caused less attention. "Where did you get this?"

"Have you forgotten? She's the reason I'm here. This classic beauty belongs to my client. A 1956 Maserati. Runs like she came from the factory yesterday. She's one of several vintage automobiles my client asked me to transport to Budapest."

"And your client allows you to drive it?" I looked across the plaza for any signs of the Russian and spotted him standing beneath the Hauptbahnhof's big Neo-Gothic portal, the entrance to one of Europe's biggest train stations. He had a cigarette in his mouth, and one hand cupped to light it. Viktor's eyes narrowed as he caught sight of me. He tossed the match to the ground. *Checkmate.* I glanced back at the Maserati. If Viktor was here to eliminate me, I would have to work fast if I hoped to convince him I was nothing more than a travel journalist on assignment, meeting up with old friends.

"We were out for a spin when you called. Isn't good to let a car like this sit idle in a garage. Get in. You'll enjoy the ride." Sandor opened the passenger door.

I wasn't about to object. Not with a target on my back. I crawled into the car's narrow backseat while Aanika settled next to Sandor. As we pulled away from the station, I looked over my shoulder. Viktor hailed a cab and pointed in our direction.

I didn't imagine a cab would be any match for the Maserati or Sandor's lead foot. The sound and vibration of the car's engine—like a predator's growl—trumped my worry, and for the moment, I felt safe with Sandor behind the wheel.

I clutched the back of Aanika's seat. "Do you two have time to join me for a little sightseeing?"

If Viktor did manage to keep up, I was happy for Sandor and Aanika's

CHAPTER TWENTY-FIVE

company and planned to make myself as public as possible, doing touristy things. The more I remained in the open, the safer I thought I'd be.

"That depends." Aanika looked over her shoulder at me. "How long can you stay?"

"I only planned for the day."

"Stay the night," Sandor said. "You'll need at least two days to see everything."

"You can stay with us." Aanika looked pleadingly. Pregnancy and the cool weather appeared to agree with her. "We have a castle."

"A castle?"

"More of a manor, really," Sandor said. "Right below Kaiserburg Castle. It belongs to my client. He offered to let Aanika and me stay in exchange for closing things up for him here."

"It's given us a little time together before the baby comes." Aanika put her hand on her stomach and smiled at Sandor.

I glanced into the side mirror. The cab had been forced to stop at a red light while Sandor continued on, turning right through the Frauentur Tower, a rock archway, and into the Old Town. I was immediately taken by the change of scenery, the half-timbered buildings, and the narrow cobblestoned streets. I felt like I had instantly been transported back to the Middle Ages. Convinced we had lost Viktor, I relaxed into the Maserati's soft leather back seat while Sandor explained the area's history.

Kaiserburg Castle, also known as the Imperial Castle, was a thousand years old and had once been the main seat of the Holy Roman Empire. The Old Town or Alstadt, and the medieval wall surrounding it, had been destroyed during the war. But today, many buildings and much of the wall had been restored, making the area a big draw for tourists.

The manor, where Sandor and Aanika were staying, had once been a coach house, and like the other half-timbered homes, had been built with split logs exposed to the outside with spaces in between filled with white plaster. Once the royal stable and later a youth hostel, it was now the residence of Sandor's well-to-do client, or as Sandor said, one of several such residences his client owned.

Ground level, where the royal stables had once been, were four large wooden garage doors, while above were three stories of windowed living quarters.

"As you can see, we've plenty of room. Come, I'll show you." I followed Aanika up the stairs to the residence.

The manor was comfortable in a modern, very medieval, hunting-lodge sort of way. The main room included living and dining areas, a large wood-burning fireplace, and a huge wrought iron chandelier. Beneath a raised beam ceiling, with square curtainless windows, was a couch, a loveseat, two overstuffed chairs, a coffee table, and a designer rug that covered most of the living room's wooden floor. To the left of the living area were a dine-in kitchen with a blue enameled gas stove, an industrial size refrigerator, and a table that could easily have sat a dozen people. Antique floor runners lined the two stairways, one off the kitchen, the other off the main living area, both leading upstairs to two separate bedroom wings, where I guessed there to be at least six suites.

Aanika showed me to the master suite. The bed was piled high with baby clothes, little pink dusters, toys, and blankets. "So, you'll stay the night? There's plenty of room, and we can pick up anything you need in one of the small stores. Say yes." Aanika put her hands on either side of my face and nodded my head up and down. Pregnancy had made her determined to have her way.

"Yes," I said. How could I not? The more time I spent with Sandor and Aanika, the safer I felt, and the easier I hoped it would be to convince Viktor that I was nothing more than a travel journalist on assignment who had run into old friends.

"Good, then it's decided. We can visit the Christkindlmarkt tonight. It's crowded, and you'll want to see it with its lights and take your time. But I need to have lunch before we do anything else." Aanika took my hand and led me down the stairs to the living room. "I'm starving."

* * *

CHAPTER TWENTY-FIVE

The cobblestoned streets below the castle were wet with melted snow and crammed with tourists. Sandor did his best to keep Aanika from slipping on the cobblestones while he pointed out the town's highlights as we worked our way down narrow streets, through the town's center, toward the river. When we passed the Burggarten or the castle garden, Sandor stopped and pointed to several bunkers. Here was where the Nazis had hidden art in old beer cellars, and further on, across the river, was the Palace of Justice, where the Nuremberg Trials were held.

When we reached Albrecht Durer Square, Aanika insisted on stopping to catch her breath. I wandered the square and took a couple of photos of Sandor and Aanika as they paused beneath the statue of Nuremberg's most famous Renaissance resident and another of Saint Sebald Church. Then, as I prepared to take another candid shot of the two of them together, I stopped. In the lens of my camera, standing in the alleyway behind Sandor and Aanika, was Viktor. He had taken off his Russian hat, probably in an attempt to blend into the crowd of tourists, but I recognized his bulbous nose and dark brows. I snapped a quick picture, refocused my lens, and clicked off several more shots. Enough to prove the Russian was in Nuremberg.

I reminded myself to look like I was on assignment. That I had met a colleague, and we were enjoying the afternoon shopping and noting the attractions. I returned to Aanika, and when she was ready, we linked arms and wandered ahead of Sandor. Several times, we stopped to look in the store windows while I took photos and picked up brochures, stuffing them in my bag as we worked our way through the town. I wanted there to be no doubt that I was on assignment. *Nothing to see here, Viktor. Move on.*

We paused, and I was looking at the map when Aanika grabbed my arm and pulled me ahead. "Hurry, we need to get to hospital." With one hand on her belly, she pointed toward a building partially built over the river.

"Hospital? Are you okay?" My concerns about Viktor suddenly took a backseat to Aanika.

I looked back for Sandor. Aanika wasn't due for three months.

Sandor hurried to her side. "She's fine. It's not the hospital she's talking about, it's the restaurant, Heilig-Geist-Spital. It used to be a hospital, but today it's a restaurant, Aanika's favorite. She's been there nearly every day since we arrived."

"I get cravings. I love their sausages. Sandor and I'll go ahead and get a table. Kat, there's a pharmacy next door. You can get whatever you need. We'll meet you inside."

Aanika scurried ahead with Sandor behind her while I ducked inside the pharmacy to buy a few personal items. I had just finished paying and was about to leave when I noticed Viktor standing in the doorway. He had followed me inside and was now blocking my exit.

"Meine Liebshin. My darling. I am so sorry." Viktor stepped forward, took hold of my upper arm, dragged me toward the back of the store, and pushed me up against a wall like a child who had misbehaved. The clerk, busy with his next customer, paid no attention. Anyone watching would have thought Viktor and I had had a lover's spat and weren't about to get involved.

"Let go of me." I struggled to remove his grip, but Viktor was twice my size, and with his thick sausage-like fingers, he grabbed the sides of my face and kissed me on the lips. His breath was like day-old fish, hot and stinky. I wanted to gag.

Viktor whispered in my ear, his hand vice-like on the back of my neck. "You make a scene, and I'll snap your neck and be gone before anyone can help you."

I wiped my mouth with the back of my hand. "What do you want?"

"I want you to go home."

I wanted to punch him, anything to get away, but no amount of strength on my part would have penetrated his thick lamb's wool coat, and there was nothing I could grab off the shelf to use as a weapon. Viktor tightened his grip on my neck. I put my hand on top of his and dug my nails into his fist. "And just why would I do that?"

"Because you and I both know you're not a journalist. You're a spy. You go home now, and I'll let you go. If not—"

"If not, what?"

Viktor squeezed his hand tighter around my neck and pulled me closer to him. "Because if you don't, your friends here might not do so well."

CHAPTER TWENTY-FIVE

"What are you talking about?"

"You heard me. You hang around, and your friends here might get hurt. No reason for you to pretend anymore, Ms. Lawson. Or do you prefer Kat? You go home now, and you won't have to worry." Viktor dropped his hands from my throat, then turned and walked away.

With my hands on my throat, I watched Viktor walk out the door. Then, to my surprise, the German agent, who had sat across from me on the train, appeared from between the aisles and, without so much as a nod in my direction, followed him. I swallowed hard. *Yeah, I get it. You're undercover. What were you going to do, let him kill me?*

I wanted to yell at the bulky Russian and tell him what a bastard I thought he was, but I didn't dare. It had never occurred to me that Viktor might harm Sandor or Aanika. I couldn't tell them about Viktor. If Sandor had any idea about the Russian or knew that he had threatened me, Sandor would go after Viktor, and I wasn't about to endanger my friends.

Chapter Twenty-Six

Sandor stood up as I entered the restaurant. It would have been impossible to miss his six-foot-two, oversized frame. He had found a table and waved for me to join them. The restaurant was noisy, crowded with tourists, and decorated with holly boughs and mistletoe that hung from lanterns beneath the heavily beamed ceiling. I scanned the crowd for any sign of Viktor, and, not seeing him, weaved my way through the tables as best I could. I worried I had led the Russian mobster to my friends and that their lives and my own were in danger. Satisfied Viktor wasn't there, I heaved a sigh of relief and joined Sandor and Aanika at their table.

"You find what you need?" Aanika squirted a mountain of mayonnaise on top of an order of Pommes Frites—French Fries—she had ordered while waiting for her meal.

My stomach roiled. Whether it was the combination of mayo and fries or my run-in with Viktor, I felt sick.

"Yes, thank you. I didn't need much. Toothbrush, that's about it." I patted my bag to indicate I had all I needed. Once Viktor had left the pharmacy, I waited long enough to ensure he was gone, then slipped out the door and hurried toward the restaurant.

"You look pale." Sandor held out a chair for me. "You okay?"

"I'm fine." I hugged myself and rubbed my hands up and down my upper arms. "Still getting used to the cold, that's all. What's everybody having?"

I desperately wanted to think of something other than Viktor, but I couldn't keep my eyes still long enough to focus on the menu. I worried he was watching me from somewhere.

CHAPTER TWENTY-SIX

Sandor grabbed the menu. "I ordered a beer. You want one?" I nodded. "Aanika's already started. when it comes to food, I've learned not to get in the way of a pregnant lady." Sandor reached for one of Aanika's fries, and she slapped his hand.

"Very funny." Aanika squirted more mayo onto her fries. "You have to try the Nuremberger rostbratwurst, Kat. It's their specialty and my favorite. I don't know what I'll do when I get back to Budapest and can't get it. Sandor may have to truck it in for me."

I ordered the rostbratwurst. Not that I was hungry after my scare with Viktor, my stomach was still in knots, but it seemed the easiest thing to do and kept the conversation away from me and onto the topic at large; Aanika's ever-growing belly. But, even as we joked and talked about the future, my mind was spinning with thoughts about what I would do if Viktor were to approach me again.

Aanika finished first, licked her fingers, leaned back in her chair, and put her hands on her stomach. "Ahh, this was good. And now, my husband, I am full. And, Kat, I am tired. Sandor, you need to take me home. I need my nap."

I wasn't surprised Aanika was full, nor that she was tired. She had not only completed her entire meal but some of mine and a good portion of Sandor's Jägerschnitzel as well.

Sandor stood up and helped his wife with her coat.

"Wait." Aanika pointed to the kitchen. "I forgot to order the chocolate torte to go."

"If you have anything else to eat, my Luv, I'll have to call for a donkey cart to carry you up the hill."

"Don't be mean." Aanika rested her head on Sandor's shoulder and blew me a kiss. "Sorry, Kat, I think I've overdone it today."

Sandor put enough German marks on the table to cover the meal, then handed me a walking map with a tour of the Old Town. "Think you can manage alone?"

"I'll be fine. Don't worry." I whispered to Sandor I would be back in time for dinner, a promise I didn't plan to keep, then stood up and made a big deal of saying auf wiedersehen and hugging goodbye.

If Viktor were watching, I wanted him to think I was doing exactly as he had asked, bidding goodbye to old friends and leaving town. And to ensure that he had no doubt about my intention, rather than continue on the walking tour as the map instructed, I headed directly back toward the train station, thankful I had my backpack with me. I had left nothing at the manor house where Sandor and Aanika expected me for the night.

When I got to the train station, I took a schedule from the kiosk and went directly to the WC where I could be alone and called Sophie. She picked up immediately.

"Kat, it's you." Sophie sounded breathless. "I've been waiting for your call. Are you okay?"

"I'm fine. I'm in Nuremberg. Viktor followed me here."

"I heard."

I took the phone from my ear and pressed it to my forehead. Of course, Sophie had heard. The other side of her team had reported Viktor's whereabouts to her.

"He tried to kill me."

"I warned you, Kat. This is a high-stakes game. People disappear. Things happen. There's only so much I can do to protect you. But, on the bright side, you did tell me you could handle yourself, and from what I hear, you did quite well."

"So that's supposed to make me feel better? The fact that Viktor didn't kill me, and you've got some German undercover agent following him around? Who isn't interested in me or about to interfere if I'm on the losing end of any altercation." I exhaled. I didn't want Sophie to lose confidence in me, but this was as close as I had come to the Russian, and whether I admitted it to Sophie or not, I was worried. "Look, I get that you and your secret alliances don't like to share identities, but this was a little close."

"You did say you didn't want to go home. Has that changed? It's not too late."

"I'm not leaving. But, yes, things have changed. Viktor threatened my friends, Sandor and Aanika. They have nothing to do with this, and—."

CHAPTER TWENTY-SIX

"Calm down. Where are you now?"

"At the train station. I wanted Viktor to think he had scared me off and that I've left."

"Good, that's exactly what we want him to think."

"But what about Sandor and Aanika? I've put them in harm's way. If anything happens to them—"

"Nothing's going to happen, Kat. If Viktor thinks you've left, he's not going to bother with them. But I need you to listen to me and do exactly as I say."

"I'm listening."

"Go back outside to the tourist kiosk. Pick up a brochure for one of the international airlines. Doesn't matter which one. But I need you to make a big deal of looking at it, then acting as if you're calling the number. If Viktor's watching, he'll get the idea. Then go back inside the train station and take the next train to Augsburg."

"Augsburg?"

"There's an international airport there. Meet me at the Hotel Adler. It's a two-hour train ride from Nuremberg. And Kat?"

"What?"

"You're sure about this?"

I closed my eyes. I could still feel Viktor's gloved hand on my neck, the stench of his foul breath in my face. He could have killed me in an instant, but I wasn't about to give up.

"I'm not going home."

"Good. When you get to the hotel, ask for Miss Thompson."

"Who's Miss Thompson?"

"Who do you think?" Sophie laughed. "I'll see you in Augsburg. Stay safe, Kat."

I said goodbye to Sophie, returned to the outside kiosk, and picked up several international airline brochures. All but one, I stuffed awkwardly back into the rack so Viktor would know what I had been looking at. Then, with one pamphlet in my hand, I took my cell from my bag and looked at it as I called Sandor. If Viktor were watching, I wanted him to think I was booking a flight home. Instead, I told Sandor I had to leave suddenly, that something had come up. Couldn't be helped, I said. But I promised to call again and planned to see them both back in Budapest before heading back to the States.

When I hung up, my phone buzzed. It was Inga. Sophie's instructions rang in my head. *Don't. Tell. Anyone.* I let the call go to voicemail.

* * *

It was nearly four-thirty p.m. by the time the train pulled into the Augsburg station. It was dark and raining, and I grabbed the first cab I could get and called Sophie immediately. She met me outside the hotel with a big umbrella, shielding me from the rain and any potential onlookers. Like a mother hen, she ushered me through the lobby toward the elevators before anyone could see us.

We were alone in the lift before she spoke. "I'm glad you're here, Kat. Our contact—"

"You mean your German spy friend? The one who followed Viktor to Nuremberg?" The words tumbled out of my mouth. Accusatory and bitter. I was angry the German spy had done nothing to interfere with Viktor's assault, and I didn't care if Sophie knew it. I had had time to think about Viktor's threats on the train, and I was tired of not knowing who was involved in the mission and having little to say about it. "What's his name? I think I deserve to know that much."

Sophie pushed the lift button again. I could see she was upset.

"His name is Karl Meyer. He works with Interpol."

I rolled my eyes. "Well, at least I have a name. I don't suppose you'll tell me anything else?"

"I can tell you that Viktor waited at the train station until he saw you at the kiosk and then board the train to Augsburg. Once you left, he took the next train back to Munich. Our hope is that Viktor thinks he's frightened you off. But we'll need you to stay here for the night to be safe."

The elevator arrived on the fourth floor, and Sophie led the way to a small room at the end of the hall. Inside, the room was dark, and the curtains were

CHAPTER TWENTY-SIX

closed. Sophie waited to switch on the lights until she had closed the door behind us.

"We need to work on changing your look and getting you a new passport." Sophie pointed to the bed, where she laid out a new identity for me, a grey wig, a pair of black-framed glasses, and a dowdy-looking tweed coat.

"What's this? You want me to look like an old lady?"

"If it's going to save your life, yes. Don't you? Or would you prefer Viktor break your neck?"

I tossed my backpack on the floor. "If Viktor thinks I've gone home, what problem is there?"

"It's called playing it safe, Kat. We can't be certain what Viktor's thinking. We don't know who or how many people Viktor might be working with. He very well may be alone, but if he's not, and someone else is following you, you need to be careful." Sophie took the wig from the bed and handed it to me. "Here, put this on. I need to get some pictures."

I stuffed my dark hair beneath the wig. Sophie handed me the glasses, and I put them on and looked in the mirror. Even my mother wouldn't have recognized me.

"The coat, too." Sophie took a camera from her bag and snapped a couple of shots. "I'll be back in the morning with your new passport. Meanwhile, I've arranged for you to pick up a rental car tomorrow. Soon as you get to Hans' chateau, as long as you haven't been spotted, you can leave the wig in the car." Sophie walked to the door and stopped. "Oh, one more thing. I thought you might be hungry, and since you can't go out, I picked up a McDonald's burger and fries. They're on the dresser. I figured by now you might be missing something American."

I looked inside the sack, a small bag of soggy fries and a greasy burger that looked like it had been sitting on the dresser for hours. *Some dinner.*

"Thanks," I said.

"Get some sleep, Kat. You're going to need it."

Sophie closed the door behind her. I took a fry from the bag and sat down on the bed. I had yet to listen to Inga's message. I pushed play and wished I hadn't.

Chapter Twenty-Seven

I spent a restless night replaying Inga's voicemail. Her voice was shaky, barely audible in parts, and I felt responsible. Inga was terrified, worried about what Viktor might do to her if he knew we had spoken. Listening to her triggered thoughts of Viktor's following me into the pharmacy, dragging me to the back of the store, his foul, fishy breath, and threat to harm Sandor and Aanika. All of it kept playing over and over in my mind, robbing me of any chance of sleep. I had promised Inga I would help her escape the Russian, and now, I was stuck in a hotel room in Augsburg with strict orders not to call anyone or do anything that might alert Viktor that I was still in the country.

When Sophie arrived the following day, I was so anxious about Inga that I scarcely looked at the newly forged documents she had brought with her.

"Sit down. You need to hear this." I waited for Sophie to put her things down and take a seat on the bed, then pulled my cell phone from the pocket of the hotel's robe and put the phone on speaker.

"Kat, where are you? Viktor says you left! Please, don't leave me. I need you. Everything is falling apart here. Hans is gone. I've tried to call him, but he doesn't answer, and Erika is acting crazy. She's not come into the museum, and she's not taking any of my calls. Viktor will dump me with his friends in Prague if she fires me. Please, Kat, don't leave me. I'm all alone. Help me!"

Sophie took the phone from my hand and held it. "She's not your problem, Kat."

"What do you mean she's not my problem? You can't expect me to ignore

CHAPTER TWENTY-SEVEN

her? What's she going to do, wait for Viktor to sell her like he might a painting to the highest bidder? I'm sorry, but I won't do that. She reached out to me."

"Need I remind you, the girl mugged you. Took your purse and—"

"She returned my bag, Sophie. She's an asset, not just some collateral damage I can walk away from."

Sophie got up and went to the coffeemaker on the dresser and began to make herself a cup of coffee. "You're not going to give up on this girl, are you?"

"No. I'm not."

"Alright then, here's what's going to happen. I take it you haven't checked out of your hotel in Munich."

"I never expected to be away overnight."

"Good. If I recall, the room at the Hotel Schlicker's is a double. Once you leave here, call Inga from the car, and tell her to go to your hotel and wait for you there. I'll call ahead to the hotel, tell them I'm you and that I'm expecting a colleague, and to give her a key to the room. But whatever you do, don't give Inga my name or mention me. If she needs anything, have her order room service."

"Then what?" I asked.

"Then," Sophie took her coffee cup from beneath the brewer and crossed the room, "based upon whatever happens between you and Hans at the chateau, we'll figure out what to do with her. Or at least I will."

"Promise me you will." I didn't like that Sophie had doubts about my future, but I couldn't ignore the possibility that Sophie might be correct. If I had misjudged Hans, my return to the chateau might be a setup. "I'm that girl's only chance out, Sophie. You've got to help her."

"Enough about Inga." Sophie put her coffee down on the nightstand next to the bed. Then from within her bag took a small paper sack and handed it to me. "I picked up a few things I thought you might need. Hurry now. We need to get you dressed. You've got a big day ahead."

I showered quickly, found a new pair of undies and deodorant in the bag Sophie had brought me, and, feeling refreshed, got back into the same clothes

I'd worn the day before.

"You're going to need these, too." Sophie handed me the wig and eyeglasses she had brought with her last night. "After you get to the chateau, you can do whatever you like. But from here to Oberammergau, we don't want anyone to recognize you."

I brushed my hair into a ponytail and pulled the wig on like a swim cap, pushing any loose hairs up beneath it. Then finger combed the bangs and added the black framed glasses.

"How do I look?" I turned to Sophie for inspection.

"Like a retired schoolteacher from Salt Lake, on holiday."

"And my name?"

"Katheryn Little." Sophie handed me my new passport and an Amex card. "The card works like it did before. If you're in trouble, use it. We'll be notified right away. And if you're stopped for any reason, make sure you use this passport, not your own."

"Let's hope I don't need to."

"You may need more than hope, Kat." Sophie reached into her bag and handed me a small handgun. "I trust you know how to use it."

"Do you think I need it?"

"If you're wrong about Hans, and he has other ideas and wants to get rid of you, maybe."

I took the gun and put it in my bag. "Well, let's hope that's not the case."

"Kat, this mission was never intended to put you in harm's way. It's not too late—"

"Hey, stop it. I've got two men, Hans and Viktor, who you seem to think might both want me dead. I don't agree with you on that—at least as far as Hans is concerned—but I'm not quitting. Not until I see this through to the end."

"I like your style, Kat, although right now, I don't think it's your smartest move." Sophie picked her bag up off the bed. "But, if you want to turn around anytime between here and the chateau, it's okay. We'll get you on a flight back to the States, and you'll be fine. But, once you're inside the chateau, you're on your own. There's no cell service inside, and we won't be able to

CHAPTER TWENTY-SEVEN

help you. Your only hope will be that you're right about Hans."

"Oh, come on, Sophie, give me some credit, will you? Where's your sense of romance?" I needed to lighten the scene. All this talk of trickery had me second-guessing myself, and I couldn't allow that. I didn't have a choice. I had too many people depending on me. Inga for one, and Hans for another. That is, if he was being honest with me. I put one hand on my hip, one behind my ear, and flashed her a campy model's pose. "You think Hans isn't going to want this? Wig or no wig, believe me, this isn't going to be a problem. Trust me."

"That's why I hired you, Kat. But, things can go wrong, and very quickly. If you're right about Hans, I expect you'll spend a steamy weekend—the details of which I don't care to know—and by Sunday night, you'll have something to tell me regarding the location of Gerhard's Hoard, and we'll celebrate."

"And if it's not?"

"And you're still alive?" Sophie raised a brow. "Then I think you'll have to admit this has been a very expensive exercise and nothing more than an excuse for Hans to lure you down for a romantic weekend. And if that's the case, you can take the car back to Augsburg and fly home. There'll be a ticket for Katheryn Little at the American Airline's desk."

"And after that?"

"There is no after that, Kat. This either works or it doesn't. If it doesn't, we're done."

* * *

I liked the small, black sporty BMW sedan Sophie had reserved for me. As far as European cars go, it was low profile, just one of many like it on the autobahn, and responsive. And despite my inexperience with driving in the snow, the roads had been plowed, and I felt safe behind the wheel. I checked the map Sophie had given me. Oberammergau was an hour's drive, and once I left the city with the morning rush hour behind me, the road opened up, and so did the view.

I stuck to the autobahn's far-right lane and checked the rearview mirror to see if I was being followed. I had learned my lesson about driving in the left lane, which in my opinion, was for those foolish enough to consider the autobahn their private raceway. A farmer's truck loaded with sugar beets was the only thing going slower than me. Satisfied Viktor wasn't following me, and if he were, that Sophie's Interpol friends would be on to him, I picked up my cell and called Inga.

"Kat. You called. Thank God!"

"Where are you?"

"I'm at the museum."

"By yourself? There's no guard?"

"No. Sometimes, Fritz is here in the morning, but I don't know where anybody is right now. They haven't been around."

"What about Viktor?"

"I don't know. He went out last night and didn't come back. But he'll kill me if he finds out we've been talking!"

"He's not going to find out, but you must listen to me and do exactly as I tell you. I need you to get yourself to my hotel. Tell them at the front desk you're my associate and that you've arrived early and want to freshen up. They'll expect you and give you a key to my room. Go now and wait for me there. And don't tell anyone where you're going. I'll be in touch."

"But if Viktor thinks I've tried to escape, he'll kill my mother. He told me so."

"She's in Berlin, right?"

"Yes, but Vitor has friends."

"Call her. Tell her to leave town. Is there somewhere she could go?"

"She has a sister outside Berlin in Potsdam. We used to go there when I was little to visit."

"Good. Then tell your mother to visit her sister and not come back until she hears from you again."

"Kat?"

"What?"

"Are you okay?"

"Don't worry about me. I'll be fine. Do as I say, and don't tell anyone

CHAPTER TWENTY-SEVEN

where you've gone."

Chapter Twenty-Eight

The closer I got to Oberammergau, the more magnificent the mountains, with their jagged snowcapped peaks reaching for the sky, covered with clouds. Fresh snow had fallen, and I slowed to a crawl as I crossed the Ammer River Bridge. The early morning cold had a stillness about it. The town looked sleepy, with only a few locals out for their early morning errands. I plowed slowly through the fresh snow, past rows of frescoed cottages, searching for the small roadside memorial that marked the turn-off to the chateau. When I found it, I checked my rearview mirror to see if I had been followed. If Sophie's agents were behind me, I couldn't see them. But I wasn't about to wait. Ahead of me, evidence of another car's tracks in the melted snow suggested Hans had already arrived, and I was eager to join him.

I pressed my foot on the accelerator a bit too hard, and the car fishtailed, its tires spinning in the snow. I eased off the gas, my stomach tight. *Easy does it.* This portion of the road hadn't been plowed since I had left a week ago, and the hardpack snow, now like ice beneath the fresh fall, would make the drive up the mountain extra tricky. I clamped my hands on the wheel and, with the sound of snow crunching beneath my tires, took each turn no faster than I might walk. Finally, a glimpse of the chateau through the fog, its iron gates open. After clinging to the mountainside and giving myself as much room as possible from the sheer rocky cliffs with their icy slopes, I downshifted and made my slow final ascent to the top.

As I rolled through the gates and onto the compound's grounds, I could see Hans' big SUV parked in the drive. My heart raced at the sight of it. He

CHAPTER TWENTY-EIGHT

must have arrived just moments before. I whipped the grey wig off my head, grabbed my bag, and, careful not to slip in the snow, hurried from my car and up the steps to the chateau's front doors. To my surprise, the front doors were ajar.

"Hans? Hi, it's me, Kat." A gale of cold air followed me inside.

There was no answer.

I shut the door behind me. "Hans?"

The chateau was quiet, and the house was freezing. I thought Hans might have left the front door open, his hands full of groceries for the weekend, and I would find him in the kitchen. I wandered from the entry into the great room. Then stopped. Something was wrong. The heavy velvet curtains were closed, and a fire had recently been lit in the big fireplace. But all that remained were a few dying embers and the smell of cooling ash. The fireplace irons that Hans had kept so neatly next to the hearth lay scattered on the stone floor.

"Hans?" I patted my bag to feel for the gun Sophie had given me and took another step toward the kitchen. A bottle of red wine and a pair of wine glasses were on the counter.

"Hans, what's going on? Answer me?"

Silence.

I took the gun from my bag and, with both hands on the handle, stepped further into the kitchen. The back door leading to the ice pond stood open. My eyes swept the room. The barstools where Hans and I had sat at the kitchen counter with Baret had been turned over, and two of the copper pots that had hung above the stove had fallen. One had crashed to the counter; the other had rolled towards an open cellar door. I picked up one of the wine glasses, held it to the light, and noticed a lipstick stain on the rim. I replaced it on the counter and crept lightly toward the cellar door.

"Hans?"

The padlock used to lock the cellar door hung loosely on the latch. I pushed the door open, stepped onto the landing, and peered over the railing into the darkened cellar below. I would need a light. I felt for a light switch by the door and, finding none, stepped back into the kitchen and rummaged through the kitchen drawers until I found a flashlight. Then with the gun in one hand and the light in the other, I returned to the top of the steps and slowly, the staircase creaking beneath my feet, took one step at a time. I stopped halfway. In the light of my scope, a rat with its long hairy tail scurried across the floor. I grabbed the railing and steadied my breath. *Come on, Kat, you can't let a stupid rat spook you.* I shined my light further across the cellar's rocky floor. Baret was right. The chateau did have a dungeon, and to a small boy, this cellar, the foundation upon which Hans' mother had built the family home, was, by all means, a modern-day dungeon.

I continued to the bottom stair and shuffled across the dungeon's earthy floor, careful not to trip on its rocky surface. Ahead of me, my light cast itself on row after row of wine racks with bottles of wine. I pulled a bottle from one of the racks. A 1967 Chateau Lafite Rothschild Paulliac. *Nice. And expensive.* I was about to put it back when I noticed the rack appeared to have been moved, and behind it, a tattered piece of black canvas had been tacked to the wall.

Why would anyone want to cover a rock wall in a dungeon basement? Unless there was something to hide. I put the gun back in my bag and, resting the flashlight on another rack so that I could see what I was doing, began to remove the bottles, stacking them on the ground in the middle of the room. Once I had emptied the rack, it was easy enough to move away from the wall, and as I did, the canvas fluttered. I tore at the canvas, pulled it away from the wall until it fell to the floor, then reached for the flashlight. I couldn't believe my eyes.

In front of me, on wooden platforms, in a space that couldn't have been more than eight feet deep and maybe ten or twelve feet wide and piled from the floor to the cave's ceiling, were stacks of gold gilt-framed paintings. Some had been covered or simply draped with tarps. I lifted a tarp from one, a Van Gogh, then another, a Renoir, and a Monet. I shifted my light to another small wine rack in the corner, this one full of the rolled canvases. I unrolled several, then stopped. In my hand, I held a Rembrandt sketch, a self-portrait. Sophie was sure Gerhardt had stolen Rembrandt's lion sketch from her father's study. If it was here, I had to find it. Carefully, I pulled another

CHAPTER TWENTY-EIGHT

canvas from the rack and then another. And then found it. Rembrandt's Lying Lion.

I rerolled the Rembrandt sketch and put it in my bag. I planned to give it to Sophie, proof I'd uncovered Gerhardt's Hoard and that Hans had been telling me the truth. I started for the stairs, then stopped. Beneath the staircase, my light caught a bulky shape, partially covered with a blanket. I focused the flashlight deeper beneath the stairway and approached, thinking this might be another hidden piece of artwork, perhaps a sculpture. But the closer I got, I began to realize this wasn't some long, lost piece of sculpture. The ground beneath it was wet, and while I couldn't make out the color of the liquid, it had a distinctive coppery, iron smell and was sticky. Blood. And I had walked right through the bloody pool and smeared it across the floor. My footprints were everywhere.

I tip-toed around the bloody pool. Whatever lay beneath the mound, I couldn't leave it. Part of me wanted to think it was some animal carcass Hans had shot while hunting and had stored in the cellar. But with the chaotic scene upstairs, I knew better. Cautiously, uncertain of what I was about to unveil, I leaned down and tugged at the blanket. At first, the blanket didn't budge. It was stuck, wrapped too tightly around whatever bloody horror was hidden inside. I tried again, this more firmly, and when I did, the blanket came loose. I stood back. From within the blanket's bloody folds, a body rolled out and onto the floor. I screamed. Staring up at me were the dead eyes of Hans Von Hausmann.

Chapter Twenty-Nine

I dropped the flashlight and stumbled up the stairs. It clattered between the wooden steps and landed on the floor below, illuminating Hans's gaping mouth and black eyes. I took the remaining steps two at a time, gripping the rail for support, then slammed the cellar door shut behind me. With my hand on my stomach, I leaned against the door and tried to imagine what had happened.

Hans told me he didn't plan to be back from Zurick until later in the day, but clearly, he had come home sooner than expected. I checked the open back door and windows in the kitchen. There was no sign of forced entry. Instead, it appeared Hans had come home early, started a fire in the fireplace, probably to take the chill off, then gone down to the cellar and selected a bottle of red wine. Then someone arrived, and Hans invited them inside. Either that or the murderer had a key to the chalet and had surprised Hans.

But who? Viktor? Had the Russian beaten me here? Followed Hans up the mountain road and into the chateau? Was it Viktor's black Mercedes, whose tire tracks I thought had belonged to Hans, that I had followed up the mountain? Viktor could have easily surprised Hans. Hans might have tried to reason with the Russian, perhaps even shown the hidden cache beneath the chateau, when the Russian pulled a gun and shot Hans. Or was it Erika and her husband, Fritz? Had they come to talk with Hans after he had taken Baret to Switzerland, and an argument ensued? Erika might have had a key to the front door. This was the house she had grown up in. The relationship between Hans and his sister was strained, and Fritz did have a gun. Or could it be something else entirely? Was the heated dispute I had witnessed

CHAPTER TWENTY-NINE

between Hans, Ozan, and Cahill over more than an unpaid bill? Hans told me they would lock up before I got here. Which meant they would have had a key to the chateau.

I left the back door open and went from the kitchen to the great room. The drapes had been drawn across the windows. The only light, was what spilled in from the narrow windows by the front doors, and the room was cast with shadows. Nothing was as it should have been. It was hard to think Hans would have invited anyone inside without the house looking like it was ready for a photo shoot. Hans had a curator's curse. Everything in its place and a place for everything. But the room was a mess. Pillows on the floor. Books thrown from the shelves. The fireirons scattered on the floor. Whatever had happened, my guess was that it had begun in the kitchen. Hans had poured a glass of wine, then been lured into the great room by his guest or uninvited intruder, who grabbed one of the fire irons and used it as a weapon. Hans must have followed suit and tried to defend himself. But it would have been of no use. His intruder had a gun and used it to force Hans down the stairs to the cellar—where he was fatally shot.

A gust of cold air rushed through the house, and the back door suddenly slammed shut. If whoever had murdered Hans was still on the property, I wasn't about to stick around to find out. I bolted toward the front door, hopeful I might see the two Interpol agents Sophie had assigned to follow me. But the only cars parked in front were my rental and Hans' black SUV. I took the gun Sophie had given me from my bag and ran fast as I could for the car. I don't know how I got down the mountain safely. My foot was heavy on the gas, and the car fishtailed like a bobsled across the hardpacked snow, careening from one side of the road to the next. When I finally reached the bottom of the road, I pulled over next to the small wooden memorial that marked the road leading to the chateau, and with my head resting between my hands on the wheel, I closed my eyes and exhaled. Thankful I had made it down alive.

My heart was still pounding when my cell rang. I fumbled for my phone inside my bag.

"Hi." I must have sounded breathless.

"Kat? Hi, you sound funny, it's Kirsten. Where are you?"

"Where are you?" I put the palm of my hand on the dashboard, dizzy from the shock of everything I had seen.

"Working, where else? Peter and I are finishing up a new story. He seems to—"

"Kirsten, stop! Listen to me. Hans is dead!"

"What?"

"He's dead, Kirsten. Someone shot him. There was blood everywhere. It was horrible—"

"Kat, what are you talking about?"

"He's dead, Kirsten. I found him. He's—"

"Kat, Stop! Whatever you do, don't say anything else. You need to get back to your hotel. Do you need me to pick you up at the train?"

"No." I closed my eyes. I couldn't get the picture of Hans out of my head. "I didn't take the train. I drove."

"You drove?"

"I rented a car."

Kirsten paused. "Are you okay to drive?"

"I think so."

"Good. Call me when you get back to Munich. We'll figure something out."

As I hung up, a black Mercedes pulled up slowly behind me. In the rearview mirror, I watched as a man got out of the car. I rested my foot on the gas and gripped the wheel. If it was Viktor, I planned to gun the engine and make a run for it. But I didn't have to. The man walking toward my car was Karl Meyer, the same agent who had followed Viktor to Nuremberg. I sat back and waited for him to approach. He signaled for me to roll down my window.

"You okay, Ms. Lawson? My partner and I saw you come down that hill. You were going pretty fast."

"Hans is dead. Someone shot him."

"What?" The agent winched. "You sure?"

"His body's lying in the cellar inside the chateau. It's a bloody mess up

CHAPTER TWENTY-NINE

there."

The agent looked up at the sky. I figured he was calculating what to do next, then tapped the side of my car. "You need to get out of here. Call Sophie. Tell her what happened. We'll take care of everything here. Now go."

It wasn't until I had crossed the Ammer River again that I picked up the phone and called Sophie.

"Sophie, it's me."

"Kat?" Sophie sounded surprised. "I wasn't expecting your call so early. Everything okay?"

"He's dead, Sophie. Hans is dead."

"What?"

"Someone shot him before I got there."

"Who?"

"I don't know. Viktor? Erika? Her husband, maybe? I don't know. It might have been one of the men Hans has working for him at the chateau. I overheard them arguing."

"What about?"

"Money, maybe?" I pinched the bridge of my nose. I wasn't thinking clearly. The shock of seeing Hans' dead body beneath the stairwell was more than I could process. "I'm not sure."

"Where are you now?"

"Outside Oberammergau. The agents you had following me caught me as I was leaving the chateau. The driver told me to go and that they would secure the place."

"Good. Don't go back to the chateau. Not under any circumstances. You got that?"

"Yeah."

"I need you to go back to Munich, to your hotel. I'll meet you there. Meanwhile, I'll call the rental company and tell them you're returning the car in Munich. And, Kat," Sophie paused, "be careful."

The drive from Oberammergau to Munich should have been a little more than an hour—but it took me much longer. I stopped at a comfort station to find a ladies' room to freshen up. I had just splashed cold water on my face when my phone rang. Now what?

"Kat, it's Kirsten. I thought I should give you a heads-up. After we got off the phone, I called Erika."

"What? Why would you call Erika?" In my confused state, I didn't think I heard her correctly.

"Hans is her brother. She deserves to know." I reminded myself Kirsten had no idea I thought Erika might be a suspect. Of course, Kirsten would call Erika. Kirsten was loyal to those who cared for her, and Erika had certainly done that. "Kat, Erika's a wreck. She wants to know if Baret was there. Please tell me you didn't also find Baret there as well."

"No." I pressed the phone to my ear. "Baret went to Switzerland with Hans. Erika knows that. Hans had just gotten back. Kirsten, what's going on?"

"Erika's called the police. That's what's going on. And she didn't say anything about Hans taking Baret to Switzerland. But she told them you were at the chateau."

"Why?"

"I don't know why. But now that the police are involved, I'll have to report Hans' death to the paper."

Damnit. I had hoped I would have more time before news of Hans' death was made public. Sophie would be livid. The last thing she would want was for news of Hans' murder to be splashed across the front pages of tomorrow's paper.

"I need to think," I said. "I'll call you back."

I tried to call Sophie again, but she didn't pick up. The call went straight to voicemail. I figured she must be on the train to Munich, and reception through the mountains could be intermittent. I left a message and told her to call.

Chapter Thirty

It was late afternoon, and the sun had set by the time I returned the rental car and took the subway back to the Marienplatz. I stopped briefly in the plaza and purchased a half dozen Gingerbread cookies from a street vendor. I hadn't eaten anything since last night. Sophie had tried to get me to eat something that morning, but I was too nervous, and now, after seeing Hans' dead body, I had no appetite. But I knew I had to keep going. I had no idea what awaited me with Sophie or Inga back at my hotel. The girl was on the run. Just like I feared I might be once news of Hans' murder became public. I stuffed the sack of cookies in my bag and hurried toward my hotel.

As I crossed the street, I heard the unmistakable warble of a European ambulance. *Nee-naww nee-naww.* Its flashing red lights reflected in the Hotel Schlicker's windows as it whisked past me, splashing wet snow on my boots as its wheels went up onto the sidewalk and down again before coming to a stop in the street. I cowered against a storefront with a crowd of anxious onlookers and watched as a team of paramedics pulled a gurney from the back of the wagon. Ahead, a policeman had begun to cordon off the area. From where I stood, I could see a frail, gray-haired woman sitting crumpled in the snow, holding her head, her eye makeup streaming down the sides of her face. She looked dazed.

Sophie?

I shoved anxiously through the crowd, pushing aside strangers to get a better look. But a policeman blocked me with his baton before I could break through the restricted area.

"Please, I think I know that woman."

"Sorry, miss, you need to wait here."

"But, she's…she's my friend. I need to help her."

"Step back, please."

The cop wouldn't allow me through, and there was nothing I could do. I stood helpless and watched as the EMTs bandaged the woman's head and loaded her into the van. I couldn't be sure if it was Sophie. The bandages made it difficult to tell.

I watched as the ambulance disappeared, its lights and wailing siren fading into the dark night. If it was Sophie who I'd seen lying in the street, I'd know as soon as I returned to the hotel. She promised she would be waiting for me, and if she weren't? I closed my eyes and tried to shake the thought from my head. I couldn't take losing two people on the same day. I didn't want to think about it.

* * *

"Kat? Kat, is that you?" I turned to see Kirsten running toward me. "Are you alright?"

"I-I don't know." Kirsten put her arms around me, and I buried my face in the fur collar of her coat. It felt good to see a friendly face. "I think the woman, the one the EMTs just took away. I think it might have been Sophie."

"Sophie?"

"My boss—"

"Your publisher? She's in town?"

I slapped my hand over my mouth. I had said too much. I had promised Sophie I wouldn't say anything about her being in town, but after finding Hans dead, and thinking the woman whose body the paramedics had just loaded up into an ambulance might be Sophie, the words had slipped from my mouth without thinking.

"She called yesterday and surprised me. She said she had an opportunity to meet with old friends, and we agreed to meet for dinner later this week." I touched my head. It was pounding. "Ugh, I hope it wasn't her. I couldn't

CHAPTER THIRTY

take another death. Not today. Did you see what happened?"

Kirsten put her hands on my shoulders and looked me in the eyes. "Kat, I am so sorry. I was in a hurry to get to the hotel. I saw you had called, and I wanted to get here fast as I could."

I glanced back at the street. Already shoppers had begun to fill the area where the paramedics had picked up the old woman and taken her to the hospital.

"If it helps, I did hear a scream. And I saw a car come around the corner. I don't know if it was the same car that hit her, but the next thing I knew, she was lying in the street."

"What kind of car?" I could barely get the words out of my mouth fast enough.

"A black Mercedes, I think."

My eyes swept the street. Every other car on the road was a black Mercedes. "Do you see it here now?"

Kirsten shrugged. "Kat, whoever was driving may not have known they hit her. It gets dark early, and the streets are busy. People step into the crosswalk without looking. Sometimes drivers stop. Sometimes, they…just keep going." Kirsten took my hands in her own and squeezed them. "Are you going to be okay?"

"I think I'm going to be sick."

"Come. You'll feel better if you have something to drink. And if you want, I can call the hospital to find your friend and ask how she is. But right now, you and I need to talk about Hans. The police are calling. They're asking questions. I'm going to have to talk to them."

"The police?"

"Erika gave them my number. They're going to expect me to talk to them. But first, let's get you inside. It's cold, and you're shaking." Kirsten put her arm through mine, and we headed to the hotel.

Once inside, I stopped at the front desk and asked for my key. The clerk informed me I had a guest in my room and checked the register. "She said you were expecting her. Her name is Inga Bruan."

"Inga's here?" Kirsten looked surprised.

I took the key from the clerk and led the way to the elevator. "She's afraid of Viktor. The man's a pimp, Kirsten. She called me. She's scared to death of him, and I suggested she come here."

Kirsten punched the call button. "I feel awful. I wasn't sure, and I didn't want to upset—"

"Your relationship with the museum or Erika. I know, I get it."

When the elevator arrived, we stepped inside, and Kirsten waited for the doors to close. "Do you think Viktor killed Hans?"

"I don't know, but I think there's a good chance he did."

* * *

Inga was napping when we came into the room. She had curled up on the second king-sized bed with her cell phone cradled beneath her head. When the door closed, she woke with a start and pulled the eiderdown up around her shoulders. "Kat?"

"It's okay. It's just me." I reached out and touched the foot of the bed. "How're you doing? Has anyone else been here?" I was hopeful Inga would tell me Sophie had been here and gone out for food. That the woman I had seen lying in the street wasn't Sophie, but some other poor soul, and any minute, Sophie would come through the door.

"No." Inga shook her head, then pointed to Kirsten. "What's she doing here?"

I took my coat off and put it on the end of the bed. "Kirsten's here to help me. Don't worry. Everything's going to be okay. She's not going to tell anyone about you, are you, Kirsten?"

Kirsten put her bag on the desk. "Inga, I'm sorry. I didn't realize things with Viktor had gotten that bad. I apologize. I should have said something."

Inga sat up and hugged her legs to her chest. "I don't care. Just don't tell anybody. I'm not going back there, ever!"

I locked eyes with Kirsten. "Let's table this discussion for a bit, shall we? I need you to call the hospitals to find out if Sophie Brill's been admitted, and if so, where?"

CHAPTER THIRTY

Kirsten took her phone from her bag, then crossed the room to the window, where she had more privacy.

Inga looked at me, her eyes searching mine. She knew something terrible had happened. "What's wrong?"

"Hans is dead."

"No!" Inga began to rock back and forth. Holding herself like a small child. "Don't say that. It can't be true. D-did Viktor kill him?"

I sat on the bed next to Inga and put my hand on her shoulder. "I don't know. Things weren't good between them, but I have a couple of questions. You told me this morning that Viktor went out last night and didn't come home. But have you seen him again? At the museum, maybe?"

"No. I don't know where Viktor is. He doesn't tell me where he goes."

"What about Erika? When did you last talk to her?"

Inga pushed the hair from her face. "I can't remember for sure. Yesterday maybe? Whenever it was, she was upset."

"Who was she upset with?"

"Hans or maybe her husband. Erika's always upset about something. I remember her saying how angry she was that Hans wasn't around. But that wasn't unusual. Hans didn't like that Erika monitors him all the time." Inga got off the bed and went to the minibar. "Do you have anything to eat? I'm starving."

I pulled the sack of Gingerbread cookies from my backpack. "I picked up some cookies on the way here. Help yourself. Or, if you want, I can order something to be sent up. Maybe something hot?"

"That would be nice. But first, if it's okay, I want to take a shower."

I waited until Inga closed the bathroom door, and I could hear the water running before I turned my attention back to Kirsten.

"Any luck?"

Kirsten nodded to me, the phone in one hand, a pen and business card in the other.

"I found the hospital where Sophie's been admitted. She's in the ER now. They couldn't give me anything more than her name, but I wrote the number down on the back of my business card." Kirsten handed me her card. "But before you call, we need to talk about what happened at the chateau."

"I know." I templed my fingers against my brow and exhaled. I needed to depend on someone. There was no one to call. Sophie was in the hospital, and I didn't have a number for the German agents who had tailed me. Sophie had set it up that way. The less I knew, the safer she said I'd be. But without her, I didn't know who I could trust. If the police were calling Kirsten because Erika had led them to believe I might be a person of interest, it would only be a matter of time before they found me. In the meantime, I needed Kirsten to help. "Look, you're a reporter, the police are going to want to know what you know. In my country, a reporter can't sit on information pertinent to an investigation, and I'm pretty sure it's the same way here. So, you'll have to call them and tell them what you know."

"But, Kat. Anything I say won't look good."

"It's okay." I held my hands up. "I want you to tell them everything. I've nothing to hide, and the sooner you make that public, the better off I'll be."

"I don't think so, Kat. If the police suspect you, they'll arrest you."

"Not if they can't find me."

"What are you going to do, run?"

"Not run, but I plan to make myself scarce for the time being, or at least until I know who killed Hans. If I don't, you're right, the police will arrest me, and by the time they finish their investigation, Viktor, or whoever killed Hans, will get away."

"So, what do you want me to tell them?"

"Tell them the truth. That you met me at the Gauguin unveiling. I'm an American journalist on assignment covering the German holiday scene for a travel pub, and we've become friends."

"And what about Hans?"

Ugh. This was hard. How could I explain Hans without revealing who I really was?

"Tell the police that Hans was helping me with a travel feature. He invited me to Oberammergau to show me around, and I found him charming and knowledgeable." I paused and wiped a tear from my eye. Hans wasn't just my mark. He was someone I cared about, and I believed he wanted to do the

CHAPTER THIRTY

right thing and reveal the location of his uncle's stolen cache. And whether I wanted to admit it to myself or not, someone who, despite my duties as an undercover reporter, I wanted to know better. "Tell them that I interviewed Hans for the magazine, and off the record, he shared with me he was worried about Viktor Sokolov."

"That's it?" Kirsten looked at me like she expected more.

"For now." I wasn't about to say anything more, particularly about Erika and Fritz. Close as Kirsten was to them, I didn't dare share my suspicions with her that I thought they might be involved with Hans' murder. With her brother out of the way, Erika could deal with Viktor and take sole possession of Gerhardt's Hoard. In my mind, that was motive enough for murder.

"And what if the police ask me where you are? What do you want me to say?"

"Tell them you don't know. That you haven't seen me since we had coffee a week ago. That you knew I was covering the holiday scene for *Journey International*, and you've no idea where I am now."

"You want me to lie?"

"I want you to buy me some time. Look, this story will be good for you and your paper. You'll have a front-page story before any other paper in town even gets wind of it." Kirsten looked skeptical. "Peter will love you."

Kirsten sighed. "Like I really need that."

"Hey, it's your byline on the front page."

"Fine."

"Then you'll have the story for the morning's paper."

Kirsten peered out the window at the street below. "And what about Inga? What are you going to do with her?"

"She's coming with me. Trust me, the less you know, the better. When this is over, I'll be in touch. And believe me, if Sophie recovers, she'll want to offer you more than a simple stringer's position. I'll see to it."

Kirsten's phone rang. "Kat, it's the police. I'm going to have to take that."

"I know. Don't worry. It'll be fine." I hugged Kirsten goodbye and pointed to the door. "Go. Talk to them. I'll call you tomorrow."

I waited until I heard the lock catch, then turned and knocked on the bathroom door.

"Inga, hurry up. We need to leave."

"Leave?" Inga opened the bathroom door, still wet from her shower and clutching a towel. "Why? What's happening?"

"The police are going to start looking for me, and if they arrest me, I won't be able to protect you. Do you still have that red wig?"

"It's in my purse."

"Good. Put it on and hurry up. We don't have much time."

While Inga dressed, I shoved a change of clothes into my bag. I had no idea where we were going or how long we might need to lay low. But as long as I had a fake passport with the name Katheryn Little and the grey wig and black glasses Sophie gave me. I planned to use them to my advantage. With a bit of luck, anyone who spotted us would think I was an old spinster schoolmarm assigned some wayward student to tutor in a too-short plaid shirt.

"You about ready?" I hollered to Inga as I took the grey wig from my bag and stuffed my dark hair beneath it.

"Almost," she said. "Where are we going?"

"I don't know yet. But hurry it up. We need to get out of here."

I grabbed my bag while Inga straightened her wig and started to put on lipstick.

"There's no need for that." I pulled her from the bathroom mirror. "We've got to go. Now!"

Chapter Thirty-One

Rather than take the elevator, Inga and I took the concrete staircase to the lobby. I didn't want to risk bumping into anyone in the lift or that the sound of the elevator's bell might alert the hotel's clerk we were leaving. When we got to the main floor, I opened the stairway door. The lobby's bar area was crowded with guests, and the clerk behind the reception desk appeared to be talking with two heavy-set men, who I suspected might be plain-clothed detectives. I eased the door shut. Whether the men were here to query possible witnesses about Sophie's accident or to talk with me about Hans' murder, I wasn't ready to talk to anybody. Not until I had spoken to Sophie. That is, if Sophie were ever able to talk again.

Opposite the door leading to the lobby was a second door, a heavy metal door with a steal pressure bar marked Notausgang—Emergency Exit! All I needed to do was lean against it, and the door would open to the alleyway outside. But I feared if I were to open it, an alarm might go off, and the two plain-clothed detectives would come running. Instead, I pulled my Fodor's Travel Guide from my bag and, with my nose in the book, told Inga to follow me and pushed open the door to the lobby.

I should have kept my nose in the book, but I couldn't resist the urge to check that the desk clerk wasn't tracking our exit, and in that instant, when our eyes met, we were made.

"Fraulein, kommen Sie bitte." Whether the clerk had identified me in my grey wig or Inga as the redheaded girl to whom he had given keys earlier, it didn't matter. He pointed the two plain-clothed detectives in our direction, and we took off.

I grabbed Inga's hand, and we did a quick about-face and dashed back to the stairwell with the undercover agents close behind. With one heavy shove, I pushed open the emergency exit.

"Run!"

The alleyway was like an obstacle course, crammed with parked cars and slushy pools of melted snow. We dodged a delivery van, and I managed to tip a trash can over as we ran, tripping one of the agents behind us. Inga was a good runner and knew the area better than I did. When we came to the end of the alley, she signaled for us to go left, away from the Marienplatz. We must have run two blocks, my lungs burning from the cold night air, when I spotted a cab and waved him down.

"Airport Hotel," I said. It was the first thing I could think of.

"Hilton oder Holiday Inn?" he asked in German.

"Holiday Inn, bitte. Fast as you can." It didn't matter what hotel I had said. I wanted to get away from the Hotel Schlicker and the two detectives following us as fast as possible. I opened the cab door, shoved Inga into the backseat, and slid in beside her.

Inga pressed close to me, and I put a finger on my lips. From the look in her eyes, I could tell she wanted to talk, but until the cabbie dropped us off, it was better not to say anything. I removed the wool scarf from around my neck. Despite the cold, I was sweating from our run. When we pulled up in front of the hotel, I paid the driver cash and hustled Inga from the cab.

"Are we okay?"

"For now," I said.

"But what if the police find you, or Viktor finds us first? He'll kill us both."

"Trust me. That's not going to happen." At least, I hoped that wasn't going to happen. But at that moment, hope was all I had. "For tonight, we're safe. We going to stay in a nice hotel, and tomorrow when Kirsten's story runs in the paper, maybe the police won't be so anxious to arrest me, and they'll be looking for Viktor Sokolov instead."

"I hope so." Inga's voice sounded like it was about to crack. I couldn't blame the girl. Sokolov had promised her a better life, and look where it got her.

CHAPTER THIRTY-ONE

"I promise. You'll see."

But as we checked in, I had one more immediate problem. One I wasn't about to share with Inga. The hotel wouldn't accept cash, and all I had was the passport Sophie had given me and the Amex credit card for emergency use in the same name, Katheryn Little. The hotel would want both. Using the Amex card would signal Sophie's team that I was in trouble and give them my location. My mission would be cut short, and despite the FBI rescuing me, I'd likely spend the night in jail while the Germans and the FBI sorted things out. Any chance I had of helping Inga would be lost.

I slipped a hundred-dollar bill across the counter. "I know this is slightly unusual, but if you don't mind, would you not run the card until the morning? I can give you my passport, no problem, and if you like, I can leave a cash deposit for the room right now. It's just I've had problems when hotels put a hold on the card, and I prefer to see the bill before I check out. It's all quite good, I assure you."

"Not a problem, ma'am." The clerk slid the bill into his pocket and handed me back my Amex card.

When we got to the room, I asked Inga if she wanted something to eat. We agreed to order something light from room service and settled on a vegetable soup with the Brötchen, the warm German rolls I liked so much for breakfast. After dinner, Inga read from a fashion magazine she had picked up in the hotel lobby. Inga was fascinated with clothes and makeup and told me she wanted to be a runway model but was worried she wasn't tall enough. At ten p.m. I turned off the overhead light so Inga could sleep while I focused a small reading light on my notepad and continued to make notes in my journal. I must have fallen asleep in my clothes. The light was still on when my cell rang the following morning and woke me.

"Kat? Have you seen the morning paper? Your picture's on the front page?"

It took me a moment to realize I wasn't dreaming. "Sandor?"

"Aanika and I were driving back from Nuremberg and stopped at a rest stop for coffee. You haven't seen it?" I sat up and rubbed the sleep from my eyes. "You made the headlines, Kat. It says here the police are looking for you and that you're a person of interest in the murder of Hans Von Hausmann."

"No, that can't be. There must be some mistake. I was working with a reporter on a story about the murder of Hans von Hausmann. Her name's Kirsten Muller. She was going to file it last night. The person of interest should be a Russian named Viktor Sokolov."

"Her name's on the story, alright. But that's not what the story says. Says here, Kat Lawson, a traveling journalist with *Journey International*, was the last person believed to have seen Hans von Hausmann alive. And, his sister, Erika Schönburg, claims you bragged to her that you planned to visit him at his chateau, where her brother was found shot. She seems to think you killed her brother in a jealous rage."

"What!" I grabbed my bag and went into the bathroom to talk. I didn't want to wake Inga. "I'll call you back."

I called Kirsten's cell immediately. When she didn't answer, I waited for the call to go to her voicemail. "Kirsten, what the—"

I was cut off. Even with my limited German, I understood the automated prerecorded message. *Dieses postfach ist voll* was telling me the mailbox was full.

I fished in the bottom of my bag for Kirsten's business card. If Kirsten wasn't taking my call, then maybe her editor, Peter, would. My fingers shook as I dialed the paper's number. *Damnit. How could I have been so blind?* I knew Kirsten was loyal to Erika, but this was beyond loyalty. Erika had convinced Kirsten to write an article that made me a convenient scapegoat. And with Hans dead, Erika wouldn't accuse Viktor, not with her son's life in jeopardy.

I sat on the bathtub rim and rested my head against the wall. The only reason the police would have named me a person of interest was that Kirsten had led them to believe I had murdered Hans.

Whether it was Viktor, Erika, her husband Fritz, or the result of an argument between Hans, Ozan, and Cahill over an unpaid workman's bill, I had become a convenient scapegoat. Someone Erika wanted out of the way. And with Hans dead, Erika's dealings with Viktor would be much easier. Not to mention that Erika was now the sole heir of her uncle's hoard.

The telephone operator with the newspaper interrupted my thoughts.

"Guten Morgen. Wie kann ich Sie weiterleiten?"

CHAPTER THIRTY-ONE

I didn't understand a word. "Do you speak English?"

"Ja. What can I do for you?"

"I need to speak to your editor, Peter Bergman, please. "

"Einen Moment, bitte. I'll transfer you."

I waited through a series of beeps, unsure what I would say when Peter answered. When I heard his voice, I blurted, "Peter, hi. It's Kat Lawson, Kirsten Muller's friend? Look, there's a big problem with the story you ran in today's paper. I need to speak with Kirsten right away."

"She's not here, Kat. She's on assignment. Where are you?"

"That's not important. The story in today's paper, how could you? It's totally wrong."

"Would you like to make a statement?"

"A statement?" I spit the words out. "Are you kidding? You sensationalized Hans' death."

"We just published the facts, Kat."

"What facts? Kirsten knows exactly what happened. This story isn't even remotely close."

"Kirsten didn't write the story. I did."

"And yet you gave her a byline?"

"I did her a favor. She brought the story to the paper. She broke it, but like usual, it needed a good edit."

"I wouldn't call twisting the facts an edit. You made it look like I murdered Hans."

"I followed up on everything Kirsten wrote. I talked to the police and with Erika Schonburg. She told me you had gone to visit Hans in Oberammergau. You were the last person known to have seen him. Is there anything you want to add to that?"

I hung up. There was no point in arguing with Peter. Yesterday, I was an unknown travel reporter working for a small travel pub. But today, thanks to Peter Bergman, my name and picture were on the paper's front page, and I looked like a prime suspect in the murder of a celebrity curator I had nothing to do with. I had to do something. If Viktor saw the story, and he hadn't killed Hans, he'd think I had murdered him and would be looking for me and Gerhardt's Hoard. I had to keep moving. I didn't dare stay where I was. If the police didn't find me, I knew Viktor would.

I dialed Sandor's number.

"Sandor, it's me. Any chance you have room for two more in that cab or yours?" From here on, I needed to take Inga with me wherever I went. I couldn't leave her behind.

"Two?"

"Long story. I'll explain later. I'm desperate and don't have much time."

"I'll move things around in the trailer. Where are you?"

"I'm at the Holiday Inn. How soon can you come?"

Chapter Thirty-Two

Germany has strict laws on daytime truck deliveries, making it much easier for non-commercial traffic to get around. Consequently, Sandor couldn't bring his big truck into the city at this hour and suggested we meet at a popular trucker's stop south of Munich. He assured me it was easy to find in my Fodor's Guide, and finding it, I circled the location in pen.

"You could take the train, but this time of day, it'd be faster if you took a cab. Take you less than thirty minutes."

I hung up, went back into the bedroom, and dropped the guidebook on the bed.

"Inga, time to wake up." I shook Inga's shoulder.

"Go away." Inga pulled the covers up over her head.

"Inga, we have to go."

"No."

I'd had no experience with teenagers and little patience with someone I was trying to rescue ignoring me. I ripped the bedsheets away and tossed them to the end of the bed. "Get up!"

"Scheisse!" Inga did a quick dive for the sheets at the end of the bed. I grabbed them and pulled.

In any language, I was dealing with a grumpy teenager.

"Get dressed."

"Why? Where are we going now?"

"We're meeting a friend at a truck stop. He'll be there in a half hour, and we need to be, too." I slipped into my slacks and sweater, slapped the grey wig on my head, and picked up my backpack off the floor. "I'm going downstairs to settle the bill. Be ready to go when I return."

* * *

When I got to the lobby, my heart skipped a beat. The morning paper with my picture on the front page lay on the hotel's reception desk. The photo was the one Kirsten had taken of me mugging it up in front of the Galeries of Beauties at the Nuremberg Palace. I looked like a crazed criminal with my eyes crossed and a crooked mouth.

The clerk behind the counter glanced up at me. "Guten Morgan, Ms. Little. Can I help you?"

"The bill, please." I pulled the newspaper to me and folded it over. Hopefully, the clerk had been too busy to read the paper and, if he had, hadn't found any similarity to the picture on the paper's front page and the woman standing in front of him wearing a grey wig.

"Credit card on file, okay?"

"Yes, that'd be fine," I said.

My hundred-dollar bribe, asking last night's desk clerk not to run my card, had worked. Sophie and her team had no idea where I had spent the night. But now that I was about to leave the hotel, it wouldn't matter if the clerk ran the card. If fact, I wanted him to. When Sophie or her team received word that the card had been used, they would know I needed help and was on the move.

"I hope you enjoyed your stay." The clerk handed me the invoice. "Auf Wiedersehen."

"Danke." I smiled, slid the receipt and the newspaper into my bag, and then hurried back to the room.

"Inga, you ready?" Inga opened the bathroom door with the red wig in her hand. She looked half asleep, her eyes barely open, but at least she was dressed. I fixed the red wig on her head, grabbed her coat, and pushed her toward the door. "Come on, let's go."

By the time we got downstairs, the sun was struggling to break through

CHAPTER THIRTY-TWO

the fog. The early morning grey was so thick it was hard to see across the street. If one thing gave me confidence, it was the cars with their yellow fog lights. If anyone were following us, I'd know. Once we settled into the cab and I didn't see anyone tailing us, I breathed a sigh of relief.

Inga was unusually quiet and slumped back in the seat.

"Are you okay?"

"I'm tired, that's all. I just want this whole mess to be over with."

"So do I, and by the time we get to the rest stop, the worst will be behind us." I squeezed Inga's hand. "My friend's got a truck. He'll get us out of here, and once you're out of Germany, you won't have to worry about Viktor Sokolov anymore. I promise."

The cab dropped us at the rest stop. It was like several I had seen along the autobahn, a modern-looking glass structure with a view of the countryside and a restaurant and restrooms. I suggested we go inside and get a cup of coffee. Inga excused herself to find a bathroom while I ordered a quick breakfast from the buffet and found a table. But, by the time I had finished my coffee and Inga had yet to join me, I started to get concerned.

I checked the bathroom. It was empty except for one stall. I tapped lightly on the door. "Inga?"

Inga opened the door, her cell phone in her hand, and brushed by me to the sink.

"Have you been on the phone?"

"I called my mother, okay? I was worried about her."

I bit my lower lip. Viktor had threatened Inga and told her that if she disappeared, he'd go after her mother. Of course, Inga would call her mother. I had been a fool not to suspect as much.

"Has Viktor called her?" Inga didn't need to answer. I knew from the look on her face that Viktor and her mother had spoken.

"He told her you murdered Hans." Inga clutched the phone to her chest.

"You know that's not true."

"I know. But my mother's worried. And Viktor, he's paid her money—"

I grabbed Inga by the shoulders and turned her towards me. "Look at me. Did you tell her where we were going? Does she know where you are?"

Inga looked away. "I told her we would meet someone at a truck stop."

"Does she know where? Inga, does your mother know where we are?"

Inga's silence said it all. She had to have seen the map I had left on the bed. I had circled the rest stop. It wouldn't take much for Inga to figure out where we were going. And if Inga had told her mother where we were, then Viktor had to know, too. I took the phone from Inga and checked the number of recent calls. There had been half a dozen, two in the last half hour. Why hadn't it occurred to me to take the phone away from her? Of course, she would call her mother. It'd be a miracle if Viktor didn't know where we were.

"Let's go. We can't hide here all day."

"Where are we going?"

"We...are not going anywhere. *You* are going to stay here and eat breakfast."

"What about you?"

"I'm going to the parking lot to see if Sandor's truck is there. And you're going to wait for me here."

"For how long?"

"For as long as it takes. And you better hope Viktor doesn't show up here and recognize you in that red wig because if I see him with you, I'm not coming back inside."

Chapter Thirty-Three

I stepped down the restaurant's snowy stairs to the parking lot. At this early hour, only a handful of people were going in and out of the restaurant, and dressed as I was with my hoodie pulled up over my grey wig, my disguise was of no use. If Viktor was looking for us, it was only a matter of time before the Russian would find us, and I didn't see Sandor anywhere.

I worried I might have circled the wrong rest stop on the map. Sandor had said there were several along the autobahn. Maybe he was waiting for me thirty minutes up the road and wondering where I was. There were at least a dozen big rigs parked in the lot—twelve and eighteen-wheelers—with their drivers either asleep inside their cabs or gone to eat in the restaurant. I had never seen Sandor's truck, but I wasn't about to stand outside in front of the restaurant and make myself a target. I pulled my cell phone from my backpack and dialed Sandor's number. When he didn't answer, I started to walk the lot. Hopefully, I might find Sandor's truck before Viktor found me.

With the phone to my ear, I slipped between rigs and checked for Hungarian plates. I listened as the phone rang, then went to voicemail. I paused behind what I thought was an empty rig to leave a message. But when a horn blasted, loud enough to burst my eardrums, I jumped and scurried to a narrow space between rigs. The big eighteen-wheeler rocked to a stop, and a black cloud of exhaust billowed from the tailpipe. The driver leaned out the window. "Aufpassen!"

I stumbled out of the lot and backwards into the snowbank. If the driver hadn't seen me, I would have been killed. But the commotion of my near escape—the sound of the big rig's horn and the driver's scream—had caught the attention of a slow-moving black Mercedes with a gold grill and a bent front fender.

Viktor!

I ducked behind a small freestanding pavilion designed as a quickie restroom stop and held my breath. It was at least a hundred yards back to the restaurant. I'm athletic, and under normal circumstances, a hundred-yard dash would be no problem, but in the snow and with a target on my back, there was no way I could make it back across the lot without being seen. And from the position of Viktor's Mercedes, if he saw me, he'd have no problem running me down. I leaned back against the stone structure and considered my options.

I couldn't escape into the mountains behind me. I didn't know the first thing about surviving in the snow, and there wasn't time to call the cops. Even if there were, they'd arrest me, and what chance did I have of convincing them I was innocent? I had a gun in my bag that Sophie had given me. A stolen canvas from the dungeon beneath Hans' chateau. A fake passport. And I was wearing a wig. I'd be in custody long before I could negotiate my freedom, and if I moved now, I'd be dead before anyone could come to my aid.

I looked back at my phone and was about to redial Sandor's number when I heard another loud truck blast from the parking lot. I peeked around the corner of the pavilion. The Mercedes hadn't moved. The driver's window was down, and Viktor was smoking a cigar. Waiting patiently for me to make my move. And, directly behind the Mercedes was Sandor. As he entered the lot, he must have seen me dash for safety behind the pavilion. He was trying to flag my attention. He had no idea that in front of him was my would-be assassin. Or that the Mercedes, despite Sandor's inching closer to Viktor's bumper, had no intention of moving.

There was no way Sandor's rig could pass Viktor's Mercedes, and the Russian wasn't about to budge. Sandor gave another blast of the horn. The sound was so thunderous it shook the loose snow from the tree above me, and I feared it might trigger an avalanche in the mountains. But still, Viktor

CHAPTER THIRTY-THREE

didn't move. Instead, he reached out the window and gave Sandor the finger. Which was about the worst thing anyone could do, particularly to someone like Sandor, who had no patience for Russians and, by now, must have spotted Viktor's Russian sticker on the back of the Mercedes. Sandor put the big rig in reverse, backed it up twelve feet, and gunned the engine with the truck in neutral. The rig shuddered like a wild horse pawing the earth, spewing dirt and smoke from its tires.

Viktor didn't wait for the inevitable. He floored the Mercedes and peeled out of the lot in less time than it took me to exhale.

Sandor rolled forward and swung open the door. "Get in, Kat."

I ran to the truck, grabbed the outside handle, and climbed inside the cab.

"What's with the wig? Someone following you?" Sandor jerked his head, a look of surprise on his face.

"Yeah. Like I said, it's a long story." I panted. Between the cold air and my racing heart, my chest ached. "Where's Aanika?"

"Next stop up. She's waiting for us with the Maserati. You said you needed room, so I unloaded it. Someone else we need to pick up?"

"Not yet, but soon." I glanced up at the restaurant and hoped Inga would stay put. "Meanwhile," I pointed to the access road where I could see Viktor's Mercedes racing to the roundabout, heading back into the parking lot. In another minute, he'd be behind us. "That car ahead of you—"

"The one with the Russian plates?"

"He's been following me since I visited you in Nuremberg. And if I'm right, he not only tried to kill my publisher last night, he thinks I murdered Hans von Hausmann."

"Whoa!" Sandor shifted the big rig into gear as we entered the autobahn, and we started to pick up speed. "So, you're not a journalist? You're not here on assignment working on a holiday feature? You're a—"

"Spy," I said. I stared into the truck's side-view mirror. The black Mercedes was gaining on us. "And I need your help."

Chapter Thirty-Four

I explained to Sandor that Viktor Sokolov was a Russian art dealer who believed Hans von Hausmann and his sister Erika Schonburg had been sitting on their Uncle Gerhardt's Hoard of World War II stolen art. And that in addition to his art dealings, Viktor had arranged for Inga, a young Polish girl he had brought from Berlin, to work at the Gerhardt Galerie in hopes of learning more about Gerhardt's hidden trove. When that didn't work out, and Inga couldn't provide Viktor with any information regarding the treasure's whereabouts, Viktor threatened to send Inga to Prague, where he had a stable of young prostitutes, he used to entertain his friends.

"Inga came to me for help, and I agreed to hide her." I buckled my seat belt and glanced in the side-view mirror. I wanted to keep a steady eye on Viktor's Mercedes. "Sorry, I know you didn't sign on for this."

"Forget sorry. I'm fine with it." Sandor downshifted, and the rig slowed as we ascended the mountain pass. "So, where's this Inga now?"

I tilted my head back toward the restaurant.

"Viktor threatened her. Told her he'd murder her mother if Inga disappeared. She's petrified of him. She called her mother earlier today, and evidently, so had Viktor. He must have seen the newspaper and told Inga's mother I killed Hans and that her daughter was in danger."

"She thinks *you* killed Hans?" The rig jerked forward.

"Poor girl doesn't know what to think. And now that Viktor's found me and saw me jump into your cab—"

"He thinks we're working together." Sandor glanced into his rearview mirror and nodded at the Mercedes headlights. "I get it."

CHAPTER THIRTY-FOUR

"Viktor's been suspicious of me from the start." I explained that an American art collector had accused Viktor of selling a forged Gauguin and reported it to the FBI. But when the FBI didn't come after Viktor, and some unknown American journalist showed up to cover the unveiling of the same Gauguin Viktor was accused of selling, he got worried. "It didn't take long for Viktor to figure out that Hans and Erika had sold him a fake. Hans told me Viktor had been hanging out at their museum, and Erika worried he was stealing business, and she wanted him out. Truth is, I think what really concerned them was that Viktor might find where they hid Gerhardt's Hoard. Everybody in the art world knew they were sitting on it. The Russians. The Americans. Even the Germans. Viktor saw I was getting close to Hans, which was exactly what I was sent here to do, and he was afraid I would find Gerhardt's Hoard first."

"So, that's why he's following you?"

"Viktor's the reason I left Nuremberg in such a rush. He followed me there, and when he saw us together in your client's yellow Maserati, he probably thought you were here to help me steal Gerhardt's Hoard. He caught up with me inside the drugstore when you and Aanika went to the restaurant and told me he'd go after my friends if I didn't stop my search and return to America."

"Sounds like a real piece of work."

"I called Sophie. She's my FBI handler. She wanted me to leave right then and go back to the States, but I told her I had a job to do and wasn't about to give up. So, we agreed to let Viktor *think* I'd left, but obviously, I didn't,"

"And now that this Russian mobster's seen you climb into my truck, he's following us."

"I'm betting he thinks I killed Hans and managed to load Gerhardt's lost treasures into the back of your truck and that I'm making off with it."

"So, how about I help you catch him?"

Catch him? "I was thinking more about how you might help Inga and me escape. But if we go back now for Inga, Viktor will follow us to the rest stop and make a scene. And if the cops come, Viktor will intimidate Inga, and it's me they'll arrest."

"Sounds like you just answered your own question, Kat. Viktor's not going to leave you alone, and you can't go back and get Inga until you've fixed it with Viktor. So how about I help?"

"What do you have in mind?" I focused on the side mirror. The Mercedes, with its crooked headlights, no doubt from the impact of Sophie's body on the hood, trailed behind us like a wounded animal that smelled blood.

"You ever driven a Maserati?"

"You're not serious." My voice caught in my throat.

"I've never been more serious. Aanika's waiting with the Maserati at the next rest stop. About thirty minutes ahead. All you have to do is switch places with her, and when Viktor sees you in the yellow Maserati—which he will—" Sandor took his eyes off the road and stared at me, "he's going to want to catch you."

"And just how do you expect to do that? When we pull in the next rest stop, Viktor will pull in behind you and—." I didn't even want to think about what might happen. I had a vision of Viktor rushing Sandor with a tire iron in his hand and a bloody fight ensued.

"Don't worry about that. I've a few trucker friends who can help slow this Russian mongrel down." Sandor reached below the cab's dashboard for a small handheld CD radio mic and began broadcasting in Hungarian and German. After a series of short, two-way transmissions, ending with Sandor's throaty laugh, he turned to me, all smiles. "By the time we get to the next rest stop, my friend's rig will pull up behind us. It'll give you time to exchange places with Aanika. Viktor won't be able to see you get out of my cab, and by the time my trucker friend pulls out of the lot, Aanika will have climbed back into the rig with me, and you'll be behind the wheel of the Maserati. All you need to do is make sure Viktor sees you drive past him, and we'll take care of the rest."

"You want him to chase me?" I felt a chill run down my back.

"Not exactly chase, and not here, but further up the mountain. We'll take the turn-off at Rosenheim. and drive up the Grossglockner High Alpine Road. The drive gets more exciting up there. Nice road, but narrow. You don't want to meet anyone coming the other way. Lots of hairpin turns and

CHAPTER THIRTY-FOUR

a few sudden drops, but if you take it slow, you should be fine."

Should be? I had never been good with heights. It didn't matter if I was looking up at them or down; I'd get a tingly sensation up the back of my legs, and I'd feel like I was falling. As a kid, I remembered going to the Grand Canyon with my folks, and as I stared down into the canyon with its purple and orange hues, I felt as though the view before me was pulsating. I felt dizzy, as though I'd faint.

"Don't worry. Once you leave the lot, my friend, in his eighteen-wheeler, will get in between you and Viktor and slow him down. Viktor won't be able to pass, and my buddy will call the Polizei and report him for reckless driving. By the time we all get to the top of the pass, we'll have a little surprise for our Russian friend."

"What?" I asked.

"You'll see. All you need to do is stay ahead of my buddy's rig."

"And hope Viktor doesn't pass him and push me over a five-thousand-foot icy cliff."

Chapter Thirty-Five

Sandor slowed his rig as we climbed higher into the mountains and allowed another big rig to ease in ahead of us. The higher we climbed, the more the early morning fog thickened and the harder it was to see beyond the hood of Sandor's truck. Behind us, I could barely make out the orange fog lights on Viktor's Mercedes. Despite the diminished visibility, several small sports cars, impatient with our slow crawl up the mountain, sped past us like crazed race drivers and disappeared into white blindness ahead.

"Germans." Sandor checked the rearview mirror, and I did the same. A second large semi had pulled up behind Viktor, and the black Mercedes was now locked between us.

Sandor pulled a rope above his head and sounded a big air horn.

"I think it's time we did a little disappearing act of our own. Hold on tight."

I grabbed the dash, surprised at how quickly the big rig picked up speed. Then without further warning, Sandor swung the rig onto a narrow access road. With my eyes on the side view mirror, I could see Viktor's black Mercedes, the glint of its gold grill barely visible through the fog, with the semi on his tail. Viktor missed the turn.

"Nice move." I sat back and exhaled. "I take it you knew that exit was coming up?"

"Like the back of my hand. But don't get too settled. I'm not the only one who knows these rest stops. And if Viktor wants to find us, he'll double back and come looking." Sandor slowed the truck as we entered the parking lot, then stopped. "You're going to need to hop out here and trade places with

CHAPTER THIRTY-FIVE

Aanika."

"Where is she?" The lot was jammed with trucks, and I didn't see a yellow Maserati anywhere.

"Over there." Sandor pointed to a small silver camper parked above the lot. The trailer looked to be a permanent fixture, maybe a caretaker's trailer. A few trees had grown around it, and the lights were out. It didn't look like anyone was home or at least awake, and the Maserati was hidden behind it, barely visible. "It'll only take our Russian buddy a couple of minutes to figure out we tricked him and double back into the lot. And before he does, I need to get this big truck back out on the road."

"And then what?" I asked.

"You do exactly as we planned. Trade places with Aanika, wait until you see the Mercedes enter the lot, then get Viktor's attention. Make sure he follows you back out onto the Autobahn. Then, it's game on."

Sandor sounded more sure of himself than I felt.

"And your friend in the truck following Viktor, you promise he's going to be able to get in front of Viktor's Mercedes and keep him off my tail, right?"

"That's the plan. Just take your time, Kat. Make certain you see the big rig follow Viktor into the lot, then wait until he heads to the exit before you make your move. He'll be waiting for you."

"I hope you're right."

"Don't worry, Kat." Sandor put his hand on my shoulder. "I'll know the minute you leave the lot. The driver in the rig will call me, and I'll call ahead to the Autobahn police and report a reckless driver. By the time you make it to the top of the mountain, my trucker friends and I will have caused this Russian to break enough road rules the Polizei will be happy to arrest him. And once he's out of the way, we can go back, pick up Inga, and get you two out of the country until this issue with Hans von Hausmann is behind us."

I put my hand on the door handle. I wished there could have been another way, but I didn't see how I could stop Viktor without getting myself arrested as well, and if I were detained, everything I had done so far to uncover Gerhardt's Hoard and rescue Inga would be for naught.

"You ready?" Sandor leaned across me and opened the door. "You got this,

Kat."

"Yeah. Let's do it."

I jumped down from the cab and noticed Aanika was already walking toward us, the keys to the Maserati in her hands. Pregnant, in the middle of a wet-soaked parking lot, she looked more confident than I felt. I hugged her and took the keys.

"Watch the clutch. She's got a hair trigger."

"Thanks." I gave her a thumbs-up and jogged to the Maserati like I knew what I was doing.

Once inside the car, I leaned back against the soft leather seats and closed my eyes. It had been years since I'd driven a clutch. At sixteen, my then-boyfriend had a souped-up '68 Chevy Camaro with a stick shift. He taught me how to pop the clutch and burn rubber. I prayed I'd remember. I was pretty good then, but that was almost thirty years ago, and I hadn't touched a stick shift since. Hopefully, using a clutch was like riding a bike, and everything would come back to me. I inserted the key. No time like the present to find out. Then with my foot gently on the gas, the engine roared to life. The vibrations sent shockwaves up my spine.

I let the engine idle as I watched Sandor's big rig pull slowly out of the lot. I couldn't stop shaking and turned on the heat. I had a job to do. I could be cold and frightened later, but right now, I had promised Sophie I could handle this assignment, and no matter what lay ahead, I wasn't going to quit. Sophie had given me every chance to walk away, and I had refused. Initially, I thought finding Gerhardt's Hoard would be my way of making a name for myself and getting back in the game as an investigative reporter with a decent newspaper. But now I felt differently. It wasn't just a selfish motive anymore. It was the art itself. It belonged to the world, not hidden away in some private secret collection where no one but a very few would ever see it. I believe Hans had come to know that as well. The artists and the paintings deserved to be seen and understood by the world again. The art belonged to all of us. It was part of who we were and our history. And no matter how much my hands shook or my teeth chattered, I had to do my part to make that happen.

CHAPTER THIRTY-FIVE

The toot of a trucker's horn alerted me to Viktor's black Mercedes as it rolled slowly onto the lot. From my position behind the silver camper on the hill, I could see Viktor behind the wheel of the black beast. I slouched low in my seat, my eyes barely above the dash, and angled the rearview mirror to get a better view. The fog had begun to lift. Victor lowered his window, and I could see the orange glow of a cigarette hanging loosely from his mouth as he scanned the back of each big semi, looking at the plates and searching for Sandor's rig. Row after row, he zig-zagged through the lot until he came to the lane below the camper. I waited for him to pass, my eyes glued to the back of the black Mercedes, then looked ahead to ensure the big rig that had followed Viktor into the lot was waiting by the exit as planned. I rested my right foot on the gas while I pressed my left foot down on the clutch all the way to the floor. Then with one hand on the gear shift, I released the clutch, shoved the car in gear, and floored it.

Too fast! The Maserati leaped forward. I fishtailed in the snow, sliding down the hill and nearly careening into the back of Viktor's black beast. Then grabbing the wheel, I sped around the Mercedes and blasted my horn.

Viktor must have been stunned when the yellow Maserati burst from behind the silver camper and realized it was me behind the wheel. Once ahead of him, I rolled my window down and waved. *Catch me if you can!* Then, with my foot heavy on the gas, I sped toward the exit and out onto the Autobahn. I checked the rearview mirror. A big rig pulled out onto the road exactly as planned, directly ahead of Viktor. We had done it! The rig took the middle of the road and was too bulky for the black Mercedes to pass. The Russian's car was locked behind the rig, and I gave a fist bump out the window to my guardian angel trucker. *We did it!* He responded with a heavy blast of his air horn. Then I closed the window and, with both hands on the wheel, relaxed into the Maserati's leather seat and eased off the accelerator.

The Maserati was a tight drive. Her suspension wasn't as smooth as I'd like, but she hugged the road, and her engine, like a hungry tigress, begged for speed. Despite the fog starting to clear, I resisted the urge and held the speedometer to a little more than fifty kilometers per hour. I glimpsed the black Mercedes in the rearview mirror, trying to pass. But the rig's driver was good, and the road narrow. Every time Viktor would poke the Mercedes' nose to the side of the rig's rear bumper, the driver would swing the trailer wide, and Viktor would be forced to pull back. There was no way the Russian could pass. It would be suicidal to even try. One miscalculation on Viktor's part and the trailer would slam into the Mercedes and send it flying off the cliff to an icy death thousands of feet below.

All I needed to do was maintain a slow and steady pace. Meanwhile, Sandor and my guardian angel driver behind me would call the autobahn police, and somewhere between here and Sandor's rig at the top of the mountain, they'd arrest Viktor for reckless driving.

At least, that was the plan.

But, when I shifted the Maserati into low gear and started up the incline, a thin curtain of fog began to swirl on the road ahead, making it difficult to see much beyond the car's hood. I strained to catch a glimpse of the jagged mountain ridge while I slowed to a creep and hugged the mountainside. One miscalculation and the Maserati and I would slide over the cliff's rocky edge and into the abyss. I checked the rearview mirror. I could barely make out the big rig's yellow fog lights. The rig had slowed, and the space between us grew farther apart. I opened my window, and the sound of the truck's gears, metal on metal, growled as it strained against the mountain. Behind the rig, the lights from Viktor's Mercedes edged closer to the trailer's side.

Something was wrong. The big tractor-trailer stalled. The cab rocked back and forth, and the trailer jackknifed and slid into the mountain, leaving a narrow section of road wide open. Viktor didn't miss the opportunity and zoomed past the big rig and up the incline toward me.

I pressed the clutch to the floorboard and, with my eyes on the road, hit the gas like I was sixteen again and dropping rubber in a street race. I gripped the wheel. The car lurched forward and threw me back against the seat.

Ahead of me, the road made a sharp hairpin turn. My hands gripped the wheel. If I eased up now, Viktor would catch up with me, ram the Maserati, and send me to a certain death. I gritted my teeth, and with my foot on the gas, the car slid into the turn, nearly hitting the mountainside. I couldn't play it safe. I needed to keep as much roadway between the Mercedes and

CHAPTER THIRTY-FIVE

me as possible. My eyes darted to the rearview mirror. Viktor had fallen behind. The Mercedes appeared to have slowed to a crawl. And then I knew why. *Black ice!*

Like a bobsled, the Maserati slid uncontrollably across the ice toward the cliff's edge, kicking up rocks and pieces of snow-covered tree boughs and throwing them onto my windshield. I took my foot off the gas and swung the driver's wheel hard toward the mountainside. When I felt the car's tires hit hard-pack snow, I eased my foot back on the gas, thankful to have solid ground beneath me. I rechecked my rearview mirror. No sign of Viktor. The black ice had given me a lead. I rolled down my window. The fog was so thick I could only see a few feet beyond the Maserati's hood. I flicked off my fog lights. They were useless in a fog this thick. And without them, Viktor wouldn't be able to see me. He'd have no idea if I slipped off the cliff or crashed into the mountainside.

Ahead, I spotted a flashing white light. I slowed and, through the mist, spotted Sandor in the center of the road. With one hand above his head, he waved the flashlight and warned me to slow down. Behind him, the yellow fog lights of his rig barely illuminated the open cargo doors.

Sandor jogged toward me. "Hurry. Viktor's not far behind. Pull the Maserati around to the front of my rig. And stay there. Whatever you do, don't move."

"Where's Aanika?"

"She's hiding by the roadside. Hurry up. There's no time to talk."

I pulled up in front of the big rig and cut the Maserati's engine. I could only see a few feet on either side of the car due to the fog, and I didn't dare get out. Whatever Sandor had in mind, I had to trust him. And then I heard it, the awful squeal of brakes.

I unsnapped my seatbelt, my hands shaking, barely able to open the car door. I slipped as I got out, falling to my knees, then, catching my balance, ran to the back of the trailer. For a brief second, I feared Viktor might have hit Sandor, and I'd find him lying by the side of the road. But I was wrong. At the last minute, Sandor had jumped out of the way of the Mercedes and stood at the side of the road, the flashlight still in his hand. I stopped and watched as Aanika ran to his side, then looked at the back of Sandor's big rig.

Viktor had realized too late that the yellow lights ahead of him were not the Maserati's but that of Sandor's truck. And while Viktor had tried to break, it was of no use. The Mercedes slid directly up on a loading rack and into the back of Sandor's trailer.

"Is he okay?" I didn't see any movement from inside the black Mercedes. The airbag had exploded and filled the front seat.

"He'll be a little loopy. Getting hit in the face with the airbag didn't help, but he didn't hit hard. More like slid into the back of my rig. But I'll let the Germans Polizei take it from here." Sandor started to pull up the trailer ramp when he stopped and pointed to a string of flashing blue and white lights. Three silver Porche 9lls—autobahn police—came skidding to a stop in front of us.

Chapter Thirty-Six

Two of the Polizei took Viktor from behind the wheel of the Mercedes, now safely boxed inside Sandor's rig, cuffed him, then walked him down the trailer ramp. When Viktor got to the bottom, he stopped and glared at me.

I couldn't resist urging. "Didn't turn out quite like you thought, did it?"

Viktor snarled at me like a mad dog. "It's not over, Ms. Lawson."

Sandor stepped forward. The officer in charge raised his hand, a warning Sandor needed to step back.

"Ihre Lizenz, Frauline." The officer held out his hand.

Sandor interrupted. "She doesn't speak German. She's American."

"Your license, Miss."

Viktor struggled with the restraints, then spit in the snow. "You're wasting your time with that broad. Her name is Kat Lawson. She murdered Hans von Hausmann. Arrest her!"

"Me!" I wanted to hit him, but Sandor grabbed my arm.

"License and passport, bitte." The officer was losing patience.

I fished in my bag for my wallet and presented my driver's license. Forgetting that the photo on my license neither matched me nor the name on the fake passport I had just handed him.

The officer looked at the picture on my license, then back at me. "Says here, five-ten, dark hair, green eyes." He nodded to my hair. "That a wig?"

I put my hand to my head. In the excitement of the chase, I had forgotten to remove it. "I can explain."

"I think you have a lot of explaining to do." The officer took my bag from me and searched through it. "These yours?" The officer held up both my real and fake passports and flipped through them. Then looked back in my bag. "And this?"

From the bottom of my bag, the officer pulled out the gun Sophie had given me, then yelled something in German to his partner I didn't understand.

I looked at Sandor and Aanika. Aanika stood with a hand on her husband's arm, a look of shock on her face as the officer passed the gun to his partner.

"Ms. Lawson, turn around and put your hands behind your back. You're under arrest."

"What for?"

"For starters, carrying a gun without a license and for the murder of Hans von Hausman."

"Hans? That's ridiculous. I didn't kill Hans."

"Kat," Sandor interrupted. "Don't say anything. Just do as the officer says. We'll figure it out."

"May I make a call first?" The officer nodded and handed me my cell phone from within my bag.

I tried Sophie's cell. No answer. I handed my cell back to the officer, then took Inga's pink cell phone from my coat pocket and passed it to Aanika. "I need you to give this to Inga. You and Sandor need to find her. She's waiting at the rest stop where Sandor picked me up. She's blonde and young, about seventeen. Show her the phone. She'll recognize it; it's hers. Tell her Viktor's been arrested, and I sent you there to help her."

**

After my arrest, I was transported, or more accurately, my five-foot-ten frame was folded into the back seat of a Porsche 911 police car, which was insanely small, and not built to transport suspects. But after a mountain chase and the temperatures dropping, nobody wanted to wait for a larger transport. So, with my head between my knees and hands handcuffed behind my back, I was driven like a criminal to a Munich jail. Once there, I was again allowed one call. This time, I tried the hospital where Sophie had been

CHAPTER THIRTY-SIX

admitted. The attending nurse told me she was resting quietly but couldn't be disturbed. After my call, I was escorted to a holding cell and informed Viktor was sitting in a cell six feet from my own. Despite the proximity, neither of us spoke.

The following morning, the Russian was removed. I could hear the guards when they came and Viktor's grumble, all of it in German. Several hours later, breakfast arrived, coffee, and a stale roll. The guard, who spoke English, and appeared to take pity on me, informed me that after my arrest, Sandor and Aanika had returned to Munich with a police escort and Viktor's Mercedes in the back of Sandor's big rig. Viktor's car had been impounded. Sandor and Aanika were questioned and released pending further investigation of helping me to escape and advised not to leave the country.

After breakfast, I was perp-walked with a guard on either side of me to an empty room with a gray metal table and four chairs. One of the guards brought me a second cup of coffee, and I was told to sit down and wait. But when the door closed, I realized the room wasn't quite so empty. Someone had placed the Henry Rifle that Hans had shown me when I first visited the chateau in the corner. My eyes scanned the walls for evidence of a camera. There was no two-way mirror on the wall, but I was sure I was being watched and that the police had left me in the room with the rifle to unnerve me. If this was some form of psychological warfare, I intended to ignore it. What did they expect me to do, pick up the long gun, and try to shoot my way out? If so, somebody had read one too many Westerns. I ignored the rifle. Whatever their game, I wasn't playing. I sat in the chair and waited. Time passed. I wasn't sure how much, but my coffee was cold when the door opened again.

Sophie walked in with the aid of a cane and put her satchel on the table. "Are you okay?"

"I could ask you the same," I said.

"I will be. I have a nasty headache. But not near as bad as our Russian friend will have when we're done with him." Sophie leaned her cane against the table and took the chair next to me.

"I'm glad to hear it."

"I'm sure you are, but first, I need you to tell me what happened after you left Augsburg."

"I did exactly as you told me to do. I drove to Oberammergau, and by the time I got to the chateau, the front door was wide open. I went inside, and it looked like there had been a fight. And when I didn't find Hans, I went downstairs into the cellar. That's where I found his body."

"I understand all that, but what you need to understand is that the police believe you went to visit Hans with the intention of stealing some of his art. And when Hans discovered what you were up to, a fight ensued, and you murdered him." Sophie pointed to the Henry Rifle in the corner. "With that rifle there."

"We both know that's not true."

"It doesn't matter what I think, Kat. The problem is the police are building a case against you. They found two passports and a gun in your bag. Plus, you were wearing a wig, and you had blood on your boots. The police ran a DNA test, and it came back this morning with a positive match for Hans. And then there's this." Sophie took a small, rolled canvas from within her bag and placed it on the table in front of me. "Rembrandt's Lying Lion, they found it in your purse."

I looked at Sophie. We both knew the significance of the Rembrandt sketch.

"I couldn't leave it. I needed evidence. Something to prove I'd found Gerhardt's Hoard, and if I'm right, this is the sketch you said your father had in your home when you were growing up. It was hidden in the wine cellar, and I wanted you to have it."

Sophie put her hand on top of mine and squeezed it. "I appreciate what you've done, Kat. But listen to me. You need to be careful. The police know who you are, that you work for me, and that you were trying to find proof of Gerhardt's Hoard. I tried to explain it to you from the start. This is a very delicate situation. Whatever you say could get you in a lot of trouble, and—"

"Ms. Lawson." Before Sophie could finish explaining the situation to me, a plainclothes detective and the two undercover operatives that followed me to Oberammergau entered the room.

CHAPTER THIRTY-SIX

"Gentlemen," Sophie stood up. "Kat, this is Detective Chief Inspector Daniel Schulte, and Agents Karl Meyer and Stephen Wagner."

The two agents took the chairs directly opposite Sophie and me while Inspector Schulte stood behind them.

The Inspector spoke first, saying something in German and then translating so that I could understand. "Ms. Lawson, before we begin, I would like to thank you. It appears we've apprehended Viktor Sokolov because of you."

My eyes went from Inspector Schulte to Sophie. I wasn't expecting any form of congratulations, and I was suspicious. Sophie bit her lips and looked down at the table. A sign for me to remain quiet.

The inspector continued. "You'll be happy to know your friend Aanika brought one of Viktor's girls to the station to file charges. I believe you know her. Her name is Inga Bruan. She identified Viktor Sokolov as her abuser. And, as I understand it, you and agents Meyer and Wagner, along with your friend Ms. Brill here, have had Viktor in your sights for some time."

I folded my hands and sat back.

"The problem is, Ms. Lawson, we also know that Viktor Sokolov has been trying to blackmail Hans von Hausmann and his sister in an attempt to smuggle some rare pieces of art out of the country."

"You mean Gerhardt's Hoard?" I locked eyes with the inspector.

"Ahem." Sophie cleared her throat. I wasn't supposed to challenge the inspector, but I didn't care. I wasn't about to roll over and pretend I hadn't seen anything. Hans was dead, and I had already spent one night in jail.

"Ms. Lawson." Inspector Schulte paced the floor behind the two undercover agents. "I believe you must be a very bright woman, and despite my heavy accent, you'll have no problem understanding me. Am I correct in that?"

"You're accent's not so difficult."

"Good. Because you see, unfortunately, Viktor Sokolov appears to have believed the rumor that Gerhardt's Hoard exists. I'm sure you understand how absurd the idea is and how important it is that the matter not become the subject of a major investigation. Wouldn't you agree?"

This was the fine line Sophie had warned me about. From the very beginning, our job was to find and verify the existence of such a cache in hopes that those possessing these treasures would make every attempt to return them. Or at least to make them available to the public.

"What are you saying?"

"Ms. Lawson, I think you understand what I'm saying very well. You've been arrested for the murder of Hans von Hausmann. We have reason to believe you were involved with him. He invited you to his chateau for a weekend rendezvous, and you murdered him. Shot him in cold blood."

"That's ridiculous!"

"Is it? Viktor Sokolov doesn't appear to think so. You would hardly expect us to believe it was Viktor Sokolov now, would you? If it were, why would he be chasing you on the autobahn? He believes you discovered a hidden cache of artwork inside the chateau and murdered Hans so that you could access it. You see, all the evidence points to you. And this rifle here..." Schulte strode across the room, picked up the rifle, aimed it in my direction, then laid it down on the table in front of me. "We found it in the storage shed behind the chateau. It was the firearm used to murder Hans von Hausmann, and your prints are all over it."

I covered my mouth. I had handled the rifle the first time I'd visited the chateau. It never occurred to me that someone might have used it to shoot Hans.

"I must say, it would be a shame to see someone like yourself charged with murder. But with a little cooperation, I'm sure we could find a way to see those charges dropped."

"You mean you want me to shut up about Gerhardt's Hoard or the cellar full of masterpieces I saw hidden inside the chateau."

Sophie put her hand on my arm. "Hold on, Kat. Listen to what Inspector Schulte has to say."

"I think it might be better if you remembered it differently."

"And how might that be?"

"You see we think one or two things might have happened to Herr Hausmann. One, you came down to visit with Hans and had a lover's spat. And one way or another, Hans ended up on the wrong end of the Henry

CHAPTER THIRTY-SIX

Rifle he kept in the living room, and you shot him."

"Never happened."

"Alright, then. For the sake of argument, let's say you're right. That you arrived at the chateau after Herr Hausmann was shot. It's not inconceivable to think that Herr Hausmann was murdered by one of his handymen. They had access to the chateau, and according to Hans' sister, Erika, there may have been a nasty dispute over an unpaid bill."

"She told you that?"

"She's willing to think she might be wrong about you. That you stumbled upon a very tragic scene."

"I see." What I saw was Erika's hand at play. A deliberate manipulation of the facts and possible suspects, designed to draw any attention away from Erika and her husband. Like the story, Erika had convinced Kirsten to give to the paper. Erika had to know Kirsten wasn't qualified to write a hard news story. Not a murder story that would end up on the paper's front page. Everything Kirsten had written was with Erika's blessings. Kirsten had admitted that without Erika, her career would have stalled out early. All Erika needed to do was convince Kirsten to write enough that Peter would pick up the phone and call Erika to verify the facts, and suddenly, I was a person of interest.

"I'm glad you do. Because how you choose to remember what you *thought you saw* inside the chateau will make a great deal of difference in how we plan to proceed." Schulte picked the rifle up off the table and returned it to the corner.

"In other words, you'll be willing to drop the charges against me if I agree to never mention what I saw inside the cellar."

"What you saw, Ms. Lawson, was art that belonged to the Gerhardt family. They had a large collection before the war and hid what they could so that it wouldn't be destroyed by the allies' bombs. What was left, Hans and his sister inherited from their mother. And now that Hans is dead, the chateau and all that's in it will go to his sister Erika."

"And if I don't agree with you—"

"We'll charge you with murder and your friends Sandor and Aanika as accessories."

"Let me get this straight. If I promise not to say anything, I can go free. And you'll let Sandor and Aanika go as well. But you'll charge Cahill and Ozan, a couple of poor handymen, who might have had a minor billing dispute with Hans' murder."

The inspector shrugged.

"All because Germany's not ready to admit that Gerhardt's Hoard exists? No." I shook my head. "How about I make *you* an offer instead?"

The inspector laughed. "Ms. Lawson, need I remind you, you're hardly in a position to negotiate."

The inspector may have been right. I wasn't coming from a position of strength, but I wanted to clear my name and that of my friends. But, even if the charges against me were dropped and Sandor and Aanika could go home, the police would arrest Ozan or Cahill for a crime that I felt sure neither of them had committed, and I couldn't live with that.

"Look, I want two things. I tapped the corner of the Rembrandt sketch with my index finger, then pushed the canvas toward Sophie. "First, I'll agree not to say anything about what I saw in the chateau's cellar if you give this sketch to Sophie. I believe she has enough information to prove it belonged to her father—"

"Ms. Lawson." The inspector reached across the table and slipped the Rembrandt towards him. "I'm afraid it's not within my power to return stolen art."

"Actually, Inspector, it is." Sophie put her hand on top of the sketch. "According to the Washington Principals, those your country and 43 other countries signed, you're not only allowed to but encouraged to return art that has been identified as stolen to its rightful heirs. And I can easily provide proof that this sketch was in my family's home and that Otto Gerhardt took it. If you have a problem with that, we can take it up with the courts, but in the meantime, the Rembrandt stays with me."

Sophie rolled the canvas and dropped it in her bag. She wasn't about to back down.

And neither was I.

CHAPTER THIRTY-SIX

"And second, Inspector, I want twenty-four hours and the assistance of Agents Meyer, Wagner, and Sophie to help me find who murdered Hans."

The inspector scoffed. "You really think you can do that?"

"Not only do I think I can do that, but I believe I can get the murderer to confess to it as well."

Chapter Thirty-Seven

I wasn't sure how I would lure Erika and Fritz back to their Munich museum. For the second day in a row, I was headline news. My booking photo, which didn't look much better than the awful shot Kirsten had taken of me, was on the front page of the Munich papers with a headline that announced my arrest. I couldn't just pick up the phone, call Erika, and ask for a meeting. As far as Erika and her husband were concerned, I was sitting in jail, awaiting formal charges for a murder that I was convinced the two of them had committed. But Inga was a different story. And with some coaching, I believed Inga could persuade them that she had doubts about Hans' murder—knew some things she shouldn't—and wanted to talk.

Thankfully, after Aanika had returned Inga's phone and explained Viktor was no longer a problem but that I was in jail for the murder of Hans von Hausmann and could use her help, Inga was more than willing to take my call and did exactly as I instructed her to do.

Step One. Inga called Erika and set up a meeting for the following day at ten a.m. at The Gerhardt Galerie.

Step Two. Sophie and I agreed it would be best if I wore a wire and a concealed earpiece so that Karl and Stephen, the two German undercover agents assigned to us, could monitor my conversation from a van that would be parked outside the museum. If all went as I hoped, I would finagle a confession from Erika and Fritz, and my name, along with that of the chateau's handymen, Ozan and Cahill, would be forever cleared of any murder charges. Best of all, I wouldn't have to worry that if word of Gerhardt's Hoard were to *accidentally* surface after I left Germany—which I

CHAPTER THIRTY-SEVEN

was one-hundred percent certain it would—I wouldn't be extradited back to Germany for some trumped-up charge related to Hans' murder. Meanwhile, Sophie and I agreed that if anything were to go wrong while I was inside the museum, my code word would be Saint Nick. All I needed to do was utter the name Saint Nick, and Agents Meyer and Wagner would come running.

Step Three. Agents Karl and Stephen, Inga, Sophie, and I arrived in an unmarked gray utility van at six a.m., an hour before sunrise, and parked behind the museum. A light snow had fallen the night before, and the Marienplatz was covered with a white powder. Despite the serene scene, my head was pounding with thoughts of what lay ahead. Sophie and I sat in the back of the van while we waited for the agents to complete their surveillance of the area. Inga had given Sophie the security code for the museum's alarm system and the keys to the museum's back door. Once the agents were satisfied that the area was secure and their cameras and sound equipment were in place, I was allowed to enter via the alley entrance. The agents weren't taking any chances I'd be seen, and once inside, I was instructed to go directly to the small office behind the reception counter and wait.

Step Four. Inga was to stand on the steps outside the front of the museum until she spotted Erika and Fritz.

By nine-fifty-five, I heard Inga's voice outside and peered from behind the blinds into the plaza. Fritz, Erika, and their son, Baret, were headed up the stairs. Mother and son had dressed alike in puffy black snow jackets and cleated rubber boots. As Inga fumbled with the key to the museum's front door, I could hear them stomping the snow from their shoes.

Step Five. And here's where things could get tricky. Before Fritz or Erika could enter the museum, Inga had to insist that Fritz hand over his gun. I had shared with Sophie and the undercover agents that Fritz carried a weapon and would probably have it with him when he arrived. The thought of it made me nervous. I wasn't about to have an accusatory conversation with someone who had a gun and might use it against me. And the only way to ensure that didn't happen was for Inga to insist Fritz lock the gun away in the museum's safe before they entered.

I waited quietly in the office. Outside, I heard what sounded like a heated discussion in German, followed by the front door opening and heavy footfalls down the hallway. If all went well, and Fritz agreed to be unarmed, Inga would flip the light switch, signaling that Fritz had locked his gun in the safe, and we could proceed as planned.

"Hallo."

I looked out the window. Kirsten stood at the foot of the steps, her blonde hair peeking from beneath her wool hat.

Erika hollered back. "Komm schnell." Come quick.

I was prepared for Erika and Fritz and the possibility they might bring Baret. If they brought their son along, I planned to send him out for a hot chocolate with Inga. But I hadn't counted on Kirsten, Erika's pawn, and I had no time to think about it.

I waited for Inga to open the office door, then stood up. "Guten Morgen."

Erika halted in the doorway with her husband behind her, his hands on her shoulders. The three of them looked exactly like they had in Hans's unfinished portrait in his studio. In front of them was their son. Erika pulled Baret to her and wrapped her arms around him. "What are you doing here?"

Before I could answer, Kirsten pushed her way into the office. She stopped abruptly when she realized it was me behind the desk. "What's this all about? I thought you were in jail!"

I crossed my arms. "I don't know, why don't you tell me? I wasn't expecting you."

In my ear, I could hear Sophie. "Good save, Kat. Keep Kirsten in the room. Let's hear what she has to say."

Erika jutted her jaw. "What difference does it make? I invited her. Whatever you have to say, you can say in front of her."

"Well then, this is a surprise, but maybe it shouldn't be." I nodded to Kirsten. "Clearly, Erika thought you should be here, Kirsten, and why not? You've been so helpful to Erika and to the museum. All those stories Erika helped you write. Like the one on the front-page Saturday morning? The one with your byline that Peter finished off for you. Too bad you had your

CHAPTER THIRTY-SEVEN

facts all mixed up. But hey, they pay you nicely, so I suppose you just decided to look the other way. No wonder you were out on assignment when I tried to reach you. We can talk about that later, but for now, I do have a couple of questions." I gestured to the two chairs in front of the desk. "Ladies, please, have a seat. Fritz, I apologize. I wasn't expecting a crowd. But, if you don't mind standing, I see no reason why this should be a problem."

Erika scoffed. "The only problem is you."

"Really?" I nodded to Inga. "Would you mind? It might be a good idea to take Baret for a walk." Then adopting a softer tone, I spoke directly to Baret. "Is that okay if Inga took you out for a hot chocolate or to the bookstore across the mall and maybe find you another book like your uncle bought you?"

I hadn't been expecting Baret, and I didn't want whatever might be about to go down to happen in front of his young eyes.

Baret looked at his mother. "Ist es in Ordnung, Mutter?"

Inga held out her hand. "Baret, komm. Let's go."

Erika pushed Baret's hair from his face and kissed him lightly on the forehead. "Ja, mein schatz, geh. Go."

My eyes followed Baret and Inga out the door. My guess was the boy knew nothing about his uncle's murder. "You haven't told him, have you?"

"I've been waiting for the right time," Erika snarled. "Explain to me why we're here, and why aren't you in jail?"

"Because I didn't kill your brother." I motioned again to the chairs in front of the desk and sat down.

"Then who did?" Erika slammed her bag on the desk. Fritz retreated behind her, his hands on her shoulders.

"I was hoping you might tell me that. You see, I think it was you, or more correctly, you and your husband. Fritz, I'm sure, is quite good with a gun—"

Kirsten sat down, her eyes going from Erika to me and back to Erika.

"You think I'd shoot my own brother?"

"I don't think you intended to. But things got out of hand. You argued. No doubt about Viktor and what you needed to do to be rid of him. But Hans didn't care. He was tired of hiding your uncle's hoard. I think he didn't believe you had the right to hide what belongs to history and us all. He wanted to live a different life."

"You don't know what you're talking about."

"I'm afraid I know more than you'd like me to. Which was exactly what you were afraid might happen. And why you sent Baret down to spend the weekend with your brother when you knew I'd be there."

"I did no such thing. Baret loves to visit his uncle. It was a scheduled trip."

"Was it? Hans didn't seem to think so. In fact, he apologized for Baret's presence and said he hadn't expected him. But we made the best of it and had a nice weekend. Did a little ice skating. Hans made dinner. He even showed me his studio and the painting he's been working on of you, Fritz, and Baret."

"His studio is none of your business."

"You don't want it to be my business, but it is. You see, Hans showed me the Gauguin he copied so that you could set Viktor up and be rid of him. And when that didn't work, and the FBI didn't arrest him, and Viktor threatened to kidnap Baret, you promised Viktor you would give him Raphael's *Portrait of a Young Man.*"

Erika's jaw dropped.

"Oh, don't look so surprised. You knew the painting had been missing since the war, and Viktor was bound to believe it might actually be part of your uncle's collection. You also knew Hans had been working on a copy. He frequently made copies of the great masters. He was very good at it—and you were anxious for him to finish it so that you could give it to Viktor."

"I have to admit, Ms. Lawson, I'm impressed with the facts as you've laid them out. But none of what you're saying proves that Fritz and I were at the chateau. Or that we had anything to do with Hans' murder."

"You left in a hurry. The tire tracks from your car were still wet in the snow when I arrived. The front door was open, and two glasses of red wine were on the kitchen counter. The police haven't finished with their reports, but when they do, I'm sure they'll find your prints on the glasses."

"Try again." Fritz stepped forward and put his hands on the back of Erika's chair. "Erika doesn't drink red wine. It gives her a headache. Hans knew that.

CHAPTER THIRTY-SEVEN

And we weren't anywhere near Oberammergau when Hans was murdered. After Hans took Baret with him, I convinced Erika that we needed to get away. We went skiing in Salzburg." Fritz reached into his jacket pocket and threw a half dozen restaurant receipts, and several punched ski lift tickets on the table. "Check the dates if you don't believe me."

I picked up one restaurant receipt marked for Friday evening and one of the ski lift tickets and stared at the time stamp. Saturday. Ten-twenty-one a.m. If Erika and Fritz were on the ski slopes, they couldn't possibly have murdered Hans.

Kirsten started to squirm in her chair. "Erika, why are we even here? This is a waste of time. If the police let Kat go, it's probably because one of Hans' handymen shot him. You know how tight he could be with money. She's just after a story. Let's go."

I stood up. "Not so fast. I'm sure if Erika didn't murder her brother that she wants to know who did. And to be honest, I'm surprised you're not more curious yourself." Until that instant, I hadn't thought Kirsten could possibly be involved in Hans' death, but her reaction to my questioning Erika had made me think otherwise. "Tell me, what time was it when you called Erika."

"What, are you accusing me?"

"I don't know, am I?

"This is stupid. You know that. I called Erika as soon as I got off the phone with you. I thought Erika should know what was going on."

"And where were you when you called?"

"What do you mean, where was I? What difference does it make? I'm not the one accused of murder."

"Maybe you should be."

Kirsten jerked her head back like I had slapped her. "What are you talking about? I didn't murder Hans. You were the last person to see him—you admitted it to me."

"Yes, I did. Just like I admitted to you how charming Hans was."

"So—"

"You tried to warn me, didn't you? But I didn't understand. I thought you were concerned that Hans might try to seduce or force himself on me.

But you weren't worried about me. You worried about Hans. That he and I might be getting too close."

"That's not true."

"And when you knew I planned to go back to the chateau, you were afraid things were getting serious. Hans wasn't one to invite women back for repeat visits unless he really liked them."

Kirsten started to stand. "I don't need to listen to this."

"No, wait." Erika put her hand on Kirsten's arm. "I'd like to hear what Kat has to say."

"Hans was dead when I arrived at the chateau. You both knew I was going back there. Erika was understandably worried I'd find out about her uncle's collection, which we all know, despite Germany's desire to keep it secret, exists. But if it wasn't Erika and Fritz who met Hans at the chateau, it had to be you, Kirsten. You worried that Hans and I might be getting close, and you couldn't have that. Erika had made it very clear to you that you weren't good enough for the family, but you were good enough to help with a little PR for the museum, and you thought you could change her mind. So you allowed her to buy you off. You placed the stories she helped you to write. It was good for your career and kept you close to Hans, which you liked, and I'm sure it gave you a sense of purpose. But it didn't change Erika's opinion of you. Meanwhile, you fooled around with Peter, which was okay until you thought Hans might be getting serious. So you called him in Switzerland and told him you needed to talk. You knew Hans was going to make some life changes. You just didn't know what it was. I think you even thought Hans might be falling in love with me. But Hans wasn't in love with me; he was in love with his art and everything about it. You didn't understand that. All you knew was that he had changed, and it worried you. You told him you were upset, and he agreed to come home early to meet with you. It was you he poured the red wine for. He thought he could reason with you. But things didn't go so well. You argued. And from the looks of things, it got physical. Whatever happened, you took the Henry rifle from the stand and forced Hans down into the cellar, where you shot him. And then you hid the rifle in the shack next to the pond behind the house."

CHAPTER THIRTY-SEVEN

Erika looked at Kirsten and put her hand over her heart. "The Henry Rifle? The one you gave him for the housewarming?"

"You bitch!" Kirsten grabbed a small Picasso statue off the desk and lunged at me.

I backed against the wall and looked for something to defend myself, but Kirsten was around the desk in seconds, ready to strike.

I screamed and seized her wrists. "Saint Nick! Saint Nick!"

Erika stood up, reached across the desk, and tried to wrestle the obelisk away. "How could you?"

Kirsten elbowed Erika hard in the shoulder. "Didn't you hear what she said? She used Hans to find Gerhardt's Hoard. She's a spy."

"And you're an idiot." Erika backed against the door, her hand on her shoulder. "Kat was never going to find it all."

Fritz stepped in front of his wife and held his hands out. "Don't even think about it."

Kirsten held the obelisk above her head like a weapon, like a weapon she pointed it in their direction. "She's found enough. Don't you think Hans was going to give up everything? I had to kill him. I did us a favor."

With Kirsten's back to me, I had my opening. I grabbed the Picasso and tried to wrench the statue from her grip. But Kirsten held tight and backed me up into the wall.

"You're not going to pin this on me!" Kirsten turned, ready to strike. The Picasso above her head.

I crouched and crossed my arms above my head.

Suddenly, the office door burst open. The two undercover agents who had been in the van rushed in. One quickly got between Kirsten and me and wrenched the Picasso away from her, while the other wrestled her hands behind her back, then cuffed her.

I exhaled and stood up. "You're right. I'm not going to pin it on you. You did it yourself. I've got everything on tape."

I took the earpiece from my ear and pulled the wire out from within my shirt and put them on the desk.

Erika looked at the small black microphone and then back at me. "You'll never find everything. You may think you have, but you never will. Gerhardt's Hoard belongs to my family, and I plan to keep it."

I didn't answer.

Sophie limped into the room. "Are you okay?"

"She's fine." Erika grabbed her bag off the desk and glared at Kirsten as the undercover agents prepared to take her away. "Better than that money-hungry, sad excuse of a reporter who killed my brother."

Kirsten shot Erika an angry look. "I should have shot you instead."

Erika smirked. "I would have never given you the chance. You're too stupid, Kirsten. You didn't know Van Gogh from Picasso. It was a mistake to hire you. Hans regretted ever allowing you to visit him at the chateau. He thought you were a clingy bore."

Kirsten stopped at the door.

"That's not true. Hans loved me."

"He used you." Erika fisted her hand, and Fritz put his arms around his wife and pulled her back. "We all used you. You were just too stupid to know."

Chapter Thirty-Eight

Erika and Fritz filed out of the room behind Sophie and agents Wagner and Meyer while I sat down behind the desk, too numb to move. So much had happened in the last forty-eight hours and sitting alone in the small office surrounded by family pictures of Hans and Erika and mementos from their uncle's estate felt cold and oddly isolating. I had yet to process Hans' murder, and I knew it would take some time to fully understand who Hans von Hausmann was and who I believed he wanted to be. Maybe I would never know. Did he intend to reveal Gerhardt's Hoard? Was he ready to go public with it? Or did he want me to return to the chateau because he planned to murder me?

"You ready to go?" Sophie reentered the room and leaned on her cane. She looked as grey and spent as I felt.

"So that's it? We're done?" I pushed the small mic I had been wearing across the desk toward her.

"For now," she said.

"But, what about the art?"

"What about it?" Sophie picked up the mic and sat down on the chair.

"What do you mean, what about it? Are we just supposed to walk away? This is it? We're finished here?"

"Other than your report on German holiday traditions for the magazine, I'd say yes. But you've time to complete that. There's no rush."

"That's not what I'm talking about, and you know it. What about the paintings? The Picassos? The Matisse? The Monet? There were hundreds hidden in the cellar, and Erika knows where there's more. She as much as admitted it."

"I told you all along, Kat, that part's not up to us. You did your job, more than what was expected of you. Viktor Sokolov's in jail. Inga's free of him, and you helped the police nab Hans' murderer. You should feel good about it."

"But it doesn't feel right."

"It may not, at least not yet. But you proved Gerhardt's Hoard exists. You exposed it. That's all you were asked to do. You couldn't do more. The newspapers will report Hans' murder, and if there's any mention of the art in the cellar, Erika will claim it belonged to her family and that they used the chateau as a backup to the museum's vault. Whatever happens now is up to the Germans, not us."

"But there must be something we can do? We can't just walk away. That's not what Hans would have wanted. That's not why he invited me back to the chateau. He wanted to expose Gerhardt's Hoard. I'm sure of it."

"It's not up to us."

"But what about the Washington Principals the Germans signed? Wasn't it agreed that any work stolen by the Nazis should be identified and, whenever possible, the heirs be notified?"

"It was, but Kat, you're dealing with international politics. And even if the Germans chose to identify the works, there are no provisions in the principles that apply to art stolen from families like mine with private collections. And if those who hold such art today have proof of sale, unless it can be shown the art was sold under duress, the work belongs to the holder. The Washington Principles only address those works of art that are hung in museums. And, believe me, museums worldwide aren't anxious to return such art, despite their questionable provenances. Even in the US, we're slow to respond to such requests. And what makes it even more difficult is that it's up to each country to enforce those principles—not us."

"So, the principles have no teeth, and Germany doesn't really have to do anything." I picked up the Picasso that Kirsten had tried to hit me with and ran my fingers over its odd shape. If the statue could talk, its story would be as interesting as the art.

CHAPTER THIRTY-EIGHT

"Give it time, Kat. The Germans know the world is watching. Things will happen. Other hoards will be uncovered. You'll see."

"Excuse me." Inga walked back into the office. "Kat, can you talk?"

Sophie stood up. "You and I can talk later. Don't forget you promised me that Schwarzwalder Kirschtorte."

"The German cherry cake? I'm looking forward to it."

"Call me." Sophie ambled to the door, paused, and whispered something in Inga's ear, then patting her shoulder, gave a slight wave goodbye.

I put the Picasso statue down on the desk. "You were a big help today, Inga. You were very brave. Thank you."

"It's me who needs to thank you. I never could have gotten away from Viktor without your help."

"But you did. You took the chance to escape, and you made it. You're a good person, Inga. I couldn't have done what I needed to do without you."

"I'm sorry I doubted you. It's just—"

"I know. I understand. You were worried about your mother. Have you spoken to her?"

"She's okay. She's going back home, and now that Viktor's in jail, she'll be fine."

"That's good. And what about you? Will you go home?"

"No. Erika asked me to stay on. She says with Hans gone. She's going to need me. And if I stay, she'll help me get into college. I could study art. She says she wants to help me."

"That sounds like a nice offer, Inga."

"And your friends, Sandor and Aanika, asked me to visit this spring before the baby's born. Maybe I'll see you again if you're there then, too?"

"I'd like that."

"I was thinking I could keep an eye open for you, too. Like I did for Viktor... about the art?"

"That might be a good idea." I suspected my discovery of Gerhardt's Hoard had been a close call for Erika and that it wouldn't be long before she might move it, and it wouldn't hurt if Inga and I remained in touch.

I walked Inga to the door, hugged her goodbye, and watched as she crossed the plaza with Erika and Baret. When she got halfway across the plaza, she and Baret turned and waved goodbye. I waved back. "Awf Weidersehen."

"Ms. Lawson?" From behind me, I heard Fritz. When I turned around, I noticed he had my hat in one hand and his gun in the other.

"Excuse me?" I held my hands up. If Fritz intended to shoot me, there was no one around to stop him.

"You forgot your hat. And me, I forgot my gun." Fritz handed me my hat, then tucked his gun back inside his jacket.

"Thank you." I put the hat on my head, relieved he had no intention of shooting me.

"Are you leaving Germany soon?"

"I have a few things to finish up with the story."

"The story?" Fritz adjusted his hat.

"The Christmas feature I'm working on."

"Well, then, I suppose we won't be seeing you again. But I wanted to thank you."

"Thank me?" It seemed like an odd thing to do, particularly since Fritz knew I was aware Gerhardt's Hoard was hidden beneath the chateau, and his wealth and future were tied to it.

"For helping us with Viktor. Without your help, things might have ended up differently. He might not ever have left us alone."

"Mind if I ask a question?" I looked out at the plaza. The protester, the farmer's son who Erika had bilked of the Gauguin, was back, and this time I knew it wasn't a German agent in disguise.

"What?"

"You ever going to give that Gauguin back to its rightful owner?"

"Do you mean to the American who believes he owns the original or the farmer's son, the protester in the plaza that Erika stole the Gauguin from?"

"Let's start with the farmer's son. I'm sure Viktor convinced the American he had the original and that the museum's Gauguin is a copy. You and I both know that's not true. When it comes to art theft and copies, there's probably more hanging on the walls of private galleries and museums than we know, and I doubt it will make a difference. But it might to him." I nodded to the

CHAPTER THIRTY-EIGHT

protestor. "And I happen to know there's another very good copy of *Fruits on the Table* inside the chateau. Suppose you return the original and hang the copy."

"Would it get you off our backs if I did?"

"It'd be a beginning," I said. The beginning of a good story I was already starting to format in my head. I may not have been able to change history, but I could make a difference by exposing what I knew, and like Sophie said, making the Germans unhappy with the knowledge of their hidden hoards might force their hand to free those last prisoners of war.

"And you wouldn't tell Erika?"

"I doubt Erika will ever want to talk to me again."

Fritz offered me his hand. "I'll consider it, Ms. Lawson. Auf Wiedersehen."

"Auf Wiedersehen, Fritz."

* * *

It was well past noon when I got back to my hotel. Sandor and Aanika were in the lobby waiting for me. Several coffee cups, napkins, and crumbs from sweets sat on the table in front of them.

Sandor stood up when he saw me and motioned for me to sit down. "So, how did it go?"

"I'm still trying to sort it out. But thank you. I might not be here if it weren't for you."

"I'm glad I was able to help. Did you get a confession?"

"Yeah, just not quite the confession I expected, but it's over, and I'm free to go." Kirsten's confession had been a surprise, but the more I thought about it, the more I realized how desperate she was to hang on to Hans and how threatened she was when she thought I might be getting close to him.

"Then you're coming back to Budapest for Christmas?" Aanika put her hand on mine. "Like we planned."

"I hope so. I've some things to clean up here for Sophie, and I need to get back to Nuremberg for a few pictures for the holiday feature I'm working on, but give me a couple of days, and I'll be on your doorstep. I promise."

Sandor put his arm around his wife. "Bring some Nuremberger rostbratwurst with you when you come, will you? By the time we get home, Aanika will have eaten what we have, and I don't imagine she can make it through the holidays without them."

"You can count on it," I said.

"And next spring, too." Aanika touched her belly. "I want you there when the baby comes. You're the Godmother, and you must be there."

"I wouldn't have it any other way."

* * *

It was several days before I saw Sophie again. We met at a small konditori on the plaza and splurged on the German chocolate cherry cake I'd promised her with coffee, followed by an Eierlikor, a German liquor made with egg yolks, cream, and rum. I asked her how Kirsten was doing. I was still trying to figure out how the argument between Kirsten and Hans had gone down. Sophie explained she had learned from the investigators that Kirsten had called Hans when he was in Switzerland. She demanded Hans return home earlier than expected so they might talk. When Kirsten had arrived at the chateau, Hans had just set the fire to take the chill off the house. Kirsten was upset when she came in, grabbed one of the fire irons, and started to poke the fire with it. Hans took it from her hands, threw it down, and suggested they open a bottle of wine and talk. When Hans went to the kitchen, Kirsten took the Henry Rifle from the stand and forced him down into the cellar.

"They found shotgun shells in her bag and the rifle behind the chateau in the ski shack."

"Which explains why I didn't see it when I found Hans." I took a sip of Eierlikor. "And how about Viktor? How's he doing?"

"Adjusting to life behind bars." Sophie tipped her glass to mine. "Thanks to you and Inga."

Sophie sighed and played with the stem of her glass.

"What's up? There's something you're not telling me." I put my glass down.

"You're not going to like it."

CHAPTER THIRTY-EIGHT

"Hit me," I said. "I think by now you know I can handle it."

"Erika's closed the museum. She's arranged to move the collection and everything beneath the chateau to a museum in Bern, Switzerland."

"Can she do that?"

"She's legally entitled. Everything she and Hans owned transferred to her upon his death. There's no reason she can't do with it what she wants."

"Which means what exactly?"

"That Gerhardt's Hoard is no longer Germany's problem."

"I'm sorry. I was optimistic things might work out differently."

"We've known this would be a long road all along. Hopefully, one day, some of the art will be repatriated to those from whom it was stolen. In the meantime, maybe some of what we thought had been lost to the world will be on display in a museum in Switzerland."

"Let's hope," I said.

Sophie nodded. The look in her eyes was distant. I imagined she was thinking back to the home she had known as a child and the art on the walls that might never be seen again. I was comfortable with the silence between us. So different from our first meeting when she barked orders at me. I had seen some of her world, and I wanted the rest of the world to see it too.

"So, what's next?"

"Keep your bags packed, Kat."

A Note from the Author

As a young woman, I lived in a small medieval Bavarian town not far from Munich, Germany. I was an Air Force wife, and it was the early 70s, a little more than twenty-five years after the war had ended. Most of the Germans I met were maybe just a few years younger than me, and those older, anxious to look forward and not back at a time that had reflected the worst of their country. At the time, I remember being asked by my then-husband's commanding officer if I might join a group of wives to host a luncheon for some local women who wanted to practice their English. It was a luncheon that turned into a regular monthly coffee klatch—one of the highlights of my years there—with six or seven German housewives who liked to bake. We'd meet monthly, either at one of their homes, usually apartments, or when the weather prevailed, for a garden party at one of the community gardens. It was always delicious. And fattening! I don't think there ever was such a thing as a low-fat German dessert. Everything was made with real butter and lots and lots of cream. There was no way I could get away with just sampling each woman's cake. It might have been an international incident if I did. Instead, I ate a healthy portion of each, and in addition to the desserts, drank lots of black coffee splashed with schnapps and finished off with an eier liqueur, German eggnog, that had I been wearing socks, would have knocked them off.

I left Germany in 1976. I had learned enough shopper's-Deutsch to navigate my way around medieval villages, where early on, I had managed to find some porcelain factories that set up their kilns inside barns to make ends meet. I even bought a porcelain chandelier that once hung above a cow stall and, to this day, hangs in my mother's apartment. My travels allowed me to start a shopper's newsletter for military wives looking to buy gifts like

A NOTE FROM THE AUTHOR

hand-carved wooden nativity scenes, nutcrackers, candies, and Christmas ornaments while visiting places off the beaten path that tourists might not know about.

My experience in Europe opened my eyes not only to a country of beautiful lakes, mountains, and people but of secrets that, until years later, I had no idea existed. It wasn't until 2012, nearly thirty-seven years after I had left Germany that I heard a story about a routine customs check at the Swiss border, a border I had passed through many times, that would lead to the discovery of 1500 hidden works of art in a Munich apartment. Blocks from my old stomping grounds.

And thus began my research...

The result of that research is the book you hold in your hands. *Passport to Spy* is loosely based on the life of Hildebrand Gurlitt, a once-successful museum curator, one of four of Hermann Goering's authorized art dealers, who worked with the Nazis to destroy what Hitler considered to be degenerative art while looting select masterpieces from some of Europe's best museums and the homes of wealthy Jews.

After the war, Gurlitt argued that he only did what he needed to survive and had helped save art that would have otherwise been destroyed. However, records—and the Germans did keep a detailed accounting—show that the sale of such piece of art was used to help finance the Third Reich. And what the Nazis didn't sell or destroy, Goering secured for what was to be the Fuhrer's Museum while skimming select works for himself and his wife. But, there is no honor among thieves. And while Goering siphoned off works by Raphael, Van Gogh, Monet, countless tapestries, and sculptures, Gurlitt was not shy about taking what he wanted for his equally impressive collection of masterpieces.

As the war dragged on and the allied bombing increased, the Nazis hid their treasures in mountain caves, salt mines, and castles like Neuschwanstein—a castle I had frequently visited.

All might have been lost were it not for groups like the Monuments Men, who secured what today art historians call The World's Largest Art Heist in an attempt to return what they could.

At the end of the war, Gurlitt avoided prosecution at the Nuremberg Trials, claiming to be one-quarter Jewish and a victim of Nazi persecution. But rather than walk away, Gurlitt had one final trick up his sleeve and a lot of moxie. He managed to track down the allies' collection center where those works of art Gurlitt had stolen were being housed, and with a stack of forged papers, approached those in charge and claimed the art in question belonged to his family. Shockingly, he was allowed to truck hundreds of stolen masterpieces away.

Under German law, it wasn't illegal to own stolen art, and Gurlitt believed the spoils of war were indeed his, and upon his death in 1956, the entire collection was passed on to his son, Cornelius Gurlitt. It was Cornelius Gurlitt who attracted the attention of the Swiss/German border police, that ultimately led to the discovery of a hidden cache of stolen art in a Munich apartment.

The story was one I couldn't stop researching. Gurlitt's Hoard wasn't the only cache of hidden treasures found after the war. Still, when it was reported in the press *two years* after the initial find—the Germans appeared to be in no rush—it blew the lid off any chance of secrecy and, ultimately, forced Germany and the rest of the world to reexamine how to deal with stolen art.

When I finished my research, I couldn't help but think back to my time in Germany and wonder how close I might have come to stumbling upon some hidden cache while researching little-known shopping sights. I believe the story picks the writer; in this instance, Gurlitt's Hoard picked me, and *Passport to Spy* is a ripped-from-the-headlines attempt on my part to fictionalize the tale while keeping the essence of the story very much alive.

Thank you for reading *Passport to Spy*, book 2 of the Kat Lawson mysteries. Please consider leaving a review on Goodreads or Amazon. And if you'd like to email me, please feel free; Nancy@NancyColeSilverman.com

Acknowledgements

Over Christmas dinner, my son told me he had found a new online program that used AI (Artificial Intelligence) to write a book. And to prove his point, he asked the program to write a 500-word short story. I have to say I was surprised. The story was pretty good. Not great…but not bad either. Admittedly, it caused me to pause. Could Artificial Intelligence replace writers in the future? I'd like to think not, and let me explain why.

I believe writing is a gift from a higher power, with a kind of conditional clause; a use it or lose it type of affair. It's why I spend hours each day alone researching and plotting…what I call mental flossing…while creating what I hope will be a story that my readers will find entertaining and insightful. And while writing a novel—at least the type of novels I write—is a solo sport, I also know it requires a team effort to bring a book to fruition. For that reason, beginning with the Big Guy upstairs, I'd like to thank the following for helping me bring this book about.

My father, Dave Bowman, whose experiences in WW2 inspired *The Navigator's Daughter* and the Kat Lawson Mysteries. My husband, Bruce Silverman, who makes all I do possible. My family for never questioning my sanity, particularly when I need to run a few crazy ideas by them. They may roll their eyes, but I can still attend family functions. My mother, who at ninety-nine and a retired English teacher, is still as sharp as her red pencil and equally supportive. My good friend, hiking partner, and always my first reader and editor, Rhona Robbie. I don't know how many miles Rhona and I have logged, but she never failed me when I needed an ear and/or a good set of eyes as the story developed on the page. And to my publisher, Shawn Reilly Simmons, and my editors Verena Main Rose and Harriette Wasserman Sackler. Together you have all provided the type of feedback and cheer squad this writer appreciates. I don't think any AI program could have such a fabulous, supportive team. Thank you.

About the Author

Nancy Cole Silverman spent nearly twenty-five years in news and talk radio, beginning her career in college on the talent side as one of the first female voices on the air. Later on the business side in Los Angeles, she retired as one of two female general managers in the nation's second-largest radio market. After a successful career in the radio industry, Silverman retired to write fiction. Her short stories and crime-focused novels—the Carol Childs and Misty Dawn Mysteries, (Henery Press) are both Los Angeles-based. Her newest series *The Navigator's Daughter*, (Level Best Books) takes a more international approach. Silverman lives in Los Angeles with her husband and a thoroughly pampered standard poodle.

SOCIAL MEDIA HANDLES:
   https://www.facebook.com/NancyColeSilvermanauthor/
   Twitter: @nancycolesilver

AUTHOR WEBSITE:
   www.nancycolesilverman.com

Also by Nancy Cole Silverman

The Carol Childs Mysteries

The Misty Dawn Trilogy

Numerous short stories